BEYOND
THE
Millennium

BEYOND
THE
Millennium

PAUL MEIER
AND ROBERT WISE

A JANET THOMA BOOK

THOMAS NELSON PUBLISHERS
Nashville
Printed in the United States of America

Published in Nashville, Tennessee, by Thomas Nelson, Inc., Publishers.

The Bible version used in this publication is THE NEW KING JAMES VERSION. Copyright © 1979, 1980, 1982, 1990, Thomas Nelson, Inc., Publishers.

Library of Congress Cataloging-in-Publication Data

Meier, Paul D.
  Beyond the millennium / by Paul Meier, Robert L. Wise.
    p. cm.
  ISBN 0-7852-7196-1 (pbk.)
  1. Michael (Archangel)—Fiction. 2. Spiritual warfare—Fiction.
I. Wise, Robert L. II. Title
PS3563.E3457B49 1998
813'.54—dc21   97–36564
                                                                              CIP

1 2 3 4 5 6 QPK 03 02 01 00 99 98

Printed in the United States of America

DEDICATION

For our newest angel
Robert L. Wise II

"They finally named one right"

MEMORANDUM

TO: **Michael, Guardian Angel**
RE: **Records in the Archives of the Hosts of Heaven**

Further clarification is sought for the final years of planet Earth. Your original report, filed under the heading, *The Third Millennium,* left a number of issues unresolved. Please give additional information on how the ultimate scenario played out from your personal perspective.

We wish to preserve the heavenly view of the final struggle and to chronicle the strategy of the demonic forces; therefore, we require a more detailed description of how you personally conducted spiritual warfare. Now that the legions of Evil are banished, we want a record of their role in the constant disruption of human events.

Specifically, our records do not reflect the role played by Guardian Angel Seradim. We wish to record his service and activities. Please give us the inside story.

CHAPTER
1

Michael listened and knew this call was different. The angel understood the summons was personal, particular to him. Other angels might observe, but none could do so out of the totality of their being. This singular expression of Logos was for him.

The Great Light churned and boiled, rolling forth in brilliant dispersion of pure energy. Then the Creator spoke one word: "Seradim."

Michael turned toward the Center of all things and was instantly in the presence of glorious light, encompassed by a rainbow of incalculable hues. The angel both saw the sounds and heard the colors. The blending of sight, sound, and perception into a wondrous whole was all absorbing and completely fulfilling. As did all the angels, Michael basked in the moment, each moment, as the essence of all eternity, an encounter without beginning or end.

In an instant, the Father's will surged through Michael's mind with complete and total clarity. Seradim, a member of the Seraphim, was being reassigned as a guardian angel.

Michael suddenly knew his personal assignment: to be a tutor and mentor until the angel was ready to fulfill his destiny. "The burning ones," the Seraphim, were expressions of pure love and their affections so brilliant, they came forth like holy fire.

"Seradim," Michael thought, and the angel heard. "I am your companion and teacher. I have been called to instruct you about the coming battle on the other side."

"Battle?" Seradim puzzled. "I do not comprehend."

"Your whole existence has been to stand nearest to the heart of God, responding in love, praise, and worship," Michael explained. "The very purity of your vocation makes such a notion virtually impossible to understand." Michael pointed out beyond the reaches of heaven. "You have been reassigned to my order of guardian angels. Our job is to fight and work for human beings. You've been called to leave the very heights of heaven and travel to the dark depths named Earth."

"Earth?" The angel absorbed the instruction. "And I will intervene as light in that place?"

"No. As strange as it now sounds, you will become tangible in more solid terms," Michael continued. "A great war is just ahead in a place very different from ours. We will go there after I teach you something of this realm."

Seradim looked across eternity and saw no beginning or end, no limits or boundaries. Completeness was all he knew.

Michael understood at once. "You cannot yet imagine a place where there is something called time, limitation, dying. Of course, it will be painful for you to experience a world of incompleteness and finality, but this is where you will intervene."

For the first time in his existence, Seradim felt the sensation of not knowing. He frowned.

"Good!" Michael answered. "Now you are beginning. You must apprehend the nature of that other world. Trapped in finitude, those creatures must learn the meaning of eternity—a far more pleasant task than yours: to discover the nature of time and the dimensions of space. But that will come later, after other matters are sorted out."

"Earlier? Later?"

Michael nodded. "At this moment, you can only know sequence, but when we cross into that other place, distance and time will be added."

Seradim looked puzzled. "A battle?" he thought. "What is a battle? Sounds pleasant to me."

Michael frowned. "It is not pleasant. Let us learn of war." He took the angel's hand, gazing deeply into his being. "Let me tell you of strife." Michael remembered the beginning.

Immediately Seradim saw two brothers standing before a stone altar. One seethed with anger; the other was serene. Suddenly the angry brother picked up a stone and struck the other on the head. When his brother slumped, the attacker beat his head again and again with the pointed rock. The attacker hit repeatedly, until the life was pounded from his victim.

Seradim flinched and tried to push the image from his mind, but Michael would not allow it. New images filled his awareness. Seradim saw warriors racing toward each other, hurling spears and shooting arrows. Cries of hate rang through Seradim's consciousness; he tried to shake the thoughts away.

"I am sorry," Michael answered, "but you cannot intervene in what you do not understand. The world to which we must go is filled with far worse than what you have seen. War is an ugliness none should know. Yet the Holy One called you forth from the highest realm of heaven to send you into the strife. You are needed during Earth's final hours."

Seradim held his head in bewilderment. Another wave of images emerged. Great balls of fire exploded and hot metal showered down on combatants. Bodies were torn into pieces and limbs fell to the ground, cropped from the torsos of soldiers. The carnage filled Seradim with an unidentifiable sensation, making the wonder around him fade.

Michael responded, "Pain is also part of your instruction. Unless you understand its function, you cannot help. Do not worry. You will not be consumed, but you must know of the forces driving this world we will visit."

"You keep saying, 'world,'" Seradim wondered.

"Yes. Another place of unreality. It will be hard for you to understand separateness, but this is the very essence of the realm beyond."

"Why?"

"The Creator made it for Himself, but because the place is of another order, the world had to be of a different nature from heaven."

"Where is . . . the place?"

"On the other side of the wall of time."

Seradim quickly looked in every direction.

"You can't see the partition, my friend. We must experience it as a dramatic transition beyond eternity. I will teach you how to cross over."

"I'm prepared for whatever is ahead."

"No, not yet." Michael shook his head. "You must understand our enemy. We have an adversary on the other side, waiting to destroy us."

For the first time in Seradim's existence, fear shook his entire being. "An . . . enemy?" his thoughts scrambled.

"Never forget it. We have a nemesis bent upon our total annihilation."

"Enemy?" Seradim kept thinking over and over. "Enemy."

"Since you have never known anything but love, you cannot yet grasp the meaning of hate. I must teach you."

Seradim's consciousness slowly filled with a sense of pride and inordinate self-centeredness. The emotion expanded into greed and a desire to possess. The angel staggered backward, clutching at his throat. Without an immediate object to seize, his feelings twisted into anger, and black hatred spread across Seradim's awareness. He cried out in horror.

Michael immediately stopped his instruction. "Forgive me for causing you such severe pain, but the enemy has bathed the good creation of the Father in this kind of brokenness. The creatures of that world become infected with these same feelings and soon accept them as normal. We call such an experience sin. When left unchecked, the disease soon controls them. Unless intervention occurs, the creatures are hopelessly mired into the chaos that slowly destroys them. Only an outside force can set them free."

"That's our task?" Seradim shuddered again.

"Not exactly. The Father Himself has already offered a solution. Long ago the Creator struck our enemy with a fatal blow, but he still is able to work his diabolical schemes. We are part of God's plan to establish the final and total victory."

Seradim worried for the first time. "How do we face this enemy?"

"Our weapon is love, and you are already quite well equipped, for that is your very nature. You burn with love. Our task is to remain grounded in charity while fighting against the onslaught of evil."

"Why haven't I known about this world before?" Seradim thought.

"Because you've stood at the top of heaven's hierarchy," Michael responded, "doing nothing but worshiping the Most High. You've never really been in touch with what some of the other orders of angels do."

Seradim looked around. Multitudes of beings swept across the expanse of heaven. Some were huge, almost filling all the space above and below them; others were quite petite. Many seemed to be swirling creatures of energy, moving through space like meteors, leaving trailing trains of fire. The sound of singing swelled from small tones of simple concord then quickly expanded into multiple chords of perfect harmony. Pure worship swept in from the flying hosts with a gentleness that still had the impact of an overwhelming force. The vast diversity settled into a singular expression of praise.

"Holy, holy, holy, Lord God of hosts. Heaven and earth are filled with your glory." The words resonated into the deepest regions of the angel's being, and automatically Seradim joined in singing, "Holy, holy, holy is the Lord God Almighty."

A great golden throne encircled by a rainbow emerged from the center of worship. The One seated there had an appearance of jasper and carnelian. Seradim saw other lesser thrones around the great throne. Lightning and peals of thunder exploded and seven lamps of fire came forth.

Four strange creatures covered with eyes in front and back flew back and forth, crying again and again, "Holy, holy, holy is the Lord God Almighty, who was, who is, and who is to come." Sacred love burned in Seradim like a holy, incandescent light, and he became immersed in the praises of the highest hosts of heaven.

"Sorry," Michael interrupted, "but I must draw your attention away to the lower levels. You know, of course, the highest choirs of angels: the Seraphim, Cherubim, and Thrones, the juridical powers who contemplate the divine judgments. But you have never fully experienced the downward dimension of the work of our angelic hosts."

"I've always known they were there," Seradim mused, "but just didn't think about their assignments. . . ."

"The task of the next three choirs of angels is more related to the universe we are to visit," Michael instructed. "The Dominions carry the commands from the throne to those under them, the lesser angels. The Virtues help the universe operate according to the directives of the Dominions. Understand?"

Seradim nodded enthusiastically.

"Then the Powers fight the evil influences that would oppose the instructions of the Virtues. As you can surmise, we are getting closer to our enemy."

The new trainee rubbed his chin and frowned. "I can guess that trouble is just ahead."

"Now we are almost to the point where we connect with the earth. The last three choirs of angels are directly involved in human affairs. We are the Warriors or Guardians."

"We?" Seradim thought.

"Every single person in that world has a guardian angel to look after him or her. You're going to watch after some very special people during the final days of human history. I have been working at that job for what people call centuries."

"Really?" Seradim was amazed. "What is a century?"

"Time is a dimension of their world. Because we are eternal, time has no meaning for us; but on Earth they measure events in days, months, years, and finally, centuries. Understand?"

Seradim shook his head.

"Of course not." Michael smiled. "You have to go to Earth to get the idea. As a matter of fact, humans are now in their last seven-year period, a period that the Bible calls 'Daniel's Seventieth Week.' We are going to enter time and space at the start of the fifth year before the end."

Seradim smiled without comprehension.

"We work with the last two orders of angels—the Archangels, who carry the big messages to humanity; and the Principalities, who oversee the well-being of cities, nations, and empires. Together we help humans stand against the onslaughts of the Evil One."

Seradim pondered his new instruction for a few moments. "Awesome," he concluded.

■ ■ ■

Far across the galaxies from Michael and Seradim, another conversation was unfolding. Not in eternity but just beyond time, two other beings of similar but twisted nature stood behind the sweep of human affairs, looking in on unfolding history.

"Events are escalating," Malafidus thought.

"Exactly," Homelas added. "Remember when humans could only move with the speed of beasts, riding horses?"

"Their machines have made them travel almost as fast as we do. The fools only rush to their own destruction."

"I find it to be much more fun than it once was," Homelas reflected. "Remember when people only killed one at a time? Now the numbers are incredibly encouraging.

For a while, I thought they might blow up the whole planet with the big bomb."

"Those fool Russians spoiled it when they catered to the United States," Malafidus erupted. "If they'd just hung on another decade or two. . . ."

Homelas added, "All those evil prayers for peace and conversion spoiled everything. Consider how many souls could have been siphoned off into the fire with just one good exchange of missiles." The demon swore.

"Nevertheless," Malafidus reminded his comrade, "the final great battle cannot be very far ahead. All the pieces in the puzzle are coming together. The Man of Lawlessness is now in place: Damian Gianardo, the president of the United States. Just the man we've been expecting for centuries. We surely don't have long to wait."

"I believe our immediate assignment is related to the Great Plan. We are to use some young man for the devil's purposes. Who is this Jimmy Harrison we are supposed to corrupt?"

Malafidus pointed toward the West and the coast of California came into focus. "A fallen son of a Christian minister has been picked out as the vehicle for our main concern. Look, there he is."

Homelas thought and immediately saw Jimmy Harrison walking from a bar toward a shiny classic Corvette. He had the swagger and arrogance of a self-assured young man bent on nothing but his own pleasure. After draining a can of beer, Harrison crumpled the aluminum in his hands, threw the can at the curb, and leaped into the Corvette. His car shot into the oncoming traffic, causing several people to swerve, barely avoiding a wreck. Jimmy glanced in his side mirror and swore at the fools getting in his way.

Moments later the Corvette was on the freeway, flying down the coast.

"What do we need that slug for?" Homelas wondered.

"We want to help him corrupt a young Jewish girl. The message I got was that headquarters wants us to bring this girl down as the first step toward destroying her family."

"No problem. I've been doing Jews in since the Romans ran the scurvy lot out of Jerusalem when they burned the city. Why so much interest in this girl?"

"His infernal majesty, our leader, fears her family might have some strategic role in the final struggle. They must be eliminated before the war starts."

Homelas frowned. "Her old man is a general? They're Messianic Jews?"

"No," Malafidus answered, "Larry Feinberg is a psychiatrist with zip interest in any Messiah. They are basically a nonobservant Jewish family."

"So, why waste energy on them?" Homelas shook his head. "I'd much rather be back on assignment in Washington, D.C., influencing legislation to kill babies or push assisted suicides. We can harvest far more souls through bad laws or promoting a culture of death."

"You know better than to question headquarters. Nothing makes our leader angrier than being defied or second guessed. Anyway something big is already working in the White House and fully covered by our boys. If the assignment is only destroying one kid or knocking off a family . . . then that's all there is to it."

"Okay," Homelas shrugged, "what's the angle? Where's the opening?"

"Currently, the girl is in a rather typical teenage-rebellion frame of mind. Her name is Ruth Feinberg, and she's willing to lie a little, which gives us plenty to work on. She's already got a lust going for Harrison, so we have the usual perfect entry point. I think our boy Jimmy will be a good bet to get to her on all counts. Just needs a little encouragement from us."

"Who knows?" Homelas smiled wickedly. "We might get a quick pregnancy out of this one. An extra abortion. Might even be able to drive her to a suicide."

"Put your mind to it, pal. Maybe we can get you back to work in Washington in six months to a year. We're scheduled to hit her on New Year's Day. Let's go for it!"

CHAPTER

2

We have a difficult battle ahead. Now is the time to tell you more about our foe." Michael settled back, resting against space. "He was once one of us. Called the Light Bearer, the enemy held the very highest rank, second only to the Triune God. As incomprehensible as it sounds, the Light Bearer is the ultimate enemy of this entire realm."

Seradim seemed mystified. "How could any creature be opposed to the Almighty? Isn't every emanation from the Center a complete expression of love? I don't think it is possible to—"

"You are not listening," Michael interrupted. "Hear my heart. I want you to receive an image. Every past moment still exists in the eternal now. We simply bring it before us again. You must be there and experience the explosion just as I did."

Seradim frowned and blinked rapidly, unsure of what was unfolding.

"We called the Light Bearer, the greatest of us all, Lucifer. His beauty and magnificence were awesome, the splendor of pure light. But that was not enough for him."

"How could anyone want more?"

"Lucifer desired the place of the Creator."

Seradim immediately started to protest.

"Of course, the very idea sounds like absurdity, but pride and ambition created their own form of insanity. Sin is madness deliberately chosen over sanity and health. Tragically, Lucifer's decision spawned a plague that immediately infected other angels."

"Us?"

Michael shook his head. "Lucifer's distemper contaminated many of them. In a single choice of their free will, they joined his rebellion, and the war was on. You must see the explosion."

Seradim's mind filled with images of great clashes of pure energy and discharges of vast light. Then the shape of a great hideous dragon breathing fire and belching smoke appeared. The dragon's enormous tail swung left and right, knocking angels aside.

The guardian angel directed Seradim's attention toward an image flying through his consciousness. "That angel is the other Michael, the Lord's chief warrior. Watch!" The great Archangel Michael drew a magnificent sword of light and attacked the dragon. The collision shook heaven.

Lucifer's army lined up behind him and the rest of the hosts of heaven moved into rank with Michael. A third of the angelic hosts charged forward with Lucifer. Angels tore at each other with the force of mountains splitting and continents colliding. The foundations of eternity shook, but slowly the dragon was forced into inevitable retreat. The angel who had presumed to displace God Almighty could not even stand against one of his own kind. Suddenly the hosts of Evil flew backward, hurling out into the vastness of eternal space.

"God expelled the dragon and his followers from heaven," Michael explained. "They were cast down to Earth, and that poor planet became a place of unending warfare. The sin of Lucifer was his inane desire to be the head of something lesser rather than to remain the servant of the Greater."

"But why would one of *us* even conceive such a preposterous thought?"

Michael nodded gravely. "As the Father was laying out His plans for all eternity, He confided in the inner circle of angels. His intention was to create a totally different race called humanity, and to eventually incarnate Himself as one of them, so they might be made complete in love."

"Humanity?" Seradim puzzled.

"They inhabit the earth," Michael continued. "Lucifer considered such an idea too undignified and smacking of weakness. He was appalled by the idea of the Almighty taking on the terms of flesh and blood. From that one conclusion, his leap of arrogance and pride was only a small step."

The newest Guardian slumped, putting his face in his hands. "My mind is spinning, and I feel very strange. I don't understand what is happening, but I feel disconnected."

"Earth people call the sensation craziness. When truth is bent, distorted into deception and delusion, we feel disconnected. Sin does that to people, because it's basically a form of insanity. Lucifer was eternity's first expression of madness."

Seradim shook his head. "To exchange heavenliness for hellishness, how could such be?"

Michael agreed. "Unfortunately, humans do it all the time. That's why the Father sends us to help them overcome."

"If I could help one person escape this problem, I would be the happiest angel in heaven."

Michael laughed. "You will help far more than one person. By the time we are finished, you will see Lucifer's entire scheme vanish like fog at dawn."

"Fog?"

"The time has come to take you to the frontier between us and them. Think with me, and we will travel to the edge."

Seradim locked his mind to Michael's and they whirled toward the boundaries of heaven. While the journey was accomplished in an instant, Michael's instruction made it feel as if they were traveling over a boundless amount of time.

"Heaven represents the very inner domain of God, the extension of the omnipresent Creator's mind," Michael explained. "We travel in Him, by Him, with Him, through Him, and yet the Almighty remains distinct from us. We always remain apart from Him, lesser than Him."

"Of course," Seradim understood.

"But humans are actually superior to us," Michael continued. "Because the Almighty came among them as Yeshua, the God–Man, they were able to receive divine life. Human beings who accept this wonderful gift become a part of the very being of the Creator. They can become the family of the Messiah, His brothers and sisters."

Seradim marveled at what he could not truly grasp as he became aware of a barrier arising before him. Like a vapor, the curtain of many layers moved from pure energy into substance. At the far end was the amorphous shape of a vast universe of whirling galaxies, asteroids, planets, the incredible beauty of physical space filled with countless objects.

Michael pointed at the nebulous veil. "The creatures on the other side will not be able to see us unless we assume their shape. We appear only as pure energy to them."

"Then how do we make contact?"

"Because we are energy, we can put our thoughts into their thought processes," Michael explained. "And we can also disguise ourselves as one of them. We can put on their skin like they wear a coat. You shall see."

"I can just walk through?" Seradim winced. "The enemy might be waiting to attack."

Michael extended his hand. "Take my hand and follow me. Lucifer can no longer return to eternity, so he stays away from the veil. Besides, he's too busy trying to run Earth to pay much attention to who comes across. Ready for the plunge?"

CHAPTER
3

New Year's Day broke across America with the traditional promise of every new beginning. On the eastern seaboard, howling blizzard winds hurled sleet and snow against the White House. The president of the United States silently studied the bleak winter scene from a window in the Oval Office. Damian Gianardo appeared to need little rest and observed no holidays. No one stood in the way of the man with the deep scar on the side of his head.

A tall man of commanding presence, President Gianardo had the uncanny capacity to accurately read the intentions of his opponents. His ability to intimidate was legendary. Yet he felt completely at ease with his vice president, Jacob Rathmarker, a man cut from the same cloth and one of the few people Gianardo trusted.

"Unusual to do business on New Year's Day." Gianardo continued to stare out of the window into the dawn breaking over the country. "But I wanted a totally confidential environment."

"I'm your servant." Rathmarker sat on the edge of his leather chair. "When you need me, I'm here."

Gianardo smiled. "That's what I like about you, Jacob." The president turned and then pushed a file across his desk. "You'll notice most of this material is in my handwriting to ensure total secrecy. I've identified ten countries, mostly in Europe, that I intend to force into a new alliance with us. We've discussed the plan previously, but now I want you to head the negotiations to weld these nations into a union. They will be the cornerstone for my move to world domination."

Rathmarker opened up the file and thumbed through it quickly. "Yes," he mumbled, "just as you indicated earlier. The ten most significant nations in the world." The vice president closed the file. "Brilliant strategy."

"I intend to go for the jugular." The president picked up a dagger-style letter opener from the top of his desk and twirled the point slowly on a memo pad. "They will never know what hit them," he sneered. "By the time we've worked out the details of the political union, I'll have our military power in place. No one can stop us from being able to control the world." He smiled and suddenly plunged the dagger into the memo pad.

■ ■ ■

On the other side of the country, seventy-two-degree weather and bright sunlight bathed the residents of Southern California in warmth and hope. Joggers and families strolling their pets patrolled the beaches. Hordes of RVs and multitudes of tourists headed toward Pasadena and Disneyland. With the Rose Bowl parade starting later in the day, the southland was a vast theme park of entertainment and celebration. Birds-of-paradise, geraniums, ice plants, and rose bushes covered the landscape. The possibilities of the coming year seemed boundless.

In Newport Beach, Joe and Jennifer McCoy did not get up until well past 9 A.M. Joe Jr. and Erica were already watching the parades on TV with the family dog, Barkley, curled up in front of the set. Like the rest of the families in the tract-home neighborhood, their stucco house with its manicured front yard embodied the American dream of affluence and security. Inside and outside the Spanish-style two-story, the McCoys had it made.

"Great party last night." Joe yawned and pulled Jennifer closer. "We shouldn't have stayed till one o'clock." He blinked his bloodshot eyes and stared at the silk canopy above the four-poster bed.

"You shouldn't have drunk those three extra glasses of champagne. A little libation and you're ready to dance all night."

Joe chuckled. "Well, it was a great party." He rubbed his eyes. "But I guess I did overdo it a bit."

"You guess?" Jennifer asked playfully. "You were doing great until that last drop kicked in, and then you nearly went to sleep at the table. I had to drive us home."

"Oh, yeah." Joe grinned. "Well, in spite of the pounding in my head today, I believe this is going to be a great new year. The nation is in good shape. The president is a powerful leader and will keep the economy strong. People keep pouring into Southern California. The value of our house *has* to go up. Who could ask for anything more?"

"Yeah, we've got it all. Great house. Great kids." She nudged Joe in the ribs. "As long as you keep the bucks rolling in."

Joe stretched. "This is certainly the right time and place to be the comptroller for a growing computer company."

Jennifer threw the covers back. "I guess I ought to go downstairs and make some breakfast. I'm sure the kids are hungry." She stopped to brush her hair, taking a long look in the mirror. New wrinkles were forming around her mouth and lips. Pouches of skin bulged under her eyes. She felt the side of her cheek. Her skin was no longer velvety soft.

"You know," Joe called from the bed, "we ought to make some New Year's resolutions today. That's the traditional thing to do."

"And I'll fix black-eyed peas for good luck." Jennifer frowned and new lines rippled across her forehead. She was quickly leaving any appearance of her thirties behind.

■ ■ ■

Several hours later Joe and Jennifer McCoy sat at their dining room table. Jennifer held a pad and paper. "I guess your New Year's Day resolutions have to do with finance."

Joe grinned. "You do know me well, dear. But everything I do is for the family."

"Sure." Jennifer patted his hand thoughtfully. "I just worry that sometimes you work too hard for us. You drive yourself with such long hours at the office."

"That's the American way." Joe shrugged. "Let's get the kids in on this." He turned toward the den. "Erica? Joe Jr.? Where are you?"

"I'm in here," a soft feminine voice answered.

"Get your brother and come in," the mother called.

In a few moments Erica appeared in the doorway. The gangly fifteen year old had the awkward look of a typical teen. She kept her lips tightly closed to hide her braces. "Yes?"

"Where's Joe? We want to talk with you and your brother," the father answered. "Go get him."

"I can't." Erica rolled her eyes.

"And just why not?" Jennifer asked.

"Well, I'm not supposed to tell." Erica looked down.

Joe pushed his chair back. "I insist on knowing this second!"

"He, uh, slipped out to go to the video arcade."

"I have forbidden him to go to that place!" Jennifer stood up. "I will snatch him baldheaded when I find him."

"No, no." Joe shook his head. "You're going to the movies with Sharon Feinberg. I'll go get him." He turned to Erica. "We'll talk with you later. Right now your mom and I need to have a little talk."

Jennifer waited until Erica had left the room. "You want New Year's resolutions? Well, maybe this year we ought to think about the spiritual side of life more often."

"Spiritual?" Joe grimaced. "Are you serious?"

"Our kids have never even been in a church. At least we attended when we were their age."

Joe smiled. "Life was certainly different in the Midwest. Your parents took you to the Methodist church and mine made sure I was in the Presbyterian Sunday school every week. Do you realize we've been going together since we were sixteen?"

"We're sure not in Peoria, Illinois, anymore," Jennifer said thoughtfully. "I know we didn't take the teaching and preaching too seriously, but at least we picked up some values here and there. Values I wish our kids would pick up."

"Yeah." Joe frowned. "Wouldn't hurt Joe Jr. to learn a few Bible stories. Maybe it'd give him some perspective on those sadistic, violent video games he chooses."

Jennifer turned around and faced her husband. "And after all, Erica is fifteen. We've had the mother-and-daughter sex talk, but . . . well . . . I know her friends influence her. Kids today are just more loose than we were."

"Have to be." Joe nudged his wife. "You thought you were the Virgin Mary. Remember?"

Jennifer blushed. "I did learn something about morality in that little country church. The same lessons wouldn't hurt Joe and Erica."

"You've got a point." Joe kissed his wife on the cheek. "Okay, we'll add a spiritual dimension to our resolutions."

"I'll talk to Jane McGill this week. She and her husband are big church people."

"And I'll go get that wayward son of mine."

■ ■ ■

In Lake Forest, fifteen miles to the south, New Year's Day began at the crack of dawn for Frank and Jessica Wong. Business at the Golden Dragon was always good; few other restaurants stayed open on this day, and the immigrant family always put the dollar ahead of any other considerations.

Carrying a tray of lettuce, cabbages, and bean sprouts from the cooler, Frank hurried through the large kitchen in the back of the restaurant. "Jessica, it is almost ten o'clock," he said in Mandarin Chinese. "We must be open in an hour."

His wife laid down her dicing knife and wiped beads of perspiration from her brow. "We will be ready, good husband. We always are."

Frank set the tray down and checked one of the steaming kettles of rice simmering on the big stove. "Is it possible we have lived here for nearly twenty years?"

Jessica stared out the small window opening into the alley. "Twenty years . . . and we never speak of our parents or our relatives anymore."

Frank looked pained. "I try to put them out of my mind. The memories are . . . too . . . torturous . . . still."

"Do you think any of them escaped?"

Frank sat down on the stool next to his wife. Uncharacteristically, he searched her face as if seeking some hint of emotion. "We were Chinese in a Vietnamese country. I just don't know. Maybe the family migrated back to China. After all, the clan came south because we hoped for a better political climate. Once everything turned Communist, what choice did any of us have?"

Jessica's inscrutable face offered no hints of her feelings. She picked up a large silver knife and began dicing water chestnuts. Jessica recited the lines she'd said a thousand times before. "We only did what we had to do. The boat was the last chance to escape. We couldn't wait for the others. There was no alternative but to get on and hope the family made it." She chopped the vegetables with increasing fury. "I am only glad my father, Chin Lee, died before this terrible time."

"Yes." Frank clenched his jaw, his head tilted back in a pose of steely resignation. "There was no room left on the boat. Remember? Capacity was supposed to be for fifty. One hundred and fifty of us got on." He put his hand on Jessica's waist to slow down the pace of her chopping.

"And most of them died at sea. . . ." Jessica's voice trailed away. "I didn't think we'd survive the refugee camp." She quickly scooped the chestnuts in a pan and hurried to the sink to wash them.

"And now another year has come around. We are older, and honorable family is farther from us."

"At least we have Cindy." Jessica looked at their daughter's high school picture in the center wall of the kitchen. "She is all we have left."

Frank turned slowly toward the picture. His daughter's skin was smooth like porcelain china—a warm olive tint with a blush of color in her cheeks. Her heart-shaped mouth was perfect. Except for a slightly unfocused look, her sightless brown eyes looked completely normal. "If only she could see . . . if there was a cure for her blindness. I so often worry about what we did wrong." He trudged back to the cooler to pick up another tray of vegetables.

"What more could we do?" Jessica beat the drain pan against the sink. "We have made hundreds of offerings to our ancestors for her well-being. Cindy was just born blind. Is there a Daoist or Buddhist temple in this state in which we have not burned incense for her? You paid the monks well to pray constantly for our daughter." Jessica dropped the pan into the sink, and a dull thud echoed across the room.

Frank clutched his fists. "Our religion was for the old world. It does not work here. Maybe this year we find a new way."

Abruptly the swinging doors opened and Cindy shuffled into the kitchen behind Sam, her guide dog. "I have wrapped all the silverware in napkins," she said in English. "I think we have enough sets to take us through the evening." She laid a book on the counter.

"Excellent, good daughter," Frank answered in English. "You are a most dutiful child. A joy to your parents."

"I'm sure you would rather be celebrating the holiday with your friends," Jessica added.

"No." Cindy felt her way to the wooden chopping block. "I would rather be with my parents than anyone."

"You make our hearts full," Frank answered.

Cindy placed her braille book on the counter. "Maybe I will read for a while."

"Of course," Jessica insisted. "We have an hour before the doors are open."

Cindy's nimble fingers glided across the myriad of raised dots but her mind slipped away. The voice of Ben Feinberg floated through her thoughts. Never had a boy given her so much attention.

Ben is different, she thought. *He's sensitive and seems to care about me. Heaven's sake, I can't imagine what the boy would see in me. Of course, I can't imagine what anyone can see. I must guard my feelings. After all, I have so little to offer. I don't want any boy feeling sorry for me . . . or toying with my emotions.*

"You are reading?" Jessica asked. "I don't see your fingers moving."

"Giving them a little rest, Mama."

"What are you reading?" Frank Wong asked in Chinese.

"Last year in my discussion group at the library, this book was recommended. It is called the Bible." Cindy's fingers again ran across the raised dots of the braille.

"Bible?" Jessica Wong began stirring herbs into the special sauce she was making.

"Christians believe this is a holy book," Cindy explained. Her small voice matched the petite features of her lovely face.

"Indeed." Frank continued to speak in Chinese, his eyes so narrow they were barely slits. Most of his hair was gone, and he was slightly humped forward. "We must always respect such things."

"Especially because we are in a country where the majority are Christians," Jessica added. "We must offend no one."

"Are the teachings like those of the Buddha?" Frank stared down at the blank page filled with the raised dots.

"The first part is the history of the Jews," Cindy told her parents. "But the teaching of Jesus is in the second section."

"Jesus is like the Buddha?" Frank asked.

"Sort of," Cindy puzzled. "He was a Jew also. I really don't understand a lot of the story."

"Maybe you should talk to a Jew," Jessica observed. "Do you know any?"

Cindy smiled. "As a matter of fact, I do know a Jewish boy. He is one of our best customers."

"Really?" Frank began sorting the bean sprouts.

Cindy's grin widened. "In fact, you've not been too happy about the time I've spent talking with him when he was here. Remember Ben Feinberg?" Cindy bit her lip to keep from being too obvious.

"The big boy?" Frank looked at his wife. "The one who eats the Kung Pao Squid every time?"

"Exactly." Cindy nodded.

"For heaven's sake!" Jessica threw up her hands. "Why didn't you tell us that you were discussing religion?"

"Indeed!" Frank shook his finger at Cindy. "We highly respect such discussion. After all, we can learn from all religions."

"A Jewish boy," Jessica mused. "How interesting."

"Does Jewish boy understand the Bible?" Frank asked.

"I must have more conversation with him." Cindy tried to cover the widening grin with her hand. "I hope you will not worry if we have more discussion times."

"Of course not." Frank picked up a handful of mushrooms. "We want our daughter to be as well informed as any American."

"Then I will continue my religious meetings," Cindy said with a straight face.

One of the waiters burst through the kitchen door. "A young man ask for Miss Cindy. Very large boy."

"His name?" Frank's voice became stern.

"Something like Fine . . ."

Frank nodded his head to one side in deference. "A fortuitous moment. You must continue the religious talk with the Jewish boy."

"If you insist." Cindy bowed in respect to her father. Her guide dog led Cindy out of the kitchen.

CHAPTER
4

Piercing the veil of time left Seradim disconcerted and disoriented. The endlessness of eternity turned into a universe of boundaries and finitude, confining and restricting. Although he was invisible to the world of animals and people, Seradim stared at the endless variety of tangible shapes everywhere. Time left him feeling chained, inhibited by an unseen force that hung around his very essence like a ponderous weight.

"The earth is really quite a beautiful place," Michael said. "Don't let the limitations confuse you. Water, mountains, trees, humans of infinite variety—the place can be quite intoxicating. The Creator does all things well."

Seradim saw the earth both kaleidoscopically and in particular at the same time, like a television screen within a television screen. "Yes, it is a wondrous and good place, though very strange to me. How could there be warfare in a place like this?"

"Let me show you something else before we cover that dimension." Michael pointed toward the continent of Africa.

"Follow me." In an instant Seradim stood in the heart of the Serengeti Plain around Mount Kilimanjaro. "Watch." Michael gestured toward a herd of giraffes loping through the trees.

Seradim shook with laughter. "What strange creatures! Absolutely amazing."

"Now, look toward the mountains."

A family of gorillas lumbered out of the rain forest, babies swinging from beneath their parents' chests. They chomped on bamboo and tree limbs, serenely unaware of their observers.

"These are humans?" Seradim marveled.

"No, no, gorillas and giraffes are animals, another aspect of creation."

"I'm very confused," the reassigned angel confessed. "Where do humans fit in?"

Michael nodded understandingly. "The earth is made up of three orders. Plants cover the planet with greenery and provide food. The beasts live off the plants and each other and roam the forests and plains. But humans are the highest order, living off both plants and animals." Michael pointed toward the north and snapped his fingers.

The ancient city of Cairo appeared before them. Teeming multitudes milled through the streets and marketplaces. People of many races drove wagons and cars through town. Children played on the sidewalks. Babies nestled against their mothers' breasts.

Seradim was speechless and could only point in wonder.

"Quite something, aren't they?" Michael beckoned for Seradim to follow him into the city. "Humans are a part of the physical world like the beasts." He pointed at a man walking a dog down the street. "But they also have the capacity to be spiritual, to touch and experience our dimension."

"Never could I have imagined such a thing!"

"Frankly, I envy them," Michael confided. "They have the ability to enjoy the best of both worlds, heaven and earth. We don't have the same capacity."

"We can't become like them?"

"Nor they like us," Michael answered. "The Father plans eventually to give them fully completed and glorified bodies, looking something like what they already have. But we're really only their eternal servants. We look in on their world but can never experience the earth as they do. In a spiritual sense, humans were actually made in the very image of God."

Seradim stared at the people. "So what am I doing here?"

"The Father is giving you the opportunity to help these creatures endure the final great tribulation period that is coming soon."

"All of them?"

"No, we are only responsible for a particular family. The Larry Feinberg family are Jews and have a very important role to play in the impending tribulation events. We will guard them."

"These people are in danger?"

"As a matter of fact, we're just in time to meet them and their enemies at the same moment." Michael looked toward the West. "We're going to a place called California. We'll stand a safe distance just above their house in order to watch what's going on. Ready?"

Seradim attuned his mind to Michael's thoughts. "I'm hanging on."

Instantly the two angels hovered just beyond the Feinbergs' living room in Newport Beach, looking down on the scene unfolding below.

"Ruth?" Ben Feinberg called to his sister. "The football game is about to start. Ruth?" The young man turned on the television.

"There's one of our charges," Michael pointed out. "You're going to find Ben to be quite a courageous and remarkable young man."

Seradim studied Ben's eyes for a moment. "Obviously, he has a very good heart."

"We must protect him."

"Look." Seradim pointed to the fireplace. "What are those ugly, knurled things? They don't look like animals or people, but they're certainly not one of us."

Michael nodded. "They're demons, fallen angels. They're part of the answer to your question about how warfare happens on this planet. Because you are seeing them through moral vision, their ugliness is particularly pronounced."

"What grotesque creatures! Surely, they're not like us!" Seradim protested.

"Yes and no. They can take on quite handsome forms when they want to, but you are seeing them from an angel's point of view. They are really no more tangible to humans than we are. Yet they are more like us than them."

Seradim studied the wrinkled creatures with shrunken red eyes and twisted bodies. Their arms were thin projections sticking out of their bulbous greenish-black bodies; on the end of their skinny fingers were sharp, protruding spikes. Each face was a convoluted expression of pure malice and envy.

"Who are they?" Seradim asked.

"A couple of ancient manifestations of malice," Michael explained. "Homelas's specialty is subverting young women. He has always fed on lust like people eat food. His insatiable desires turned into a hatred for what he can never

completely consume. Consequently, Homelas enjoys trying to destroy beautiful women. No end to what he's willing to do, either!"

"The other . . . thing?" Seraphim pointed at Malafidus.

"He fell along with the lower angels that came down with
Lucifer, but he never quite got the memory of the goodness of heaven out of his system. When the mindless wretch
encounters a good person, he feels a deep twinge of guilt.
His warped mind reasons that destroying the virtuous will
set him free from his pain. Malafidus is the embodiment
of misery created by acting against one's higher self."

"How could creatures of light have become such expressions of repulsion?"

"Sin infects creatures," Michael explained. "Utterly
destroys. Frightening, isn't it?"

"Let's get him!" Seradim doubled his fist. "I'll wring that
ugly snake's neck and—"

"No!" Michael restrained his charge. "Don't be impulsive. You have too much to learn before you start mixing it
up. Just listen until you get a much better feel for what the
world is like."

Michael thought into Seraphim's consciousness. "The
demons have no idea we are listening. Their infernal arrogance causes them to be so self-absorbed, they seldom notice
until we are within striking distance. Thinking themselves
to be omniscient, they end up being quite stupid."

"Do we attack now?"

Michael smiled broadly. "No, we bide our time. We know
a secret that Evil can never grasp. Lucifer and his minions
only exist because the Father allows it. Even their schemes
and attacks can be used in the plan of God. We give them
plenty of rope, and eventually they hang themselves."

Ben sat down beside his father. "I thought maybe Ruth would watch the game with us since UCLA is playing."

"Maybe Ruth took a stroll down to the ocean," Larry Feinberg observed.

Seradim looked confused. "Where is the girl?"

"She lied to her family and went out the back door to meet a young man," Michael answered. "Ruth is putting herself in jeopardy."

"Then let's go help!"

"Not yet, Seradim. Ruth is one of those creatures who learns best through pain. We'll simply stand back and let those two rotten characters turn up the heat. When the time is right, we'll do what we can."

■ ■ ■

The two demons listened carefully to Larry Feinberg and his son discuss Ruth's disappearance.

Homelas laughed coarsely. "There we have it! Just the right beginning. A few lies to start the adventure rolling. Let's cut out of the family scene and see what sweet little Ruthie is really up to."

Being essentially energy without physical substance, Homelas and Malafidus could stand in the midst of human history and watch events unfold while remaining invisible to people. Yet the two demons operated with the same intention and sense of physical presence as any other person in the world. As angels did in heaven, they simply "thought" themselves to wherever they wished to be.

"I'll locate her." Malafidus closed his eyes tightly to access the central gathering focus of evil intelligence. Instantly, the interconnection of diabolic awareness scanned the world for information. The response came with the speed of light. "Well, well, sweet innocent Miss Feinberg is off being a naughty girl with our old hero Jimmy Harrison. Where better to have a secret rendezvous than the amusement park out there in the bay? Let's go to Balboa Island." Instantly, the two evil emanations reappeared in the center of the amusement park.

"Are you slick or what?" Jimmy Harrison pulled Ruth closer to him as the Ferris wheel made its final turn.

Ruth looked out over the park and the ocean surrounding the island. "Most fun place in Southern California." As the wheel settled toward the ground, she watched people getting off other rides and entering the little amusement shops around the island. "But I think I like you better."

Homelas and Malafidus perched on the edge of the bucket seat behind Jimmy and Ruth and watched over the couple's shoulders. "Going to be a piece of cake." Homelas chuckled.

Jimmy laughed. "How did you shake free of your family on New Year's Day without them blowing a gasket?" He slid his hand down her arm and into her palm, nestling against her.

"They think I'm at the movies with my college roommates, Heather and Amy. The old man would blow his mind if he knew I was taking a spin with the guy who sold us my car last week."

Jimmy smiled and bit her ear teasingly, but he didn't like the implication. From the moment the Feinbergs wheeled their big black Mercedes into the car lot, he knew his place in this rich family's scheme of things. Obviously, the mother and father saw him as a cut beneath them and certainly beneath their lovely, indulged daughter. To Jimmy the challenge of seducing Ruth was as intriguing as wringing the top dollar from their eel-skin wallets.

Homelas leaned over and whispered in Jimmy's ear. "You're just as good as the Feinbergs. Teach those pretentious snobs a lesson. Get the girl. She's insecure. . . . Make her feel important. Call her a real woman."

"You're my kind of woman." Jimmy grinned and watched Ruth's eyes light up when he put a heavy emphasis on *woman*.

The Ferris wheel came to a stop and the happy couple got out and started across the park. The two demons fell in at their side.

"Just what is your old man's line of work?" Jimmy put his arm around Ruth's waist.

"He's a shrink. Thinks he's God when it comes to sizing up people. Can you imagine, we were barely out of your car lot when he told us you were some kind of character disorder, a con-man type."

Jimmy's smile hardened. The psychiatrist's diagnosis cut through his facade and made him nervous. He felt uncomfortable, inferior, being only a twenty-five-year-old, dishonest used-car salesman.

Homelas concentrated intensely to push an image into the front of Jimmy's mind. He imagined a little boy sitting on the front pew of his father's church, feeling small, obvious, and insignificant. People were staring at the child and increasing his sense of being an outsider. The little boy desperately wanted to be important but was sure he wasn't.

For a few moments Jimmy forgot where he was and stumbled into an empty baby stroller parked on the midway. "Oh!" He grabbed his shin. "Some idiot left the wheels in my way."

"You all right?"

"Sure." Jimmy hobbled forward, trying not to swear in front of Ruth. "Let's truck over to my car. I've got a couple of joints hidden under the seat of my Corvette. How about a little grass to loosen us up?"

Ruth caught her breath. She had never used drugs before. The idea frightened her.

Malafidus watched Ruth's eyes drop toward the ground. Although tall, she easily tended toward the heavy side. Her weight had always been an issue. The demon instantly pushed an impulse toward her mind. "You won't get many chances like this one. Don't blow the promise by being a prude. The last thing a real man like Jimmy wants is an uptight little prig. After all, everyone smokes dope today. Just go with the flow."

"Sure." Her voice oozed hesitancy.

Instantly, Jimmy knew Ruth hadn't done marijuana and might get high quickly. "Well, let's give it a try."

The couple cut across the park, winding their way past popcorn vendors and men selling balloons. Straight ahead the ferry was bringing another load of cars across.

"My father's a real pain!" Ruth suddenly blurted out. "He's so self-confident all the time!"

"Tell me about it," Jimmy sneered. "I hate my old man. What a big-time jerk."

"What does he do?"

Jimmy froze. That was the one question he hadn't expected, and the answer might blow everything. Jimmy gazed into Ruth's innocent, all-accepting gaze. She was really on the hook, but Ruth was Jewish.

"Come on, honey," Ruth cooed. "There isn't anything you can't share with me."

Jimmy's eyes narrowed. He let "honey" roll around a moment. No question Ruth was going for him. "He's a Christian minister," Jimmy answered haltingly. "Has a big church in Dallas, Texas. My old man's a big daddy in Big D."

"Seriously?" Ruth asked incredulously.

"Turns you off, doesn't it?"

"No, no." A sly grin crossed Ruth's face. "I've just never been around preacher types."

"I avoid him at all costs. . . . The fanatic spent his whole life saving souls at the expense of me and my four brothers. He was so busy making God happy, Mr. Holy wouldn't even take in one of our baseball games. Don't worry. Reverend Big-Time has taken care of any interest I'll ever have in God or religion. I don't buy anything the old creep is preaching."

Homelas quickly whispered in Ruth's mind, "Your head-shrinking father didn't spend enough time with you growing up either!"

Ruth stopped and abruptly kissed Jimmy passionately on the mouth. She reached up and ran her hands through his hair, breathing heavily. "I like everything about you. Don't worry about some family hang-up. My world's not any different."

"Wow!" Homelas rolled his eyes. "I thought we were going to be in trouble. Slid past that sticky wicket just in time."

"Great turn of events." Malafidus's black eyes danced. "I was only counting on a little teenage rebellion mixed with good old-fashioned lust, but we've got some deep layers of emotional pain here. Maybe we'll be able to wreck the life of the seducer himself. Two for the price of one."

CHAPTER
5

Our immediate task," Michael said, "is to help you understand how evil operates. Only then will you become effective in combating the enemy."

Strolling along the edge of the ocean, Michael pointed out across the deep blue. "Demons fear water. It reminds them on a subconscious level of the depths of their own depraved thoughts, feelings, and motives. Water also suggests cleansing, healing. Demons avoid both like the plague."

"So we're not likely to run into the adversary down here?"

Michael laughed, "Not probable." Michael motioned toward the horizon. "Too wholesome. . . . You can enjoy the glorious beauty of the coast while I instruct. God didn't give people any better gift than the ocean."

Seradim watched the endlessly changing pattern of waves breaking over each other. Brilliant orange sunlight blended into the blue sea and suddenly changed colors, becoming a sparkling mass of red, purple, and aquamarine constantly drifting apart, then the dark blue-green of the deep broke through the whitecaps again.

"Water makes me feel peaceful," Seradim thought. "No pattern or rhythm exists in the endless changes, and yet the movement is completely with order."

Michael completed Seradim's thought. "And such is how God's plan operates. Often events do not appear to be part of any ultimate scheme, and yet everything occurs within the parameters of the Father's grand design. Even those ugly instigators of chaos cannot escape the divine context."

Seradim pondered the explanation. "Since the Father is orderly, such consequence would follow. Tell me more about how these evil creatures work on humans, causing them so much trouble."

"Demons use several basic strategies. Those two conniving creeps are undoubtedly employing one of their most common and successful methods right now. Manipulating human beings' feelings and imaginations, they will try to tempt the girl and her boyfriend to act on lustful images the demons conjure up in their minds. Couples often make the mistake of assuming that inner emotional tugs are real and not merely a momentary device to create imbalance or distort perspective. Unfortunately, the approach works quite well."

"What else is possible?"

"They create unfounded fear or use anxiety in exaggerated doses to panic the frightened into a self-protecting course of action at the expense of others. Fear is as effective a prod as thunder is in stampeding cattle."

"Humans overreact?"

"Most of the time." Michael watched the waves crash against the breakers just ahead. "Their survival instinct turns into apprehension when they are threatened. Children have to develop the ability to trust and have faith. Some never do and are constantly targets for chaos. Unfortunately, a few are permanently infected with paranoia and live their entire lives diseased with dread. The only remedy for fear is to learn to have constant confidence in God's provision. Fear will either make or break a human!"

"Simply describing dread gives me a tingling sensation of apprehension." Seradim shivered.

"Lucifer often uses another method on the more devout," Michael continued. "One of the Evil One's favorite disguises is to appear as an angel of light, deceiving people through false revelations. Church folks tumble for that old scheme all the time."

"Church people?"

"Some humans are already committed to the love of the Father and are His personal possessions. Remember? The people who have the life of God in them?"

"Oh, yes. The blessed ones."

"Periodically, Evil will detour these folks off on a tangent. They'll think some surge of enthusiasm is a divine revelation. Much like a runaway imagination, spiritual deception can create even more havoc than plain old temptation."

"Our enemy is quite crafty and capable."

"Seradim, never doubt his tenacity. Lucifer's brilliance often turns into stupidity and his intelligence into madness, but he doesn't stop. If given the opportunity, Lucifer will invade and completely take over a human life. At other times, people don't even realize they are being sucked into the vortex of his intentions."

The new Guardian watched the waves creeping up the beach. "Like the tides pulled in by an invisible force?"

Michael nodded his head. "Evil is sometimes subtle, like gentle waves, and other times as obvious as a hurricane. Lucifer's diabolical storms work on three levels. Of course, everyone is tempted. That's just part of the human condition. But when demonic forces find a really effective good person, they attempt to oppress the individual. Their assault creates depression and overwhelming sorrow, especially if they can generate some bitterness in that person toward himself or toward others."

"That's when we step in?"

"We are called on to help drive Lucifer's forces out," Michael explained, "but the spirits only look for new territory. Because demons never die, they have a way of hanging around for centuries, just waiting for a new opportunity to attack again. The worst kind are the most persistent and destructive."

"Give me an example."

"Molech is a good case study. The demon hated children. After centuries of spiritual intrusion in weak and perverse people, he finally got himself recognized for several centuries as a false god in Canaan. The ancient Canaanites practiced child sacrifice to Molech.

"When the Jews entered the land, they destroyed the idols and put an end to appeasing Molech, but the diabolical creature's pursuit of death was relentless. The demon moved over to Tenochtitlán in Mexico, and got a similar system going with the Aztecs, using young maidens as sacrifices to satisfy his appetite. The Spanish conquerors stamped out the practice, and Molech went north to bide his time. For a while, Molech's spirit worked overtime in the Nazi death camps. Today the demon is behind the abortion mills across America. Get the picture?"

Indignation welled up in Seradim as only righteous wrath can in the innocent. "I will seize Molech by the throat. By all that is holy, I will bring an end to his influence!" The angel kicked a spray of sand across the beach. "Bring on this vile thing!"

"All in due time, Seradim," Michael said, laying a hand on his young charge's shoulder. "The important thing is to make sure *we* are part of God's divine plan and don't go off on our own ill-conceived tangents. As angels we must remember that we are part of something much larger than our own sense of outrage. We are members of an army and must stay under our commander."

"But you're always by yourself, Michael."

"Oh, far from it! Most of the time I've battled as one of the Lord's legion. . . . Let me show you a story." Michael recalled the era of Elisha, the prophet of Israel. Once again he saw Elisha's servant standing at dawn in the ancient city of Dothan. Seradim immediately experienced the scene as if it were happening for the first time. The high walls of the city rose above the horizon. Palm trees swayed in the hot summer breeze.

Seradim pointed at images dancing in his imagination. Rank upon rank of chariots driven by armed soldiers bore down on the city gates. Archers put arrows to their bows. Men with spears were poised. "A war is about to begin," Seradim exclaimed. "The people in the city are in great jeopardy."

"Listen carefully," Michael instructed, "and simply watch."

Elisha's servant burst into his master's simple room in a watchtower perched high above the fortress city. "Wake up!" he shouted. "The city is surrounded by chariots, horses, men with spears. They have come for you. We can't escape. What shall we do?" He wrung his hands and pulled his dark brown robe tightly around his shoulders.

Throwing the sheet back, Elisha calmly walked to the window and looked down on the city walls. "As you say, we are outnumbered."

"Oh, my Lord, the king of Aram hates you. The Arameans will slay you. All hope is lost!" The servant put his hands to his face and wept.

"Now, now." Elisha put his arm around the young man. "There's no reason for panic. We are more than they who are with them."

The servant looked out the window again and then down at the emptying streets as people ran for protection. *Fear has affected his mind,* he reasoned. *Elisha retreats into madness.*

The prophet pointed to the hills. "Son, you must learn to trust the angels." Elisha bowed his head and prayed. "O Lord, open my servant's eyes, so he may see."

As the scene flashed through Seradim's mind, he saw the prophet's servant begin to blink rapidly and then look over the walls again. To his amazement, countless chariots of fire appeared, standing behind the enemy soldiers' lines. Suddenly, the hosts of the Lord raced down the slopes toward the Arameans. Seradim instantly recognized the lead charioteer.

"That's you, Michael! You're leading the Lord's army."

"One of my finest hours. We struck the king of Aram's men blind and Elisha led them like helpless babies to the King of Samaria. The result was so dramatic, the meandering bands of Aram never returned again."

"Wonderful!" Seradim applauded.

"But did you see how many angels were there? Keep looking! Quite an army. Don't ever forget that we outnumber the grains of sand on the seashore. Don't forget it! Our job is to help humans remember."

CHAPTER
6

"Follow me." Michael's thoughts guided Seradim toward Balboa Island. "I'm going to give you some field experience in how the demons influence humans. We'll check in on those two fiends, Homelas and Malafidus. By now they're already hard at work on Jimmy Harrison and Ruth Feinberg."

Seradim and Michael saw the couple walking lazily through the crowds at Balboa Park. Homelas and Malafidus hovered at their side, oblivious to the surveillance going on just above them.

Michael pointed to the two young people and the ghouls following them. "Let me explain a few things about what you are seeing. You need to understand perception.

"Humans fundamentally perceive through their five senses. Of course, they are capable of spiritual vision, but often only the poets and artists use the ability very well. Consequently, Jimmy and Ruth don't know we are here." He pointed at the demons. "You and I see moral reality.

The despicableness you see in the devil's errand boys is a true reflection of their very essence."

"Why don't they see us?"

"Creatures of evil have a natural aversion to goodness. Basically they avoid looking in our direction much like humans turn away from bad odors. If they perceived our presence, the vile perverts would quickly discover we're here and see us as bright shining lights. In due time, they'll discover we are on their trail. Right now we need to concentrate on the young couple."

Ruth took Jimmy's hand. "My parents have got some rich Jewish doctor or lawyer staked out for me." She paused and tossed her long black hair. "But a long time ago, I realized that my father lives his life by the book. All I ever get out of him is what the latest psychiatric party line is. I figure out what he wants to hear, and I just feed it back." Ruth's eyes snapped with fire. "I'm sick of being analyzed by him every time something goes wrong." She thought for a moment. "I'm going to have to go to the movies to cover my tracks. I think I'd better not do a joint today. Maybe next time."

Jimmy smiled.

"Watch carefully," Michael instructed. "Our bad boys are pushing images into each of their minds. While the demons can't read their thoughts, those two jerks can impress ideas on them in response to what they see going on. Right now they're pushing lust."

Jimmy squeezed Ruth tightly and kissed her neck. "Next time, we'll make sure that we have plenty of uninterrupted time. I'll call you at your apartment at the university."

"You bet." Ruth put her arms around his neck. "I hate to run, but if I don't, I'm going to get into problems with the traffic." Ruth started for her own car and then turned back. "I can't wait for us to be together again. Just maybe I'm falling in love with you, Jimmy Harrison." Ruth ran back, kissed him passionately again, and then ran for her car.

Jimmy stood beside his highly polished red Corvette and watched her drive away. He wore a self-satisfied grin.

"Our adversaries have scored points," Michael noted. "Ruth's rebellious attitude toward her parents prepared the way. Jimmy's current lascivious attraction to anything in skirts set the stage. The two young people might as well have sent an engraved invitation to attack."

"Our charges are in danger?"

"In a limited way. Right now their emotions are spinning. Unfortunately, that's how the first step is taken. Things can quickly go from bad to worse."

"Then we must charge in!"

"And do what?" Michael's question betrayed his amusement.

"Well . . . I . . . don't . . . exactly know."

The senior angel laughed. "My young friend, you're going to prove to be a great warrior, but you do need a little more preparation. No, Ruth and Jimmy don't need us just this moment. They will have to face a number of truths about themselves. Let's follow our two corrupt adversaries. If you listen intently, you can pick up what they are saying. You will naturally want to censor out much of their conversation, but fight the impulse. Everything you see and hear will be repugnant, but this is necessary to our task. Ready?"

The junior angel apprehensively shook his head. "I hadn't bargained for a walk through the mud."

Homelas and Malafidus watched Ruth drive away, and then the two demons slowly ascended above the earth.

"Piece of cake," Homelas boasted to his colleague. "This one is already in the bag."

"Don't be so sure," Malafidus warned. "Our nemesis has this weird thing about protecting Jews. They won't let the girl go easily. We must pay attention."

"Okay. But they won't pick up on the caper until we've been able to do real damage. Look. The girl's a virgin and she's got the hots for him. If we set it up right, Harrison ought to be able to get her in bed on the next go-around."

"Possibly. But I've had angels discover one of these operations and just appear out of nowhere." Malafidus swore. "After all, the girl has been raised with strong moral values."

"Forget it." Homelas pointed toward the north. "Let's take a break and really enjoy ourselves for a while."

"Where to?"

"Let's cruise up toward the Brentwood and North Hollywood area. Great porno shops up there." The sun was slowly sinking over the ocean. Shadows fell across the streets.

"I'm with you."

The two demons slowly rose above Balboa beach and then leisurely floated toward the north. Michael and Seradim ascended with them and moved back, giving the demons plenty of distance. Like feathers in the breeze, the two drifted along the freeways and over the endless rows of buildings until they settled around the Northridge area.

"Let's swoop down over the Sunset Boulevard area," Malafidus suggested and pointed south.

"Sure. Lots of action around there."

The two demons dropped down over the busy thoroughfare. A woman in an extremely tight short skirt was standing on a street corner. Her high leather boots came up to her knees, and the low-cut red blouse was sheer and skimpy.

"Look at that!" Homelas pointed at the woman. "A really good sign."

A sports car slowed at the curb. The driver made quick obscene remarks to the woman. She smiled and got in. The car sped away as she snuggled closer to the man.

"A-h-h-h," Malafidus sighed. "Makes me feel warm all over."

"Look!" Homelas pointed toward a low building with a bright neon sign flashing *Strip Joint*. "Let's try it."

The two demons shot through the walls into the topless bar. The lights were low and dim. Smoke hung heavy in the air. Men and women sat around small circular tables, watching naked women writhe in endless contortions to the loud, thumping drumbeat of the disco music. Strobe lights flashed in bright blues and greens. Men laughed crudely and hollered suggestive directions to the dancers. Wearing virtually nothing, women mingled among the customers, talking, buying drinks, laughing, and enticing.

"This *is* the place." Malafidus giggled in glee. "I've been working in and out of here for two decades. Feels like home."

"N-a-a-w," Homelas shook his head. "I didn't come up here to work. I just want to relax and absorb the atmosphere. Recharge my batteries. All this unbridled lust makes me feel s-o-o-o good."

"Yeah, sure, but it's hard for me not to zero in on somebody."

"Do what makes you happy." Homelas tossed the suggestion aside indifferently.

Far above the scene, Seradim turned away. "Let's destroy them now!" Seradim's thoughts were twinged with disgust.

"All things must run their course until the Holy One's plan is fulfilled." Michael motioned toward the boundaries of eternity. "Watch," Michael instructed Seradim. Endless scenes of past human history raced by the new Guardian like in a fast-forward motion picture, playing out the entire history of humanity in a matter of seconds.

"The Heavenly Father gave humans great promise and they have made great strides. You will be surprised to know the Father also allowed extraordinary latitude to the Evil One. Lucifer has never understood that he still has a place in the plan of God. Don't worry. The day of the final great battle will come, and then we will have our revenge. Homelas, Malafidus, and all the rest will receive their due."

Seradim stared in awe as the images of history slowly dissolved. "I can stand no more."

"My friend," Michael said in a heavy voice, "you have certainly not seen the worst."

"But I have seen all I can stand for now. Please, I want away from here."

"We can leave them," Michael concluded. "This place will keep the demons occupied for a while. I am sorry to expose you to the battle so quickly, but we don't have much time. The final conflict is not far away."

■ ■ ■

Customers poured into the Golden Dragon up to the moment of closing. "Happy New Year," Frank greeted the last patrons paying their checks. "Prosperity to you!" He waved good-bye and turned on the neon *Closed* sign. "Must have said that one thousand times! Not say again for twelve months!" He hurried back to the cash register.

The busboys quickly cleared the dishes in a frantic effort to get home or to the last party of the season. Frank cleared out the cash drawer, cramming the wad of bills into a bank deposit bag.

"Wonderful!" He chuckled. "We do very, very well tonight." He slammed the drawer shut and hustled to the private office in the rear of the kitchen.

Jessica sat just inside with her back to the door.

"Look," Frank held up the bulging money bag. "What a haul!"

Jessica slowly turned around, her eyes filled with tears.

Frank stopped, stunned. "What . . . what has happened to my honorable wife?"

Jessica buried her face in her hands.

"Please. Please speak to me."

The Chinese woman finally looked up. "I try not to think of our family. I push their faces and memory out of my mind . . . but they wouldn't stay gone today. Oh, Frank. I am so lonely. We have no friends here. Only Cindy. And I worry if any of them survived." She sobbed. "Or if they died terrible deaths."

Frank put his arm around his wife and for the first time in a very long time tears rolled down his cheeks. "Yes," he answered slowly. "We are so very alone in this land. No one stands with us." His voice trailed away. "No person, no god."

CHAPTER
7

Michael lifted Seradim up and out of the corruption on Sunset Boulevard and whisked him away. "Let me show you another method Lucifer uses to deceive the gullible and the grieving. We are going to visit a family that will have future importance to the Feinbergs. Think with me about a town called Lake Forest, California. We are going to visit a Chinese family."

The pair of angels envisioned, and were instantly transported to, a small house several blocks from the Golden Dragon restaurant. Seradim studied the simple stucco structure with a sign on the front door: Your Fortune Told Immediately. He noticed the symbols of the zodiac hung in a window and a placard on the wall that promised, "Contact your lost loved ones again!"

"Frank and Jessica Wong are inside," Michael explained. "They are Chinese immigrants. Their parents were Daoist, ancestor worshipers. The Wongs' daughter, Cindy, is the apple of Ben Feinberg's eye. Right now, Frank and Jessica are trying to get in touch with Jessica's father, Chin Lee, who died just before they came to America. She hopes to talk with him this evening."

"Talk to the dead?"

Michael nodded gravely. "Let's perch on top of the house and watch."

Seradim looked down on the Wongs, who were seated at a circular table with a bowl of green incense in the center. Gray smoke curled upward. Their eyes closed, the Wongs' fingertips touched those of a middle-aged Chinese woman across the table. Behind her were statues of dragon-headed people with frightening faces. Burning candles filled the room with the smell of hot wax and pungent incense.

"Help us, Yong Lou," Jessica Wong begged, tears running down her wrinkled and worn face. Her hair was still jet black, pulled back in a tight knot behind her head, making her plain face look severe. "Please bring back my honorable father, Chin Lee."

Her eyes tightly closed, the fortune-teller gripped the table fiercely. "Your father is coming now," Yong Lou said. "His spirit is returning to us."

Michael tapped Seradim gently and pointed knowingly at the woman's face. "Here it comes."

Yong Lou's expression slowly changed. The pleasant smile gave way to a contorted grimace. She caught her breath and rocked back in the chair. Yong Lou's lips moved mechanically, but nothing came out. Then a low guttural sound like a growling man slowly slipped through her parted lips. "My child," the new voice drawled, "I am here with you."

"Father?" Jessica Wong clenched her eyes even more tightly. "Honorable father are you among us?"

"I have come back to speak to you," the rumbling voice continued. "To tell you of my happiness where I am."

"Oh, Father," Jessica cried out, "where do you dwell?"

"In the abode of your ancestors where the great spirits rule. I have found the blessedness of which Buddha spoke, the place of complete enlightenment."

"Wonderful! Wonderful!" Jessica clamped her hands to the table. "I am so relieved. I knew you were a good man."

"I offered incense in the temples," the voice continued. "I drank the blood of the sacred snakes and always placed rice on our ancestors' graves. I have been rewarded."

"Thank you, thank you," Frank Wong joined in. "Chin Lee, we need direction to know what to believe in this new and strange land. Help us see the truth."

Yong Lou's body became rigid, and she caught her breath. The incense continued to rise from the bowl in front of her face.

Michael thought softly, "Seradim, I want you to look very carefully at the fortune-teller. Look inward through the layers of her being and see what is dwelling at the center."

To Seradim's amazement, he began to see a form within the woman's body, as if another person were wearing her body. The inner shape was ugly and gnarled like Homelas and Malafidus.

"The woman is possessed," Michael explained. "Many times séances are charades, just magic tricks made to look like something is happening when the whole thing is a hoax. Not this time."

"She can't be talking to the dead!"

"Of course not! Necromancy is an old trick of Lucifer's. He uses master ventriloquist demons to slip into the minds of fools who toy with evil. Yong Lou's family has been possessed for centuries. They have a long tradition of fortune-telling and calling up the dead. What she thought was an inheritance, a gift from her grandmother, was simply the demon moving from grandmother to grandchild."

"And now the Wongs are victims."

"Not yet, but they are being deceived. We must stop this exploitation lest they really get hooked into this calamity."

"Aren't there any warnings for such good people?"

"Unfortunately, the Wongs never read the Bible. If they had, they would know such practices are an anathema to the Holy One. The law of God forbids divination, horoscopes, psychic enchanters, witches, charmers, wizards, and necromancers. The Bible warned that these practices are condemned . . . forever!"

"We must teach the Wongs," Seradim interrupted.

"They have already heard some of the truth when their daughter introduced them to the Bible a few nights ago. . . . Now we're going to do something about this current situation." Michael pointed at the fortune-teller. "Follow me."

Michael gently descended behind the Chinese woman. For a moment he concentrated on the meaning of love. The harder he pondered, the brighter his personal radiance became. The demon inside Yong Lou slowly turned, as if distracted from his task. At the sight of the radiance of pure light, the creature recoiled and the woman shook violently.

"Away from me!" the demon protested.

The demonic words came out of Yong Lou's mouth in an explosion of agony. Frank and Jessica jumped. Their eyes popped open in a terrified stare.

"You can't touch me," the demon threatened. "Leave me, or I will destroy you!"

Frank and Jessica leaped up, their chairs hitting the floor. Yong Lou's eyes were fixed, and drool ran down the corner of her mouth.

As Michael stretched forth his arm like a sword of light, an increasing aura of goodness settled around the room.

"I have the power of death!" the demon cried. "Evil must triumph." Suddenly the demon gagged. "I can't stand the smell." The grotesque thing backed out of Yong Lou's body, and she fell face forward on the table.

Frank Wong grabbed his wife's hand. "Run! We are about to be attacked!" They bolted for the door.

The demon writhed and twisted in pain but finally detached from the fortune-teller. Michael advanced, driving the spirit in front of him.

"A-h-h-h!" the creature screamed. "I can't stand any more goodness." He shot through the walls into the darkness outside.

After a few moments, Yong Lou opened her eyes. She wiped her mouth and looked around the room. She saw the two overturned chairs on the floor. The front door was wide open.

"Oh, my." She stared at the mess. "What happened here?"

Yong Lou slowly stood up. With halting steps, she walked around the table and uprighted the chairs. "How strange. I remember the Wongs coming but not leaving." She looked around the dim room. "I need more light," she decided and switched on an overhead lamp. "Yes, what this house needs is much more light!"

CHAPTER

8

Michael pointed south of Highway 5, toward Irvine. "I want to teach you more about what humans call psychology, the dynamics behind human behavior. At the same time, I'll give you some insight into Larry Feinberg. Let's go down and watch the good doctor at work."

Seradim followed Michael's lead and zoomed down toward the Physicians Medical Building just blocks away from the Orange County John Wayne Airport. Michael led his charge down the pastel colored corridor on the fifth floor. Potted palm trees and flowering shrubs lined the hall.

"Doctor Feinberg's in session. He's seen this young woman a couple of times before. Her parents are long-term missionaries in New Guinea, where they translated the Bible into a new language.

"Unfortunately, their daughter struggles with some severe mental and emotional problems. You will notice that Larry does not have a very charitable view of Christianity. The freethinker's mind-set only applies to socially approved causes." The two angels walked through the wall.

Bookcases filled with leather-bound volumes lined the walls of the exquisite office. Above a red leather couch hung an oil painting of the surging ocean coastline. Larry sat in a large overstuffed chair across from a distraught young woman.

"Look, Dr. Feinberg." Louise wrung her hands as she struggled to choose her words. "I think about suicide all the time. I just can't get the thought out of my mind."

Dr. Feinberg nodded sympathetically. "Feels like you're trapped under a huge black cloud, doesn't it?"

"Yes!" The black-haired, twenty-six-year-old woman brightened for the first time.

"It's like morning never comes. You live in a perpetual night."

"Exactly. Oh, yes, I can't get away from the darkness."

"Louise, you're struggling with depression. You don't really want to kill yourself. Your feelings create those thoughts."

"But I've prayed for help so often."

Larry almost sneered, but instantly recovered his demeanor. "I've always found mood brighteners do a whole lot more for people than prayer," he chided. "The real need is for us to get to the bottom of your depression."

Michael nudged his young charge. "Of course, the psychiatrist is right about the cause of her self-destructive inclinations, but all humans need to feel important. They have a great vulnerability in this area. One of the reasons Larry likes being a psychiatrist is that he can be the expert for everyone. He's had lots of trouble with his kids because of this tendency."

Seradim nodded. "Obviously, a target area for the demons."

"Exactly," Michael confirmed. "Louise's problems started in her need to feel important. The need is easily manipulated. Keep watching Larry as he works."

"Seems like I've been depressed forever," Louise moaned. "Since my parents went back to the mission field six months ago, the gloom has been impenetrable."

"Did you want them to go back?"

"Of course. Their work is very, very important."

"More important than you?"

Louise looked shocked. "Well . . . my goodness . . . I never thought about . . ."

"Yes, I think you have. I think you've resented always being left behind by your parents."

"Absolutely not!" Louise's brown eyes snapped. "How could I possibly stand in the way of the work of the gospel?"

"Yes, how could you stand in their way without being a bad person?" Larry spoke gently. "But you still resent being pushed aside."

"Never!" Louise clenched her fist. "I'm not that kind of person. You're making me sound . . . selfish . . . my parents insensitive."

"You're hurt, Louise, and you're very angry with them as well as with yourself."

"No!" Louise's voice raised with more than a hint of agitation. "No! I tell you . . . I mean, I want you to know that . . ." The woman began shaking. "I can't be angry," her tone took on the feel of pain. "What kind of a person gets angry at godly parents?"

"A normal human being," Dr. Feinberg answered sympathetically. "A good, sensitive, caring person."

Louise choked and grimaced. "Good?" Tears ran down her cheeks. "How could I possibly be good?" Suddenly

Louise began sobbing so violently, Larry worried that she might slide from the chair.

As the flood of tears ebbed, he commented, "You've been very angry for a long time, Louise. Your suicidal thoughts are only one symptom of an inability to deal with your anger toward your parents."

"But I shouldn't be angry," Louise protested and dabbed at her eyes.

"*Should* and *ought* don't have a place in the world of our emotions," Dr. Feinberg explained. "We feel what we feel. It's just that simple, except we must admit to ourselves what's going on. Otherwise, we become prisoners of our past."

Michael nudged his colleague. "Larry's actually a very good psychiatrist in spite of himself."

Louise began crying again, but the sound had changed. The weeping was gentle, pleading.

"As you set the pain free, your anger will subside and the suicidal thoughts will disappear," the psychiatrist advised. "Don't worry. You won't kill yourself if you release your rage."

"I've just never felt I could admit how much I resented my father leaving me."

"Men struggle with Oedipus complexes and women face similar Electra complexes." Dr. Feinberg sounded professorial. "Or to put it another way, you've had a father vacuum."

"A what?" Louise dried her eyes.

Michael laughed. "Our boy's trying a little razzle-dazzle on his client. Freud talk. Nevertheless, he's on to something. Pay attention, Seradim."

"Your father worked alone in the jungle a great deal of the time while you were a child, didn't he?" Larry asked.

Louise nodded.

"You probably didn't feel like you had much control over your life in those days?"

Louise looked shocked. "How did you know?"

"You've been trying to control these sessions from the moment you walked through the door." Larry smiled. "It's okay, but I immediately noticed your need to stay in the driver's seat."

"Am I so transparent?"

"My job is to read the signs, Louise, and to help you accept the fact that anyone growing up under your circumstances would feel the same way."

Seradim looked at Michael. "A father vacuum?"

"A big problem in American society," Michael said, "caused more frequently by people chasing money than those helping the lost in primitive jungles. But Larry hasn't learned about the biggest emptiness of all. The God vacuum. We're going to have to help him with that one."

"But my behavior is far from normal." Louise choked her words.

"Especially when it comes to men."

Louise froze, and the color left her face.

"I have a hunch you're also depressed about your sexual behavior."

Louise began breathing rapidly, as if her heart were pounding out of control.

"Everything said in this room is kept completely confidential. You have to be able to let me help you deal with your secrets."

"You know about the men in my life?" Louise could barely speak.

"Only theoretically. But I do know that girls with a father vacuum are sitting ducks for men's sexual advances."

"I . . . just can't . . . seem to say no . . . often enough."
Louise's voice trailed away. "But I try to be a good Christian girl."

"The Christian stuff doesn't interest me, but I know that every time you violate your own moral code, you pay a heavy price in guilt and self-condemnation."

"Oh, I do. I do."

"And every time you succumb, you're really trying to fill the father vacuum with a man. Once you see what you're doing, you'll be able to get your life under control again."

Seradim turned to Michael. "I bet the demons have a field day tempting women who have that tendency!"

"Important insight," the senior angel said. "The inability to understand this need has shipwrecked legions of young people."

"Where do I begin?" Louise asked.

"Accept the fact that it's normal to resent the absence of your parents even if they are doing a good thing. Recognize anger as a normal emotion. Allow yourself to experience the pain that's behind the resentment. Then you can truly forgive. The healing comes by forgiving, but you'll never be able to forgive your parents or anyone else if you don't even know that you are angry and bitter."

Louise settled back and leaned against the chair. She stared at the ceiling for a long time.

Michael explained to Seradim, "Men have similar problems with the father vacuum. They get into homosexual relationships, trying to find the masculine image lost in their childhood. Very tragic consequences follow. When fathers neglect their sons, they set them up for a lifetime of painful struggle. Make careful note. The demons never miss that one either."

After five minutes of silence, Louise spoke. "I can't believe it. I don't feel as depressed!"

"Good," Larry affirmed. "Those dark moments will probably be back to some extent, but now you will know what to do. We'll keep working until they're gone. Remember, Louise, listen to your own feelings, admit what they are, share them with a friend, forgive, and fill those parental vacuums by connecting more on a deep personal level with good people. Then you won't be so vulnerable to men taking advantage of you sexually."

Michael tugged at Seradim. "Enough of the psychiatric couch talk for one day. Larry doesn't even know his advice works because it's biblical. Let's go across town. I want you to watch a far less therapeutic meeting going on right now. Think yourself to the Community Church three blocks from here."

When the two angels arrived in the fellowship hall of the highly successful church, four people were gathered around a small serving area at the far end of a row of tables being prepared for a Wednesday night dinner.

A tall, thin woman was speaking in a low voice. "Ed, you're the chairman of the pastoral relations committee. I think you've got to get the committee together and lower the boom."

The overweight accountant shook his head. "I don't know, Dorothy. We're playing with fire here. A lot of people really admire the pastor. He's got a large following."

A chunky middle-aged woman with frosted hair pushed her finger in the accountant's face. "I don't care, Ed." Sylvia Springer, head of the church's social committee continued, "We can't have a minister who's got trouble at home. Everyone knows Pastor Reynolds is facing the possibility of an unwanted divorce. We need to sack him before word gets out around town."

"And everyone thinks his wife is a nut," Dr. Stanton Young, a distinguished-looking man, interjected. "The woman is unfriendly and distant—and only heaven knows what she's into."

Michael motioned for Seradim to sit next to him on the edge of a small stage behind the group. "What we have going on here is an old-fashioned unofficial board meeting. You don't need demons when you've got a crew like this one at work in the church. You're going to learn one of the reasons people like the Feinbergs don't take the Christian message seriously. These church members are a bigger problem than our old buddies Malafidus and Homelas."

"Dr. Young, I always respect your opinions," Ed Parker continued. "But starting an assault on the pastor could result in a church war we might well lose."

Dorothy smiled faintly. "I've been at this a long time." The elderly woman looked as if she'd been to the plastic surgeon once too often. "I've been in many church scraps, and we'll be here long after the Reynolds family is gone." Dorothy's voice became sharp. "It's better to bite the bullet and get it over with quickly."

"Agreed!" Dr. Young said.

Michael nudged Seradim. "Remember the human need to be important? Here it is again, causing strife and dissention. Sex, power, and money. Those are the big three. Louise tried illicit sex to fill her father vacuum. But these church folks are definitely into power to feel important."

"Yes, Michael, it seems the whole bunch are on a power trip," Seradim concluded.

Michael pointed toward Dorothy James and Stanton Young. "We've got a couple of obsessive-compulsive personalities on our hands. Legalists are usually cut from this cloth. You get the nice-guy types—neat, orderly, hard working—but behind the perfect facade is a dangerous need for control. Usually these people are big into hoarding money. Unfortunately, this church is filled with money-chasing social climbers. They will listen to Dorothy and the doctor spin their yarns."

Dorothy pointed a long bony finger at Ed. "The first step is to get the facts out. Let people know what's going on at the Reynoldses' house. Once the pastor's popularity is undercut, the rest is a downhill slide."

Ed Parker's eyes narrowed. "The truth is, we're the most influential people in the church. People will listen to us."

The chunky woman smiled. "I talk to people on the phone all the time, making calls on the inactive members. A few well-placed comments can turn the tide in a hurry." Sylvia Springer glared. "I never really trusted the pastor from the start."

Michael nodded knowingly. "Sylvia is more than a tad paranoid. Had alcoholic parents that set her up to not trust any authority figure. She's a controller as well. Because Sylvia is so filled with anger, she assumes everyone else is angry with her. She sees the speck in her brother's eye instead of the log in her own eye. No matter what the pastor did for her, Sylvia couldn't trust him because she is projecting her anger onto the good man. She'll feel completely righteous trying to hang the pastor because underneath it all, Sylvia is trying to get back at her parents who failed her."

"The biggest problem will be the McCoys," the doctor noted. "Since they've joined the church, Jennifer and Joe think Reynolds hung the moon."

"We can't win them all." Dorothy shrugged. "They're new. If they don't like what's happening, let them go to another church. The town's full of 'em."

"Where do we start?" Ed rolled his eyes.

Sylvia smiled. "I've seen the pastor come early to his office to counsel a woman. He says it's the only time she can come because of her work schedule. Sounds fishy to me."

"Reynolds has left himself wide open," Dr. Young continued. "Over our objections he let that Alcoholics Anonymous group meet here. They try to keep the lid on it, but everyone knows his wife drinks too much. Well, of course, that's a rumor. But I say we start the ball rolling by letting people know the moral laxness of the man."

"Okay. Okay," Ed agreed. "You people make the phone calls, and in a week I'll call the pastoral relations committee together."

Michael sighed. "Pastor Reynolds is a very good man. . . . God has really used him, but that won't make any difference now. His real error was failing to see that all the adulation and praise heaped on him by these people was only a form of projection. They wanted the pastor to be the perfect parent they never had. Of course, no one can fill that role. As they discovered his humanity, these members started sharpening their knives. Pastor Reynolds is too good-hearted a man to see what's coming."

"Ed, that's sound thinking," Dorothy said condescendingly. "The attack must be swift and to the point. When the pastor sees the handwriting on the wall, he'll slip out the back door."

"And the AA group goes as well!" Dr. Young insisted.

"But what if Reynolds doesn't go quietly?" Sylvia asked. "The pastor can be quite obstinate." The chunky woman bit her lip. "After all, he didn't listen to us in the past."

Dorothy's eyes narrowed. "If we throw enough dirt, some will stick."

"I just worry about the McCoys." Ed looked away. "They just started attending church recently."

"Oh, well." Dr. Young smiled. "The last time we were involved in a church split there was some fallout. Just part of the process."

Seradim stared in shock. "What a terrifying scenario!"

"The actions of this small group of people will have big repercussions in the future. The Scripture warns Christians to be respectful of their leaders. Because of their opposition to the pastor, these dissidents will destroy their spiritual covering and open the door for Evil to strike their church. Their personal needs for importance, control, and domination will be the downfall of many."

"Should we do anything?"

"Not yet, Seradim. Humans have freedom. Once they invite attack, the opposition has a right to respond."

"I fear for the McCoys. They're not true believers yet."

Michael hung his head. "When you see such travesties, you know the church has to have been preserved through the centuries only by the grace of God. Any other organization would have turned to dust long ago.

"Well, Seradim, we have work to do. The world is coming to an end, and these foolish, vain people want to fight a war over who controls the keys to the clubhouse!"

CHAPTER
9

Black clouds boiled and spirit winds blew fiercely toward the eastern seaboard of the United States. At the imperial summons, demons from across the globe instantly responded. New orders were about to be issued and demonic forces repositioned. Specialists in fear management and deception swooped down on Washington, D.C. Such a gathering of evil had not occurred since Adolf Hitler's Munich putsch or Joseph Stalin's political purges, which resulted in the deaths of twenty million people.

"Something big's coming down," a huge black troll told the comrade flying at his side. "Maybe a world war is in the making. Anybody who is anybody is being called in."

"I love a great military explosion," his yellow-greenish companion answered. "Civil wars are particularly good. Relatives kill each other, and the hate lasts for centuries. Of course, chemical warfare is excellent for maiming children. Genetic defects even produce kids without arms and legs. The pain just won't quit. I hope they start slinging around some nasty viral concoction."

"Perhaps we're going to get an atomic explosion out of this one. Maybe hit Damascus or Jerusalem. What a blast!" The demon laughed at his own pun.

"Whatever. Let's hunker down to the war room and see what's cooking."

The two demons merged into a multitude of ugly creatures pouring into an enormous smoke-filled chamber. The swarm quickly blended together in a semblance of order in front of a huge opening similar to a gigantic television screen where Earth scenes were magnified for the legions of hell to watch.

A gargantuan form overshadowed the congregation of malefactors. "Pay close attention." His deep, ominous voice rumbled through the assembly. "You must carefully observe what is unfolding. We are now positioned for a major opportunity to create chaos and revolution everywhere. Millions can be destroyed!" A sound akin to thunder erupted in an orgasmic explosion of raw emotion, sending shock waves across the gathering.

"For the first time in a decade, we may be able to foment a world war and unbounding carnage! We are going to watch the president of the United States give instructions, which will set these possibilities in motion. You must be ready to give him every assistance." His hideous laughter rocked the gathering.

The inner office of the American president came into focus in the gigantic viewing area. Damian Gianardo and his vice president, Jacob Rathmarker, stood side by side in the Oval Office, listening to the secretary of state report. Occasionally, they looked knowingly at each other.

"In summary," the secretary said as he turned the final page and cleared his throat, "your suggestion to the European heads of state for a federation of ten nations has been received with total consternation. The idea of a new common market and new trade agreements with us was welcomed. However, the notion that we develop a joint military, combining all land and sea forces, was met by bewilderment. And when I talked of governmental linkage, they ran."

"Thank you, Mr. Clark." The president smiled condescendingly. "Did you bring it to their attention that we have the nuclear attack capacity to make compliance advantageous?"

Secretary Clark pulled at his collar. "Sir, they would have seen such a suggestion as an implied threat. I didn't feel that such a course was helpful."

"Not at this time . . . at least." Rathmarker smiled cunningly. "I trust all discussions have been completely and totally confidential."

"Absolutely. I spoke only with my counterparts at the top level of government. No one wanted a word of these discussions leaked."

Gianardo turned and walked to the opposite end of the office. He crossed his arms and paced back and forth. "Something is needed. Some extraordinary event must happen that will cause each of these nations to realize how much it needs my leadership. The world needs a good shaking."

"I don't understand what you are suggesting," the secretary said nervously.

The president stood with his right side to the wall. "Obviously, I am changing the political face of our country very quickly. People have learned that my leadership is flawless. On the domestic scene, we are creating complete dependence on me. We need a good worldwide disaster to accomplish the same thing abroad."

"A *good* disaster?" The secretary swallowed hard.

"Come now, Clark." Damian Gianardo laughed. "Be a little imaginative. Surely we can create a nice little crisis that will demonstrate a demand for my proposed alliance."

"I . . . I'm not sure how to proceed, sir."

Gianardo leaned over the desk, jabbing at the secretary of state with his index finger. "Assemble a top secret think tank of military experts to work on this problem. I want every aspect of international terrorism and deception explored. Study everything from the sinking of the *Lusitania* to Lyndon Johnson's Gulf of Tonkin manipulation of the Vietnam War. What would it mean if we caused the economy of a country like Italy or France to collapse? And then brought overnight restoration?"

"Frankly, Mr. President, some heads of state suggested that we seem to be trying to re-create the old Roman Empire. As absurd as it seems, they—"

"Significant choice of words, Mr. Secretary." Gianardo cut him off. "Why not?"

The secretary of state's eyes widened in dismay. Clark nodded his head mechanically. "Let me . . . uh . . . give it . . . some thought." He hurried from the room.

The scene faded from the viewing area; demons frantically communicated with each other. Steam and foul vapors arose from the heated discussions, which sounded as abrasive as a drill grinding on a tooth.

"Get the idea?" the singular massive voice echoed over the gathering. His awesome shape overshadowed the assemblage. "See the potential?"

The demonic assembly squirmed and writhed in increasing agitation. Explosions of energy sent fireballs in every direction. The swarm was clearly building to a frenzy.

"I want us to create a massive, worldwide sense of fear, dread, and apprehension," the oppressive voice continued. "We must create a climate of panic around the globe."

"Yes! Yes! Certainly!" the group echoed. "At once!"

"Give me a report from the major principalities," the supreme voice ordered. "I want an update on the social climate you are creating in the American scene."

A monstrous shape floated up from the group and drifted toward center stage. The brownish, amorphous figure changed form as the demon hovered in space. "We have successfully captured the entertainment industry," it explained. "Hollywood is the spiritual Babylon of our era. Christian beliefs and values are consistently belittled. Cherished symbols of faith are put to blasphemous use in both television and movies. Whenever a Christian character appears in a film, we make sure the person is portrayed as a fool, a liar, a cheat, a murderer, or a crazy person. Media bias promotes intolerance and materialism. Yes, we are winning the culture war."

The convocation exploded in enthusiastic approval.

"We have created a significant wall of separation between God and the screen," the head of the Hollywood principality continued. "The common Judeo-Christian values that shaped the founding of America have been replaced with moral relativism, which often celebrates the degrading."

"Give us examples," an evil enthusiast yelled.

"Back in the 1990s we had great success with a film titled *The People vs. Larry Flynt.* We were able to slip in total nudity and complete degradation under the heading of 'art.' We made the fundamentalist minister Jerry Falwell look like an idiot while portraying the porno publisher as courageous and progressive. Shortly after that event, we got a grotesque episode aired on the Fox network, portraying a series of clergy murders. Splattered dead priests' blood all over America!"

The conclave again erupted in approval.

"We have been able to suppress the fact that Hollywood has two thousand committed Christian employees. The believers never think to pray for them, so we continue to rule virtually unopposed. All we need is to make one change in a script, distort one idea in a movie, and we reshape what millions of people think and believe."

The leader of the council pointed to the opposite side of the gathering. "Tell us about the European principality," his ominously deep voice invited and demanded all at the same time.

A knurled, ancient-looking demon with great claws arose. "We've had our ups and downs over the centuries," he began slowly. "The high Victorian culture of a hundred and fifty years ago was a problem, but with the help of Sigmund Freud, we were able to portray morality as repressive and unhealthy. World Wars I and II provided the maximum opportunity to destroy restraint and propriety. Consequently, Europe is now filled with morally adrift parents and kids without any sense of spiritual direction.

"Many have found an affluent lifestyle beyond anything their ancestors could have dreamed. All we will need to do is shake their faith in the economic underpinnings that feed them and they'll fall for anything. Accept the lie. Embrace a dictator. Riot. Steal. Believe me, the world is filled with soulless rabble whose consumerist mentality leaves them totally vulnerable to the least threat to their affluence."

"But will the churches be a menace?" another demon shouted.

"They could be," an anonymous demon answered. "But most groups are so preoccupied with ski trips and basket weaving for the old folks, they never get around to the message. And many ministers are busy building their own personal empires and chasing after everything under the sun except sharing the Christian story. As long as they stay distracted with monkey business, we don't have to worry."

"In addition," a green creature said, "we've been able to profit from the national climate of disillusionment with TV evangelists. In thousands of local churches, we've incited distrust and disrespect for religious leaders. Members whisper rumors and spread stories of deceit, enabling us to discredit the clergy. Never have pastors had as difficult a time leading their flocks."

The Evil One applauded slowly and then more forcefully until the entire chamber rocked with the sound of raucous applause. Demons hissed and spit. The stench rose like the smell of manure on a hot summer day.

Another scene appeared before the conclave. Damian Gianardo continued talking to his vice president, Jacob Rathmarker, after the secretary of state had left. Gianardo was a tall, distinguished man of commanding presence. Long before the presidency fell into his hands, he had acquired the art of walking into any room in a way that demanded attention. His intimidating black eyes and penetrating stare always produced a disconcerting feeling that he knew what others were thinking. He had an uncanny capacity to accurately read the intentions and motives of his opponents. Once he grasped the other person's position, Gianardo had no restraint in the pursuit of his own ends.

"Jacob, I have little confidence in Clark's ability to do what needs to be done. He's of the old school. Ethical behavior and honorable intent. The man's out of touch with today's world. He'd be terrified even to order the CIA to assemble a hit squad and bring an enemy down."

The president's graying hair was carefully combed over the right side of his head, down across his temple and toward his neck. Even hair transplants could not conceal the reminder of the near-fatal head injury. His vanity caused him to keep the damaged side of his head toward the wall as he spoke.

Rathmarker shook his head. "I agree. We may have to take things in our own hands. Bumping Clark aside now could raise questions later."

"Yes, we must be quite prudent." The president rubbed his hands together. His perfectly manicured fingers were long, tapered, and unusually thin. Though they might have been the hands of an artist or a surgeon, the fingers had the disconcerting look of a stereotypical undertaker in a horror movie. "Perhaps history will yet play into our hands. If not, we will seize the nations by the throat and shake them until they fall into line."

Rathmarker laughed coarsely. "I admire you for many reasons, Damian. But most of all, your ruthlessness is an inspiration."

As the scene faded, the exhilaration of the hordes of evil climbed to an elevated stage of euphoric ecstasy.

"Yes! We've found our man," a voice echoed from a far corner of the conclave.

"He can lead them into the great war," another harmful creature shouted over the din.

The Evil One, the personification of every diabolical intent, ascended even higher above his legions, extending his arms into the air. "The Beast is ready," it exclaimed. "The unbridled evil of uncontrollable governmental authority is about to be made manifest. Don't let me down," it threatened. "I've waited since the beginning of time for just such a moment! We've had an antichrist in the wings in every era since Yeshua's death and resurrection. Gianardo is our man for the third millennium. No doubt about it!"

CHAPTER
10

Michael beckoned Seradim to follow as he rose aloft over Community Church and its conspiratorial committee members. He pointed toward the amorphous veil separating time and eternity. "We're going back across the great barrier. We need to let some time pass."

The two angels shot through the vaporous curtain covering the entrance into eternity. Immediately a sense of profound and ultimate completeness wrapped around them like an all-sufficient mantle of peace.

Seradim sighed deeply. "I had lost touch with the impeccability of heaven. The quintessence, the *ne plus ultra* that feels so inexpressibly awesome."

"In the mind of God, everything is in the now," Michael began. "All moments are immediately present to the Holy One because eternity is only an aspect of His Being. Time on Earth will race forward while we talk."

Seradim absorbed the instruction. "Time moves on while we are stationary in eternity?"

"A number of events must happen before we return. For one thing, Sharon Feinberg caught on to her daughter's little rendezvous with Jimmy Harrison. She didn't need our help to put the clamps on Ruth's behavior. The entire family is going for counseling with a therapist named Dr. Ann Woodbridge, an associate of Larry's who happens to be a Christian. Things are moving along right on schedule."

"Oh," Seradim nodded approvingly. "Good."

"Moreover, we must give Lucifer ample room to put a few more pieces in place for the grand scheme the devil thinks he is creating. Remember Gianardo, the president of the United States?"

"Certainly."

"During the next several months, Gianardo and his vice president, Rathmarker, will be looking for a worldwide crisis to catapult them to unprecedented power. Little do they know that heaven itself will give them their opportunity. With no idea that the Creator is working, Lucifer is actually fulfilling God's sovereign plan."

"I don't grasp what you are describing," Seradim said. "Perhaps . . . I—"

"No," Michael interrupted, "you must not think with the same patterns humans use or you won't ever be able to understand. Mortal insight is called syllogistic thinking. People attempt to figure out the world, nature, events, even the mind of God, as if reality is a path of stepping stones leading logically from one idea to the next. People fail to see the difference eternity makes in understanding existence." He chuckled. "Lucifer has also forgotten. As a result, the most brilliant minds often skip down the path of logic and end up with conclusions worse than ones drawn by humans of greatly limited capacity. Geniuses have ended up not even believing the Father exists. Now that is arrogance!"

"People are exceedingly strange," Seradim concluded. "They have such awesome potential, and yet they come to such peculiar ends as if their capacities were even lower than the animals."

"Such always follows when they ignore the divine factor in their equations." Michael pointed across heaven. "In our world all things come together. What appears to be contradictory on Earth coalesces here. Heaven is not only the place of harmony of relationships, but of ideas. Ours is the realm of paradox."

"The place where contradictions meet and kiss?"

"Excellent, Seradim. A paradox is two ideas that appear to be in collision but are actually both true. Human behavior is quite paradoxical. The best of people can do the worst of things. The most dangerous humans are capable of very altruistic thoughts and actions. Get it?"

The new trainee nodded. "And that is how even Lucifer serves the Father?"

"Lucifer's actions seem to be the result of utter contempt for the Creator, and they are. Yet he is acting right now in accord with prophecy given by the Holy Spirit millennia ago. With no insight whatsoever, the demons are performing right on schedule. Quite a paradox!"

Seradim lowered himself until he lay prone toward the throne of the Father. Spontaneous words and melody rolled out of his soul. "Holy, holy, holy, Lord God Almighty, before Your throne of glory our songs arise to Thee. Holy, holy, holy, wondrous and mighty, God in Three Persons, blessed Trinity." The words poured out in heartfelt praise and tribute.

Michael could not resist being swept into Seradim's praise. He sang a completely different melody, blending with the young angel like the countermelody in a fugue. The two angels' songs rose and ascended to the heights, blending into a mighty chorus of adoration.

Other angelic voices spontaneously joined the hymn. Seradim's simple song became a canticle of heaven, total and original yet resonate with all the glorious sounds of continuous praise and love that circulated around the Father's throne like the massive movement of clouds constantly in motion over the earth.

When they came to the end, both angels felt even greater exhilaration than in the beginning. Slowly, Seradim's melody lowered into a singular song within his own heart.

"I find it difficult to stop," Seradim confessed to Michael.

"It is truly glorious. But we must stop now because we have other work to do. Someday nothing will interrupt us.

"During our song, several months have passed on Earth and Lucifer's plan has progressed. It will soon be time for us to return. The Satanic trinity has been hard at work."

"Satanic trinity?"

"Lucifer attempts to counterfeit everything in heaven," Michael explained. "Ultimately, no originality exists except that which mirrors the mind of the Father."

Seradim's soul sighed deeply, still enraptured with the lingering melody of praise. "I have a difficult time shifting my attention to such contrary thoughts, but I know it is important for me to understand these matters. Explain the Satanic trinity to me, please."

"As the Father is the center of all things, so Lucifer is the source of all destruction, the unity behind and within all evil." Michael projected into Seradim's mind a collage of pain-filled scenes from Earth.

In an instant, the new Guardian envisioned airplanes crashing, children dying, diseases devouring healthy people, thousands starving, and people betraying each other with endless schemes of deception. Seradim put his hands to his eyes. "Stop! Please stop. I can't stand it."

"Very different situations," Michael continued, "but tied together with one strand: Lucifer."

Seradim nodded hesitantly.

"The second person in the diabolical scheme is 'the lamb with the voice of the dragon.' The devil is constantly working to create a system of apostate religion as his alternative to the work of Yeshua on the cross. Often the same biblical words are used, but Satan redefines the meanings to serve his worst purposes. See the possibilities?"

"No," Seradim puzzled. "No, I don't."

"Watch." Once again Michael recalled scenes from the past. He thought of teenage Moonies standing on a street corner, selling flowers to raise money for their cause. "Seradim, look into those young faces so innocently working for the Moon that pretends to be the Son." Michael next remembered Jim Jones and the masses who followed the preacher to Guyana and died at Jonestown. Immediately, Seradim experienced hundreds of people lying dead on the jungle floor with cups of Kool-Aid in their hands.

"Apostate religion can be deadly," Michael added. "Jesus redeemed the lost. The lamb with the voice of a dragon condemns the deceived."

"Father and Son," Seradim repeated aloud. "Lucifer and religion."

"The third person in the devil's trinity is 'the Beast,' a system of governmental power." Michael quickly switched images in Seradim's mind, unfolding the panoramic story of the evolution of the kingdoms of the world. Pictures of tribal chieftains, kings, and tyrannical despots flashed past. The concept of government expanded and Seradim saw

Caesars dispatching legions to annihilate innocent people. He saw the city-states of Europe spring up into the emerging nations of medieval times. Kingdoms turned into democracies, and kings were replaced by committees and security councils. The czars of Russia became the prime ministers of communism, and millions died in labor camps and before firing squads.

"What you are seeing," Michael instructed, "is the way in which political power can take on a life of its own. The system becomes like a train run amok without any hand at the switch. The Beast is the metaphor for corrupt state agencies and armies that have actually slipped into Lucifer's hand. Regardless of nameplates on governmental doors of authority, he alone has become the true master behind the thrones of power. At this moment the devil is turning Damian Gianardo, the American president, into the final manifestation, the incarnation of the Beast."

"Astonishing!" the reassigned angel gasped.

"But we both know the secret of how the final victory arises from what seemed to be the ultimate defeat," Michael said. Instantly he recalled the darkest day in human history. Black clouds rolled up from the deep and covered the city of Jerusalem. Tornadic winds abruptly swept across the ancient city, over the high stone walls, and down on a limestone quarry where men were hanging from cross beams tied to massive poles sticking out of the ground. Soldiers with iron spears milled about watching the crowd cowering in grief before the monstrous scene of three men having life slowly drained from them.

"A-a-a-a-h!" Seradim writhed in torment. "I can't stand to revisit this sight."

Michael kept remembering. One lone figure towered above the grotesque executions. Blood ran down His face, and bones protruded from His distended chest drooping beneath arms nailed to the rough cross-member beam. His head hung low as if no capacity for movement was left. Above the thorn-crowned head, a crude sign proclaimed in Greek, Latin, and Hebrew, "This is the King of the Jews." The Rabbi slightly raised His head and cried out, *"Eli, Eli, lama sabach-thani.* My God, My God, why have You forsaken Me?"

Seradim wept.

The image expanded in Michael's memory. Yeshua's head and body finally sagged out of control, limp and dead. Michael could hear the sounds of the great Temple curtain tearing in two pieces. An earthquake shook the earth and great boulders exploded in half. Thunder roared over the city. Lightning split trees into splinters. Michael could recall the scene no longer.

Seradim turned and stared into eternity. Slowly, far off in the distance, another image arose before his vision. A wondrous glorious shape appeared between the throne and the flying Cherubim and Seraphim. A slain Lamb, standing triumphant.

The Lamb reached out and took a great scroll. Immediately the elders of the tribes of Israel and the twelve apostles fell down before the Lamb. Angels swooped low in obeisance. The elders and apostles took up harps and golden bowls of incense, and smoke arose in the form of prayers.

The mighty chorus burst into song, "Worthy are You to take the scroll and to open its seals, for Your blood did ransom humanity for God from every tribe and tongue and people and nation. You have made them a kingdom and priests to our God, and they shall reign on earth."

Suddenly myriads of myriads and thousands of thousands of angelic voices rang out, "Worthy is the Lamb who was slain, to receive power and wealth and wisdom and might and honor and blessing!" Blending into the incredible chorus came other voices, voices of earth and sea singing, "To Him who sits on the throne and to the Lamb be blessing and honor and glory and might for ever and ever!" The elders worshiped by crying out again and again, "Amen, Amen, Amen."

Seradim smiled. "We have only to remember, the victory is already His."

CHAPTER
11

The time is right for us to reenter the universe," Michael instructed his charge. "We're going back on one of my favorite days."

"Rosh Hashanah!" Seradim caught the thought before it was completely expressed. "Yes, I can see how special holy days are for angelic intervention."

"High holidays help us keep our bearings as we move between time and eternity. I'm particularly moved by this day, Rosh Hashanah, the beginning of the Jewish New Year. Many times I've hovered above synagogues and listened for the shofar's sound, the blast of the ram horn that tells the world Jehovah Rafah has called another year into being."

Seradim looked around heaven, noticing a great change in the usual patterns of worship and the offerings of the incense prayers of the saints. A flurry of activity was building. Cherubim and Seraphim continued their usual ministries of praise, but the Thrones had shifted their major focus to directing the work of the angels under their authority. Juridical angels who constantly contemplate the divine judgment were in a high state of animation. Dominions rushed back and forth across heaven, delivering special messages and instructing the Virtues on special assignments.

"Some very unusual preparation is underway," Seradim observed. "Warrior angels are charging across the time barrier as if they are preparing for an all-out war and Principalities left even earlier. A completely new alignment seems to be taking place within heaven itself."

"For eons, we've waited for this moment to arrive," Michael answered. "Heaven is about to swell dramatically, and we will be needed on Earth as never before." Michael pointed to the barrier. "We must depart quickly; the hour is at hand. The great event will coincide with the celebration of Rosh Hashanah."

In an instant, the two angels burst through the barrier and plunged rapidly into the hectic pace of life in Southern California. Larry and Sharon Feinberg were speeding toward the counseling office of Dr. Ann Woodbridge in Newport Beach. Heading south from the other direction on Highway 5, Jimmy Harrison and Ruth Feinberg were just about at the parking lot in front of Dr. Woodbridge's building, the New Life Clinic.

"Since our departure, much has happened." Michael pointed to the scene unfolding beneath them. "The Feinberg family is trying to come to grips with a number of their problems. Ruth and Jimmy's flirtation took on a new depth of meaning. Homelas and Malafidus blew their assignment when youthful lust and rebellion turned into love and caring. We really wouldn't have had much to do but observe." Michael pointed to the five-story building. "The demons won't be around here today. Rosh Hashanah makes them nervous and the atmosphere inside the office is too

Christian. Let's go down and watch. The fireworks are about to begin."

The two angels flew above the packed 405 Freeway, gliding toward Irvine. "Let's check in on the McCoys quickly before we join the Feinbergs in their little showdown. Think yourself to Joe's office."

Joe McCoy pointed to the chart behind him. The twenty employees in the room listened carefully to his instruction.

"We must reprogram how computer routing is occurring," Joe continued. "We need to have a more efficient system for quicker response to the customer."

One of the employees laughed. "We've already got the quickest draw in the West. Our company is the original 'Billy the Kid' of the defense industry." Others laughed.

Joe shook his head. "Well," he drawled, "you just never know when the unexpected can happen. Our job is to make sure the national security radar and response systems can't be fooled. In that spirit, we have to make sure the customers buying our products have an absolute sense of instant response."

"Is anyone more up on their toes than old Joe McCoy?" another employee asked. "Go get 'em tiger." The group laughed again.

Michael beckoned for Seraphim to follow him. "Before the morning is out, the laugh will be on Joe's colleagues. Time to check in on Larry and company. Let's think ourselves over to the counselor's office."

The Feinbergs were already waiting to enter the conference room on the fourth floor when Jimmy and Ruth rounded the corner. Ben was with his parents. Their greetings were stilted and stiff. Dr. Woodbridge stood at the door, ushering the group inside.

"Watch the father," Michael said. "He'll automatically go for a chair in the center of the room to claim the power position and his wife is going to tell Ruth and Jimmy where to sit. Real controllers."

Dr. Woodbridge opened the session. "Why don't we put our expectations on the table? Let's explore the agendas that we brought with us today."

"I'll start," Ruth blurted out. "After all, the meeting is somewhat at my instigation. No one thinks Jimmy is good enough for me!"

"Oh, come now!" Larry protested. "We are very accepting."

"Absolutely," Sharon agreed. "We have friends from all walks of life." Her dark brown suit seemed unusually severe.

"I pride myself on openness." Larry shook his head. In contrast to his usual Southern California casualness, he wore a tie and sport coat.

"How do you feel about what you just heard?" Dr. Woodbridge asked Jimmy.

"I know you mean well." Jimmy tried to smile. "But you sound like I'm the gardener you invite in for a sandwich every Christmas."

Sharon's jaw tightened and Ben rolled his eyes.

Larry sat upright with his chin stuck out. "If I have any hidden agenda, it's shaped by what I know professionally. The statistics just aren't good. Ruth's dated only one boy in her life. The odds are even worse for a Jewish girl and a Baptist boy making it work."

"And what are the dangers of a girl who hopes to get a Ph.D. marrying a used-car salesman with a high school education?" Ruth added, defiantly tossing her hair sideways.

Larry shrugged. "You know as well as I do. That's strike three."

Dr. Woodbridge kept trying to smile. "At least, we're getting it out quickly."

Sharon cleared her throat. "I don't like what I need to say. I don't even know how it makes me feel to speak up, but I can't be honest if I'm not forthright." She scooted to the edge of her chair. "Maybe it's totally selfish, but I am self-conscious about how my Newport Beach friends will view any future son-in-law who is a used-car salesman. After all, we're professional people."

The room became intensely quiet. Jimmy looked down at his feet and Ruth grimaced.

Sharon broke the silence. "Yes, and I feel guilty because I didn't contribute enough of our family background to help Ruth make sure she stayed within our race when she was looking for a spouse."

"I'd like to add a word." Ben pulled himself up to his full height in his chair. "We've always been a close-knit family. We have our little rituals and ways of doing things. It's not easy to bring someone into the inner circle." Ben stopped and smiled unexpectedly at Jimmy. "But I appreciate how it feels to be an outsider. Ethnic differences shouldn't matter if we're as liberal as we profess. All of us need to get over thinking we're better than other people."

"I didn't say that." Sharon bristled.

"In fact, we did." Larry fidgeted in his chair. "It's not flattering, but that's about the sum of what we've said so far."

Michael pulled Seradim aside. "The activity you saw in heaven has great significance for what will transpire in a few minutes. For centuries, prophets and teachers attempted to help human beings recognize what's coming. Ironically, Jimmy's father is a highly respected minister who understood the scenario and tried many times to warn his son about the coming Rapture. The Feinbergs have no idea the heavenly Father is about to execute His special plan for believers. Watch."

Jimmy raised his hand. "I know it doesn't sound like much to your family," Jimmy winced as he spoke, "but I really like selling cars. Sure, it doesn't take much education to be a salesman, but I'm good at what I do. Ruth has motivated me to become honest, and I am building an excellent reputation in Laguna Hills. I've done so well, I've saved $12,000. The boss said that he plans for me to manage our new place in Laguna Niguel, and I'll get 10 percent of the profits."

Jimmy smiled weakly. "Can't your Newport friends simply think of me as a businessman? Maybe someday I'll own a chain of car lots."

"Jimmy has been very good for me." Ruth reached out for his hand. "He's the best friend I've ever had."

Ann Woodbridge seemed distracted. Her usually rapt attention faded as if she were hearing something that no one else heard. She turned her head slightly and began staring at the ceiling almost as if she saw Michael and Seradim looking down on her.

"That sound!" Seradim grabbed Michael's arm. "It's an irresistible summons calling us home to the Father. It's the last trump, blowing on the Feast of Trumpets. We must leave."

"No." Michael held Seradim's hand tightly. "Hang on. The call is not for us. The heavenly Creator is calling home an army of people like Ann Woodbridge."

"Ann?" Larry Feinberg tried to get the therapist's attention. "Ann? Are you with us?"

In the twinkling of an eye, Dr. Ann Woodbridge was gone.

"Look!" Seradim pointed as Dr. Woodbridge passed the angels. "She's going toward the time barrier! What's happening?"

Michael pointed across the face of the globe as multitudes of humans rose from the earth, flying toward the same place. "The Rapture is occurring," he explained. "God's people are being pulled out of the world before the final battle occurs. Dark days are ahead for the entire planet."

"Shouldn't we help them enter eternity?"

"No, Seradim, our assignment is to help the people left behind. We must protect the Feinbergs and Jimmy. They are important players in the final confrontation with evil."

"Oh, no!" Jimmy was the first to break the stunned silence. "No! NO!"

Ruth slid to the edge of her chair. "Ann? Ann! Is this a joke?"

"This better not be some kind of crazy psychodrama experiment." Larry stood up.

"It's happened," Jimmy gasped. "Just like Dad said it would. He preached about the Rapture."

Larry took several steps toward the vacant seat. "She was right there." He reached out to touch the arm of the chair.

"Mom was right." Jimmy moaned. "The time is at hand."

Larry spun on his heels and raced toward the offices. Ben followed but found only empty desks and chairs, with clothing and jewelry scattered across the floor. The receptionist's headset was lying on the desk next to her phone. On the other desks, pencils and papers were scattered about as if everyone had abruptly left on a coffee break.

Jimmy held to the doorjamb and stared at the floor. "My father preached this exit would happen someday. He must have figured out that Rosh Hashanah was the key to the timing of the Rapture."

"Rosh Hashanah?" Larry spun around. "Stop it. Don't add to the confusion. We've got to keep our heads."

"But they've disappeared," Sharon said. "Gone . . . just vanished into thin air."

After several heated exchanges, Larry demanded they leave and rendezvous at the Feinberg home to make some sense out of what had happened. Ruth and Jimmy took the stairs and left through a side door. Once in the parking lot, they sped off in his red Corvette without waiting for the rest of the family to catch up. Vacant cars were smashed and burning all along the way.

"Jimmy?" Ruth grasped his arm. "What were you talking about up there? What's a Rapture?"

"If I'm right, my parents will have disappeared. There won't be anybody at their usually busy church in Dallas." He veered off the street into the driveway of a convenience store with an outside drive-up telephone. An empty pickup truck had smashed into the store itself, and people were screaming in panic. Jimmy grabbed the phone and punched in a set of numbers followed by his credit card number. No one answered.

"Let's help some of these folks," Ruth said tearfully as Jimmy stared into space, totally stunned by this strange turn of events.

Michael watched the growing consternation on Ruth and Jimmy's faces. "Seradim, the chaos has just begun," he concluded. "Get ready."

■ ■ ■

Joe McCoy braced himself against the wall, his face white. He kept his hand over his mouth. Twelve of the remaining employees raced from chair to chair. Two women were crying.

"I . . . I . . . I *saw* them . . . just disappear!" Joe stuttered. "Poof! They were gone!"

The division manager kept slapping the back of one of the empty chairs. "No one disintegrates into thin air!"

"Is this a trick?" one of the secretaries asked. "Are we being put through one of those contrived security examinations? A psychology grilling to see if we will come unglued?"

"Yeah," a male programmer growled, "this whole thing smacks of a military stunt to check us out. I don't like it one bit."

Joe shook his head in disbelief. "No. No one could stage what we just saw. I was looking straight in the face of Sally Vaca. I've known her for years. She was an outstanding person. She wouldn't be part of some government plot. In an instant Sally was simply . . . gone . . . gone, I tell you."

■ ■ ■

Frank Wong held Jessica's hand in a vice grip. He kept pointing across the dining room, which had erupted in complete chaos. Couples had been split apart. Whole tables were empty. Waiters had disappeared.

"I tell you, Jessica, one minute every table was full, and in a matter of seconds, lots of these people were gone! Gone! Do you understand?"

Jessica stared. "Is not possible!"

"Even three of best waiters vanish. Best servers. Never steal."

Cindy patted her father's arm. "I can only hear what you say, good father, but it sounds like many people were upset."

"Oh, Cindy." Jessica clutched her daughter. "Stay close to us. World gone completely crazy. Nothing predictable. Stay close. We must not lose you. Ever!"

"Think of all money I didn't get!" Frank shook his head, and he looked out the window. The parking lot was snarled by cars that had crashed into each other. People were screaming.

"Oh, help us!" Jessica implored, speaking more to the empty space above her head than to any specific place. "I fear I go crazy."

CHAPTER
12

Jimmy and Ruth stared at the evening newscast. The anchorman sounded urgent. "Apparently, about 25 percent of the population has simply vanished." A picture of the Notre Dame Cathedral in Paris appeared on the screen. "Europe reports about 5 percent losses, while virtually no one is missing from Muslim, Hindu, or Buddhist nations. This factor is forcing an analysis of a possible religious component in the disappearances."

"Yeah," Jimmy drawled, running his hand nervously through his hair, "maybe they would like to factor in the disappearance of my parents and their entire congregation! Let Mr. Nightly News explain that one."

A picture of an empty podium with the seal of the president of the United States flashed across the screen. "Please stand by," the broadcaster said. "We have a live statement from the president."

Damian Gianardo walked briskly to the stand, appearing nervous and edgy. "My fellow Americans, tonight we are facing one of the strangest crises in national history.

There is no current explanation for the disappearance of millions of our citizens. Key military and police personnel are absent without reason. To ensure order and security, I am now declaring a state of emergency. National Guard and reserve units will patrol our streets until further notice."

Jimmy squeezed Ruth's hand. "For years, my parents tried to prepare me for this moment, and I didn't listen." Gianardo's voice rumbled on in the background.

"I know most of what I'm saying doesn't make much sense to you, Ruth. Give me time and I'll help you get everything into perspective. I need to retrace my steps and get back in touch with what my father taught."

"You can rely on me and my government to protect your interests and guide you through this difficult time." The president jutted his chin out and spoke defiantly. "In the name of human goodness, we will gain the inevitable victory!"

"He's wrong," Jimmy quietly answered as the picture faded. "This time the head man is completely deceived."

Ruth squeezed Jimmy's hand and grimaced.

■ ■ ■

Homelas and Malafidus intently watched the same news conference from the back of the State Department auditorium. Other demons hovered around the room or were perched on the walls.

"A couple of African nations lost nearly half of their populations," Homelas quipped. "Russia and some Eastern European nations also lost large numbers. What do you make of it?"

"An old legend once floated around about a rupture or rapture or something of the sort." Malafidus squinted his deeply shrunken red eyes and lowered his voice. "All the Christians were supposed to bail out before the big war. I don't know. Always thought it was nonsense."

"Where would we find out more about the idea?"

Malafidus pointed his skinny arms, which jutted out of his bulbous body, and jabbed his spearlike finger in Homelas's face. "Don't you dare go looking around in one of their Bibles for insight. Headquarters would clamp you down like locking up a bank vault on a holiday! No sir! Keep your mouth shut and wait for instructions from the source himself!"

"Okay! Okay, I'm not looking for trouble. But you've got to admit these disappearances are a strange turn of events."

Malafidus snorted, discounting the question. "Actually, the departures are to our advantage. Think how many problems were jettisoned out of our way. We won't have interference from all those prayer fanatics who kept messing up the airwaves. Half the time, I couldn't think straight, trying to sort out instructions from headquarters while those blasted intercessors kept breaking in. I hated them. Maybe the exodus is a sign we are winning."

"Time to get to work." Homelas pointed to the president. "Right now, Damian is a might shook up. He's always at his best when apprehension makes him mean-spirited. We need to apply pressure at his fear points to gear him up a tad more."

■ ■ ■

Seradim and Michael watched Ben Feinberg pace the floor in front of Cindy Wong. The reception area in her dormitory was empty except for them. The usually crowded sidewalks to the classrooms were sparse. The blind Chinese girl patiently listened as Ben rambled almost incoherently.

"The whole thing must have been an attack from outer space," Ben muttered. "People don't just disappear. I mean that doctor . . . counselor . . . whatever . . . that woman my parents took Ruth to just went up in smoke! I mean, you talk about weird!"

"Please, Ben. Be calm." Cindy reached out but couldn't touch him. "Yes, I'm sure my blindness saved me from the shock you are feeling, but we've got to stay calm and keep ourselves together."

"I just don't know." Ben wrung his hands as he paced. "I feel like I've gone nuts." Ben walked to the door. "Cindy, I've got to get some air. I'm going to the ocean to think. Sorry, but I need to be by myself for a while. I'll call you this evening."

"I understand, Ben. I want to go to the library and study anyway. I'm going to listen to my cassette recordings of the last lectures in biology. Keeping my mind on science for a while will help me get my mind off of all the crazy and painful things going on in the world right now! I'd rather not sort it all out yet.

"I guess that's a difference between me and you, Ben. I feel pain and confusion, so I want to escape from it—to stay 'blind' to reality until later. But you want to go straight to your emotions and dive into the truth headlong. I admire that."

Ben touched her hand as he left, then hurried toward the parking lot.

"Seradim, your hour is at hand." Michael pointed at Ben and instructed his charge. "Ben and Cindy are going to need a great amount of oversight to fulfill their destinies. The spiritual warfare is about to heat up."

"Where will the attack come?"

"It's already started. The real battleground is always the human soul. The ultimate struggle is over control of the precious ground in the center of each human life where connectedness to God begins and ends, the place where the highest affections and deepest commitments are held. If the demons can disrupt and destroy the divine linkage, they've captured the person. We have to make sure they don't win."

Seradim observed Ben carefully. "I can't read his thoughts," the angel concluded, "but I certainly sense what his demeanor indicates. Ben doesn't know who his heavenly Father is."

"Exactly."

"We must help Ben get connected."

"Very good. You make me look like an excellent teacher."

Seradim studied the young man carefully. "Ben is a good person. Lots of integrity there. Where can we expect evil to attack?"

"Not all evil comes directly from demons," Michael explained. "Most doesn't. The flesh is quite capable of an amazing assortment of delightful expressions of wickedness. Demons often play off of these themes and employ them like fishermen use worms. Of course, the world system also comes into play."

"How so?

"Greed, lust, power, immorality, enmity, strife, divisiveness, selfishness, and a host of equally destructive tendencies form webs of intrigue and seduction, trapping people much as spiders catch flies. The demons help set the ambush, so we've got to help Ben, his family, and his friends escape the snares by giving them a vision of the greater spiritual realities."

"Tell me how to make sure our charges do the right thing," Seradim urged.

"Sorry, friend. Human beings are endowed with an awesome capacity. Like the Creator, they have free will. Each person must make up his own mind to do the right thing. Even God Himself will not force the human race to do His supreme will. We do everything we can to help, but the choice is theirs."

"Then, what *can* we do?"

"Watch over them carefully! I am constantly making sure Cindy doesn't get in trouble. Blindness makes her physically vulnerable. What do you see right now, Seradim?"

The junior angel thought himself to the street corner across from the library. The sounds of traffic filled his mind, but one sound prevailed. A block and a half away, a teenager roared up the street in a red Pontiac Firebird. Going far beyond the speed limit, the car veered toward the curb. Within seconds, Cindy would be standing where the vehicle was aimed. Sam, her guide dog, unable to sense the approaching danger, kept leading Cindy toward the street.

Michael instantly placed himself in front of the guide dog. Although Sam couldn't see the invisible angel, he sensed the unexpected presence and started backing away, pulling Cindy with him. A second later, the red Pontiac's right front tire hit the curb and bounced over the sidewalk. The teenager instantly jerked the steering wheel, sending the car back into traffic. Swerving to miss a parked car just ahead, the Pontiac barely managed to keep from sideswiping a car in the second lane of traffic. People honked and shouted, but the boy only increased his speed.

"Sam!" Cindy jerked the handle on the dog harness. "What was that? Did we nearly get hit?" She listened to the sound of the car speeding away and the honking. "Is someone there?" she called, but no one answered. "Felt like a person was close," she said to herself. The noise subsided. "It certainly sounded like we were at the racetrack for a moment, and someone special was here." She urged Sam to take her across the street.

Seradim moved to Michael's side, observing Cindy as she crossed the street and went up the steps of the library. "Intuitive intelligence is everything," Michael instructed. "Trust what you 'just know' and contemplate what pulsates from the mind of God. You'll automatically know what to do."

"That miss was too close for comfort!" Seradim said. "I was really frightened."

"That's because we profoundly care for them," Michael replied. "The Creator built that capacity into us. Our love naturally flows from what we know. Humans tend to feel love. We *will* love. We choose it! The instant I saw Cindy's dilemma, everything in me moved according to the dictates of love. Don't worry, Seradim. You'll get the hang of it quickly enough."

CHAPTER
13

The disappearance of millions of people sent shock waves of chaos across the world. The catastrophe hit hard at Frank Wong's restaurant in Lake Forest, California. The Golden Dragon lost many customers and a number of its best employees. With no explanation for the disappearances, the Wongs worried and fretted constantly. Most of the time Frank and Jessica spoke Chinese and avoided unnecessary conversations with Caucasians.

The sun was going down as Frank turned off El Toro Road into the parking lot in front of a large apartment complex clubhouse. "Jessica, I . . . very . . . uh . . . glad we prepare for initiation into Transcendental Meditation before all craziness happen." He turned off the ignition and got out of the car. "We must find serenity in midst of confusion. Most difficult time."

"Honorable husband, I agree." Jessica joined Frank on the walk leading to the long, flat-topped building. She carried a small plastic sack. "T.M. promise prosperity if only follow teaching of the Maharishi Mahesh Yogi. Obviously, many people agree with us."

"After bad experience with séance, we need something more in this world than talking to our ancestors." Frank took his wife's hand at the door. "Mr. Penny is good instructor. He say reaching fourth state of consciousness is answer to our worries. News reports only make everything worse."

The Wongs cautiously entered the spacious club room filled with people. Chairs lined the back, the main area covered only by a thick rug. In the front of the room, an altar-like table featured a picture of an Indian guru. Flickering candles placed around the room threw long shadows across the walls. The smell of incense was heavy and stale. Many of the initiates were sitting on the floor.

"You have special offerings?" Frank asked.

"Yes. Teacher say bring six flowers, three pieces of fruit, and white handkerchief." Jessica held up the plastic bag. "We are ready for the offerings of life and for cleansing."

After removing their shoes, the Wongs found a place near the altar. Like others seated on the floor, they assumed lotus positions. Their teacher entered from the back of the room, smiling and nodding to the group.

Jim Penny lit a candle beside the picture and began singing a Sanskrit hymn. The Wongs bowed their heads in respect. Michael and Seradim hovered above the scene.

"We cannot be concerned for Cindy without experiencing the same love for her parents," Michael said. "Keeping Frank and Jessica out of trouble is nearly a full-time job."

"What's happening?" Seradim wondered.

"After the Wongs got the bejabbers scared out of them talking to the dead, they turned to this old Hindu hoax and paid a considerable initiation fee. Their instructor told them T.M. wasn't a religion. Little did they know the teacher was leading them into the Shankara Hindu tradition. The origin of everything they've learned is in the texts of the Hindu sacred writings—the Vedas and Upanishads—and particularly the Bhagavad-Gita. Frank and Jessica are dangerously close to connecting with the principalities and powers of this world."

Michael pointed at the picture. "The T.M. people tried to sell their system to the American schools as nonreligious, but the lawyers caught them at it. The Federal Courts consistently ruled T.M. a religion." Michael laughed. "One of the few things the Supreme Court did right during the last decade."

Seradim listened to the chanting for a moment. "I don't think anyone in the group has any idea what the words mean."

"Frank and Jessica think it's a nice chant. The Vedic hymn, the *puja*, is actually worship of Hindu deities. In the first part of the song, Penny is calling out the names of the gods. Through the mantra the people receive, the gods will be worshiped. Listen. He is saying, 'I bow down.' Scary stuff indeed!"

"Who's the guy in the picture?"

"Sri Guru Dev was the Maharishi's teacher. In just a moment, Penny is going to worship the guru because he is identified with the Trimurti—the Hindu triad: Brahma, Vishnu, and Siva. Dev was declared a personified fullness of Brahma."

A strange sensation inched up Seradim's body. He felt agitated, and an eerie sense of foreboding settled around his thoughts. "Something weird is happening. . . . I don't understand. . . ."

"Watch!" Michael pointed toward the candles. In the shape of curling smoke, convoluted forms began emerging out of the flames.

Seradim stared at their evil faces as the disembodied creatures floated up like greasy smoke.

"The Hindu gods are only the facade for demons, each name the result of centuries of seduction." Michael made a slight gesture, parting the smoke and incense rising to the ceiling. "Although the initiates don't know it, they are being prepared to worship and make contact with these demons. Sri Dev actually became the name used by a demon known to us as Dungetius, a vile creature thriving on rotten thoughts."

People stood, came forward, and knelt before the altar. The teacher bent down, whispering a mantra into each person's ear.

"These people think they are receiving a harmless sound to repeat," Michael explained. "Actually, the mantras are the names of demons. As they repeat the word over and over, the vibrations invoke the presence of the spirit."

Seradim choked at the thought.

"Look!" Michael pointed at the candles again. More spirits emerged as each person received a mantra. The ethereal horde increased, blending together in a whirling mass above the group. Like storm clouds forming a tornado, the black minions writhed together like snakes slithering over each other in a den of venomous death. Periodically, a single demon's face surfaced above the horde. Poised to strike, the horde waited for the signal to attack.

"As soon as the group starts mass meditation, the demons will hit them. Seradim, prepare yourself for battle. We must strike first!"

"H . . . H . . . How?" Seradim stuttered.

Michael dived into the center of the demonic mass. A great burst of light exploded in a brilliant flash. Demons momentarily evaporated like a campfire dissolving in a gust of wind. The stunned horde tumbled backward out across the boundless expanse of space separating earth and heaven. Unaware of the spiritual warfare exploding above them, the Wongs continued the ritual of initiation.

The demons surged back toward the room in an attempt to regroup. Seradim saw the pack returning and immediately flew down to protect Michael's back. "I'm with you!"

"Let my thoughts guide you," Michael instructed. "We must scatter this scum quickly." He paused until the scourge was nearly upon them. "Jesus is Lord!" Michael exclaimed. "You are completely defeated!"

Like a squadron of tanks screeching to a halt before a cliff, the demons stopped in consternation. A thundering voice arose out of the mass. "Who are you?"

"Angels of the Most High!" Michael shouted. "Come forth and meet your fate." Michael began glowing in an increasing aura of light.

"Our time is not yet," a demon's voice rumbled back.

As Seradim thought on the light of God, he reflected the celestial glory. The splendor of brilliant color merged into the light already emanating from Michael.

"The Light of the world has appeared," Michael answered the demon. "The darkness is overcome."

For a moment, the evil pack paused in bewilderment. Then slowly the demons backed away, moving toward the dark edges at the end of time. One by one the mass dissolved, the black energy dissipated.

"Wow!" Seradim gulped. "What happened?"

"They're gone." Michael smiled mischievously. "You did good."

Seradim looked into the empty space in amazement. "What . . . did . . . I . . . actually do?"

"Darkness cannot traffic with light. You blasted our adversaries with the splendor of God. These vile creatures can't stand the impact."

"Will they return?"

"Not tonight! However, if these new T.M. initiates continue the practice of calling forth the Hindu deities and the demons behind them, then yes, they will return to infest the people."

"What about the Wongs?"

"Seradim, let's go down and stand beside them. I think we can quickly get them out of this snare. Follow me." Michael immediately thought himself next to Frank.

Frank turned to his wife and opened his eyes. "It working?"

Jessica shrugged her shoulders. "Just making strange sound but nothing happening."

The instructor looked around the room and frowned. People were not connecting as he had anticipated. "Concentrate," Penny urged. "Let your mind go into neutral while you say the mantra over and over."

Frank closed his eyes again and started repeating the name in a low hum.

Michael looked knowingly at Seradim. "Think with Jessica while I do the same with Frank. Concentrate on the love of God. Remember how the Father wants a real and genuine relationship with all of His creatures. Help the Wongs realize the true nature of their spiritual hunger."

Michael steadily emanated the profound love of the Heavenly Father. His thoughts hung in the air like the sweet smell of spring flowers. The angel leaned near Frank's ear, sending his thoughts like beautiful music traveling through a special frequency to an inner receiver. Seradim did the same thing with Jessica.

Frank abruptly opened his eyes and looked around the room. He shook his head and looked perturbed. Jessica opened one eye. "I don't think this what we need," Frank whispered. The instructor checked the thermostat on the air conditioner.

"Atmosphere seems stale," Penny announced. "Just keep repeating your mantra and soon you will enter your new level of consciousness. Please, don't stop," Penny urged nervously.

Michael smiled. "The teacher can't make the system work tonight because we have broken the spell of the spirits. Penny doesn't know why but he knows something is missing."

"Look at him." Seradim pointed. "The teacher appears to be wrapped in a film."

"Unfortunately, the instructor is sealed," Michael explained. "Penny dabbled with the satanic elements one too many times, granting them possession of his life. In ancient times, people used a seal stamped in wax to indicate ownership. You are seeing the spiritual sign of Satan's possession. Just as Christians are sealed and protected in the baptism of the Spirit at salvation, this man is marked by the devil."

"Can't we break the bondage?"

"No, the teacher has free will. We cannot cross that boundary. Even the heavenly Father honors his right to choose. Only as the man repents and renounces evil can he be set free. In the meantime, the demon controlling him is protected from us. People who own Ouija boards, tarot cards, or dabble with astrology, Scientology, witchcraft, or visit fortune-tellers are in the same danger. They become cursed as this poor man is."

"Is there no hope?"

"There's always hope, Seradim, because Jesus Himself became a curse through His crucifixion to break all bonds of evil. But until this man accepts the gift of salvation, he is trapped like a lion in a zoo. What he thinks is freedom is nothing but a cage with invisible bars."

Jessica poked Frank in the side. "I want to go home. This is not at all what I expected."

Frank nodded toward the door. "Let's slip out." He stooped over for several feet before standing up. To his surprise several other couples joined them.

"Please," the instructor begged, "we've just begun."

"Don't look back," Michael whispered in Frank's ear. "Keep walking."

Frank and Jessica hurried through the door and toward their car. "Strange. We just can't seem to find anything that works," Jessica concluded. "Cindy is so much more satisfied with the Bible lessons she discusses with her friends. Maybe we should listen to her."

"Yes, holy book not like this silly business with candles and funny words."

Jessica nodded her head and slid into the car.

As Michael felt profound satisfaction, the feeling immediately registered with Seradim. "We did well tonight, Seradim. Very well. Now it's time to get back to Cindy."

CHAPTER

14

While the Wongs terminated their foray into the world of T.M. at the Lake Forest clubhouse, Ben Feinberg finished supper at the Golden Dragon. Cindy's questions about the Bible encouraged him to reconsider his skepticism about the Scriptures.

"An amazing number of people are converting to evangelical Christianity," Cindy told Ben as he consumed Hunan chicken. The smell of simmering vegetables and roast duck hung in the air.

"So it seems." Ben ate without looking up. Guests walked past him. Most of the tables in the popular restaurant were already taken.

"I heard one report that thousands of people in Eastern Europe and parts of Africa are accepting the ancient faith," Cindy added. "The strange disappearance of Christians has certainly left everyone in consternation."

Ben put his chopsticks down and sat back in the black ivory chair. "Apparently thousands of Orthodox Jews have suddenly embraced the idea that Jesus is the Messiah," he added. "Some discovery from a just-released portion of the Dead Sea Scrolls convinced them. The Essenes, who collected the Dead Sea Scrolls, had eight copies of the book of Daniel, a book that predicts some of the things that seem to be happening right now. They thought the events would happen in their era." He took a long drink of iced tea.

Cindy swallowed hard. "We've got to recognize something incredible is going on."

"Some Jewish converts have also come to an additional conclusion," Ben said. "They expect there will soon be another worldwide persecution of Jews, which will be worse than Hitler's holocaust."

"Oh, Ben!" Cindy stiffened. "That is too horrible to think about. Don't say such a thing."

Ben looked up at the elegant ceiling. The long figure of a dragon wound its way across the top of the dining room. "We once thought smog was the worst thing in the air. Now a little pollution seems innocuous." Ben finished eating silently and laid his chopsticks down for the last time. "Got to run, Cindy. See you tomorrow morning."

"Drive carefully, Ben."

He impulsively leaned over the table and kissed Cindy on the lips. *"Ciao!"* the youth called over his shoulder.

Cindy sat stunned for several moments before a sly smile finally inched across her face. "Well, for goodness' sake! *Ciao* to you, too, Mr. Ben Feinberg."

Tapping with her white walking stick, Cindy found her way back to the kitchen. The afterglow of Ben's romantic gesture sent her mind spinning in other directions.

A breath of fresh air is what I need, Cindy said to herself. *Ben has an amazing effect on me. Just can't think straight around him.*

Leaving Sam curled up next to the stove, Cindy used the cane to guide herself toward the back door. She stepped out into the evening alone. *The cool air means it must be dark.* Her fingers glided over the top of her braille wristwatch. *Ah, my parents should be home by now,* she concluded. She felt her way along the side of the building leading into the alleyway where trash containers were kept.

Fifteen feet away a large figure lurked behind one of the dumpsters. A man crept out, hovering close to the building. He crouched down with his hands outstretched, open, and aimed at the blind girl carefully tapping against the brick.

"Good evening," Michael abruptly barked from behind the thug, where the angel had suddenly appeared in human form.

The startled attacker slipped and fell into the wall, sprawling on the cement.

"Hello," Cindy answered timidly. "I didn't know anyone was out here."

Struggling to his feet, the assailant leaped toward Michael, only to discover him towering nearly a foot above his head. The culprit froze, stared for a second, and then charged toward a hedge at the back of the shopping center.

Cindy tilted her head, listening to the man run. "Don't leave."

"I'm still here," Michael answered.

"There's two of you?"

"No, just me. I scared off a man about to harm you."

"Oh, my goodness." Cindy braced herself against the wall. "Who are you?"

"Just a friend. Call me Michael."

"We've met?"

"Not formally." The angel chuckled. "But I've been around. I'd suggest you be more careful walking around in the dark by yourself. After all, most of the spiritual people are gone from the face of the earth. Why don't you get a quick breath of fresh air and go back inside?"

Cindy swallowed hard. "Well, I . . . uh . . . think so. I really should keep my guide dog with me all the time." She turned toward the restaurant's back door. "You said you're a friend named Michael?"

"Yes," the angel answered. "I'll be around."

"Thank you." Cindy opened the door. "We need to get better acquainted."

"Certainly," Michael answered and promptly stepped out of time into eternity, reappearing next to Seradim.

"You became one of them!" the trainee angel exclaimed. "How did you do that?"

"We have the capacity to assume bodies by thinking ourselves into them," Michael explained. "Guardians can put on a human form like people wear costumes. The shape we take is like wearing a mask. Because angels aren't born, we don't have anatomy like humans. We never breathe or eat. Of course, you can munch on a cookie if you choose . . . taste is quite an adventure, but you never get used to the feeling. Sense perception and appetite are only a vehicle to achieve our purposes."

"I can't believe it!" Seradim shook his head. "You looked exactly like one of them."

"I could have assumed any height or weight I wished." Michael shrugged. "You just think yourself into the condition. Being confined in space is an interesting experience."

"Hmmm," Seradim pondered the thought. "The idea of physical space is amazing. Strange."

"Humans have an equally difficult time understanding how place doesn't confine us. Centuries ago medieval philosophers debated how many angels could dance on the head of a pin." Michael laughed. "Not a dumb question at all! Since place cannot confine spirit, an infinite number of us could think ourselves in any one place at any time. Locality doesn't surround us as space does a human body. We can encompass an area as I did by entering into a body."

"When you saved Cindy from getting run over at the stoplight, people couldn't see you. Right? But the attacker saw you a few moments ago?"

"Exactly. On the first occasion I enabled Cindy's dog to sense my presence, so I didn't need to materialize. Actually, I can speak directly with Cindy more often because she's blind and won't realize I haven't taken on a human form."

"Why don't we just appear as we are, Michael?"

"Humans can't see or comprehend pure spirit. And people have nothing in nature to compare with our appearance; we have a beauty beyond human imagination. In the same way, people's souls are more beautiful than their bodies."

"I certainly have an incredible amount to learn," Seradim concluded. "How do you always stay on top of things?"

"While humans sleep, we watch. Often the Father directly dispatches us to fulfill His will. Of course, prayer helps us stay aware. Hear the supplications?"

Seradim frowned and shook his head.

"You are accustomed to hearing the heavenly praise. Now you must learn to tune into the special frequency that lifts the needs of people to the throne of God. A heavenly network is poised to maintain an unbroken line of communication. No prayer ever goes unnoticed."

"I'm missing something," the younger angel concluded. "I don't hear anything."

"Tune in the praises of the Cherubim and Seraphim. Now, shift your perception a little farther down and tune in the worship of Christians in this world."

Seradim concentrated with everything in his being. "I . . . think. . . . Yes, I am getting the sound. In fact, I can *see* it happening. I perceive faces of many people in small groups, large sanctuaries, and lone prayer warriors, praising God and asking for divine help, pleading assistance for people in need. Incredible!"

"Excellent, Seradim! Often we respond to those very prayers, as the Holy Spirit guides us."

Listening to the myriad of intercessions rising up to heaven, Seradim was completely distracted. "I had no idea," he said. "I never heard them before."

"As each prayer goes up, the need comes before the Throne of Grace. The twenty-four elders constantly offer up prayers in golden bowls as overtures of pure incense." Michael pointed toward heaven. "Prayers are the one human thing that can cross time and penetrate eternity."

"People are the only creatures who can pray?"

"Yes, in their minds they have a wonderful spiritual frequency transmitter capable of breaking through the limitations of the physical world. Unfortunately, most don't know they have the ability, and few of those who do work to develop their full capacities. If people knew what their prayers accomplished, they would be on their knees day and night."

Seradim nodded. "With their feet on the earth, their souls can roam the realms of heaven!"

Michael tilted his head and pointed toward California. "I want you to listen to one specific prayer going up right now. Eventually you'll become accustomed to staying attuned to prayer for our charges. Pay attention to a prayer on behalf of the Feinbergs. Hear it?"

Seradim looked mystified and shook his head.

"Joe and Jennifer McCoy are old acquaintances of the Feinberg family. The good doctor and his wife have no idea Joe and Jennifer pray for them. Before the Rapture, the McCoys knew what God expected, but didn't know Him personally. The McCoys simply didn't embrace Yeshua into their hearts. After the Rapture, at a Christian fellowship, the McCoys accepted Jesus as their Savior and Lord, so from now on they will have the presence of the Holy Spirit who is sealed within them until they get their new bodies in heaven someday. They returned to the spiritual roots of their parents. Follow my mind and I'll help you pick up their prayers."

Steadily and with increasing clarity, words filled the space between the two angels. Seradim listened carefully, and the sound became louder.

"Bless Larry and Sharon, Father. . . . We have no hope in this world without you. Please forgive us that we didn't listen all those years. But please, please, help the Feinbergs. We know they are closed to their Jewish heritage, but please help them understand how Jesus is their Messiah too. . . ."

"Hear them praying?" Michael asked.

"Amazing!" Seradim replied. "It's like I'm right in the room with them."

"Sure. If we pay close attention, the McCoys' prayers can be a wake-up call to alert us to the Feinbergs' need."

"Then the Holy Spirit uses angels and other means to answer those prayers?"

"Exactly. The Holy Spirit translates their prayers into heavenly groanings that cannot be uttered by humans. Then the Father tells Yeshua and some chosen angelic creatures, and the prayer becomes a symphony of action—divine action. Then angels deliver suggestions to other humans to help fulfill the original prayer request. An amazing process! Those prayers return to Earth with the power to touch the souls of people like the Feinbergs. The intercessions are change agents, influencing a new mind-set. Prayer creates a sense of need. Humans are deeply affected by their environment. Teenagers want loud music on the radio so they won't feel alone. Adults like the thermostats set just right to feel comfortable. Lovers try to create romantic moods. Understand? Prayers release spiritual energy, the power of the omnipresent Holy Spirit. Prayer surrounds people with the aura of God's love and compassion. Hearts are turned and inclined to the Father."

Seradim nodded slowly. "They return to the persons in need?"

"And with all the power of heaven added. . . . Let me show you." Michael thought himself and the young angel into the Feinbergs' living room. Larry was adjusting the TV, and Sharon was reading a novel.

Sharon laid her book down. "Larry, maybe we ought to turn the TV off. Since the Rapture there's nothing but violence, crime, and sex left on the screen. I didn't think much of TV before, but now the content is simply ridiculous."

"You're certainly right about that!"

"I'm concerned that we have, well . . . for lack of a better term . . . no spiritual direction in our lives." Sharon sounded apologetic. "Know what I mean?"

Larry frowned but paused a moment before answering. "I . . . started . . . to tune you out, but maybe you're right, dear. I guess . . . I . . . I just don't know . . . where to turn for help. We were never observant. The synagogue doesn't seem to be the right place now."

"I don't know why, but I feel that Jennifer McCoy might offer some help. I've known her forever. And recently she told me she'd found some spiritual answers. Maybe we ought to talk to the McCoys about this."

Larry shrugged. "Couldn't hurt anything. Who knows? Might help."

"I'll make the time to talk with her."

Michael smiled. "See how the system operates? The power of prayer really works! The Holy Spirit answers prayers with compassionate conviction, and the Holy Spirit uses us and spiritual humans as His messengers."

■ ■ ■

A week later Sharon ran into Jennifer in the grocery store and invited the couple over for dessert. Joe and Jennifer came prepared to tell their story. The Feinbergs stared in rapt attention as Joe and Jennifer McCoy answered their questions. Sharon Feinberg had been amazed at how quickly the McCoys wanted to meet with them, as if they had just been waiting for an opportunity like this.

Jennifer placed her cup on the coffee table in the Feinbergs' den. "Many Christians are meeting frequently for fellowship. Once a week on Sundays just doesn't seem enough with so much turmoil in the world after the Rapture—the disapperance of so many millions of believers. So people are getting together in their homes for fellowship and prayer."

"One of the leaders taught a short Bible study," Joe continued. "He talked about Jesus being the light of the world and how much we needed illumination in these dark times. He explained the disappearances, and it made tremendous sense."

"Yes." Jennifer nodded her head. "Joe and I had discussed our family's need for spiritual guidance for a long time. We could see the terrible moral dangers our children faced and knew we deeply wanted the hand of God in our family. The moment was right for us to say yes."

Joe smiled. "The leader said that we could have Jesus in our lives all the time. He suggested that if we didn't know that decision was an already accomplished fact, we should settle the matter at that exact moment."

"Our eyes met," Jennifer continued. "We both knew what the other was thinking. I put my hand in Joe's, and while the group prayed, we asked Jesus to be the light of our family."

"By the time we left, Jennifer and I knew something tremendous had happened. Everything about the future would be new and exciting. We haven't been disappointed."

Larry rolled his tongue around in his mouth and forced a smile. "Quite a story," he mumbled.

"But we are Jews," Sharon protested.

"Jesus was a Jew," Jennifer answered. "His name in Hebrew was Yeshua, and many Messianic Jews use that name."

"Well, yes," Larry agreed. "But for us it's more difficult." He rubbed his chin nervously. "To be honest, we don't know much of anything about what Christians really think or what the Bible says, Old Testament or New Testament."

"Hey, we were no different." Joe picked up a cookie. "We were as spiritually blind as a bat in a church belfry. But we've had an incredible time simply studying the Scriptures and going to Bible studies." He reached for a sack. "We've brought you a Bible and some study materials."

"I prepared a list of Scriptures that have really been help-ful to us," Jennifer added. "You'll love making your own discoveries."

"Thank you for the thoughtfulness." Sharon slowly accepted the material from Joe. "I promise we'll take a look."

"It will take time," Larry hesitated.

"Whenever you have questions, we're as close as the phone," Joe assured. "We won't push you . . . just be avail-able to answer questions."

"Simply let us know." Jennifer beamed.

CHAPTER
15

The national security adviser's eyes flashed with anger. "Any second now we will have to walk into his office and talk with the president," he said to his top-ranking staff member. "We don't have the answers we promised. Do you understand the seriousness of our plight?"

"He's a harsh man." The staffer looked grim. "But we've been unable to find anything but religious explanations."

"God help us if you bring that up!" Further comment ended when the president's chief of staff opened the door to the Oval Office and motioned for the two men to enter.

"Good morning, gentlemen." Damian Gianardo stood and offered his hand. "Excuse me for a lack of pleasantries. We must get right to business. We are facing an increasing financial crisis across the world. I must quiet public fears. Time is running out. Please give me the report of your investigation of the disappearance of millions of people."

"Sir," the national security chief said haltingly, "we really don't have a written report."

"A verbal explanation is sufficient for now," the president answered sourly. "I promised the world an answer before the end of the year. A quick synopsis will do."

"The problem is . . ." The security chief stopped and turned to his assistant. "You tell him, Ralph."

"Mr. President, we have found no rational explanation. We have been unable—"

"You've what?" Gianardo's neck began turning red. "I promised the world that I would have an answer. You had best not make me appear to be a fool." His black eyes narrowed, glaring as if he could burn holes through the assistant's face.

"Our only explanations are religious," the staffer blurted out. The national security chief covered his face.

"Religious!" the president shouted. "You expect me to make a sectarian pronouncement about this disaster? Financial markets are collapsing everywhere, and you want me to offer superstition to assure the masses?"

"It's all we have." The assistant held up his empty hands.

Damian Gianardo turned slowly to his national security head, his gaze so fierce the man was forced to look down. "I would suggest two things. First, you fire this incompetent fool before sunset. Second, you have a plausible answer for me in one week or prepare yourself for new employment immediately thereafter. Good day, gentlemen." The president turned back to a letter on his desk and continued reading without looking up; the two bewildered men scurried from the Oval Office with the chief of staff hurrying after the two aides.

Gianardo had no idea he was actually the subject of intense scrutiny. From the dimension existing behind time and beyond space, the demonic war council continued their ongoing examination of the president of the United

States. "What do you wish us to do, O Great One?" Dungetius humbly asked the leader. The host of demons genuflected before the Lord of Hate.

Radiating with the brilliance of the morning star, their leader brushed the question aside. "This one is my chosen man. He is almost prepared to do my total bidding." The Evil One towered above the other demons like a mountain eclipses a valley, his radiance beyond theirs as the sun is brighter than the moon. "He does not yet understand the destiny I have placed at his feet, but Damian is learning." Lucifer thought of his future intentions, and his vision instantly rippled through the hierarchy of iniquity, causing a gasp of awe and amazement. "We must help him grasp the meaning of this moment."

Lucifer's voice bristled with pure spite. "Help Damian see his options," he snarled. "I want him to throb with the same motivation and drive that worked in the bones of Nebuchadnezzar before his conversion to God. Make him pulsate with the same greed we put in the heart of Nero. My son Damian has a right to enjoy the intoxication that comes only from the joy of fulfilled hunger for power." The Evil One pointed his finger through the curtain of time straight at the president still sitting behind his desk. "Dungetius, get down there and work on expanding the possibilities of the religious explanation the aide offered. Damian needs to know what excellent opportunities are his through the politics of counterfeit religion. Get on with it!"

"Excellent, majesty!" Dungetius kept bowing and rubbing his hands together. "I can help him understand the value of the partnership between 'the beast' and the 'lamb that speaks with the voice of the dragon.' Fortunately, the Christians are gone, except for the post-Rapture converts, so we don't have to contend with much prayer opposition. Nothing is left to push our Regional Overseers out of place."

"Dungetius will require assistance!" The devil's response rumbled across timelessness. "I want the Principalities and Powers controlling Washington, D.C., to increase fortification over the entire area. We cannot tolerate a counterattack to break our grip on the capital. Work on the entire presidential staff. Mingle greed with fear! Now is the moment to send Rathmarker into the president with the book we placed in front of his face." Lucifer clapped his hands; thunder roared through eternity. "Do it now!"

Principality demons controlling the eastern seaboard surged into place. Demonic princes immediately began securing the space above the national capital to avoid a counterattack from any angels circulating in the area. Dungetius and his pack thought themselves into the White House. They found the fear and distrust permeating the staff, offering them additional leverage for their work.

Dungetius instantly found Vice President Jacob Rathmarker reading in his office. The demon stood beside the politician and bombarded his mind with intense thoughts. "Tell Gianardo about this book you are reading. Share your conclusions. Get in there and speak to him. Do it now!" Repeating it like a mantra, Dungetius kept saying over and over, "Now, now, now, now, now, now . . ."

Rathmarker put his book down and stared at the wall for several moments. He finally reached for his phone and rang the Oval Office.

"Yes," Gianardo answered sharply.

"Mr. President," Jacob began, "I think I'm on to something that might help us out of this crisis."

"Then you're the only one who's got any brains," Gianardo carped. "The rest of these idiots are completely hung up on religious answers. I am surrounded by a pack of idiots!"

"Interestingly enough, we might be able to use this nonsense to our advantage. If there's one thing we can count on these days, it's that people are incurably religious because of the turn of the millennium and the disappearance of more than half a billion people. We simply need to manipulate their tendencies."

"Come on over, Jacob," the president's voice softened. "I've been about half distracted for the last hour. Don't know why but I can't seem to concentrate."

"I'll be there in a moment."

Rathmarker quickly walked from his office into the inner office. He laid a book before the president. "I've been reading poems written by Lenin. Very interesting."

"What?" Gianardo did not hide his irritation. "Poetry at a time like this?"

Rathmarker smiled slyly. "Lenin taught me something. What the world needs at this moment is a messiah, a new Christ, a quasi-religious hero. Every major leader of the twentieth century had an inkling of this need. Think about it, Damian. Stalin, Hitler, Mao. Every one of them was fundamentally a religious figure pursuing a bigger, better hope than the churches offered. We've come to another opportune moment for a charismatic leader to take the place of God. After all, the evangelical Christians seem to be gone so we don't have to contend with their Jesus-talk nonsense to confuse people."

"What are you driving at?" Gianardo laid his pen down.

Rathmarker picked up the book of poems. "Lenin called this one 'Oulanem.' The title is the inversion of the Russian name for Emmanuel, meaning 'God is with us.' The satanists have been turning Christian words and symbols around and upside down forever. Lenin once was an enthusiastic Christian, but he became involved with the occult. That's when he wrote the following: 'If there is something which devours, I'll leap within it, though I bring the world to ruins. The world which bulks between me and the abyss, I will smash it to pieces with my enduring curses. I'll throw my arms around its harsh reality. Embracing me, the world will humbly pass away. And then sink down to utter nothingness. Perished, with no existence; that would be really living.'"

Gianardo got out of his chair and walked around to the front of his desk. "Those words strangely resonate with me. I don't know why, but it feels as if I have been waiting all morning for this moment. Bizarre! My ancestors were, like Lenin's, very religious, and I have always wanted to depart from the faith of my fathers."

"Here's one Lenin called 'The Fiddler.'" Rathmarker cleared his throat and read in low threatening tones. "The hellish vapors rise and fill the brain, till I go mad and my heart is utterly changed. See this sword? The prince of darkness sold it to me.'" Rathmarker closed the book. "Get his drift?"

Gianardo frowned and shook his head.

"Lenin wasn't an atheist. He was a God-hater! The man learned the secret of becoming an antichrist, a messiah of this world!"

Gianardo's eyes widened. The president slowly shook his head as if suddenly possessed by an idea of monumental portions.

"Look!" Rathmarker's eyes narrowed. "What if all those Christians were swallowed up by the devil? Expelled from the world! What if the deity the Christians called 'God' was actually a weak contender for control of the universe? What if the figure Lenin called the prince of darkness finally won the war?"

"Incredible idea, Jacob. Remarkable."

"Lenin, Stalin, Hitler, all knew how to manipulate the religious needs of their subjects, and obviously they had help. Just maybe Satan is waiting to empower and guide anyone willing to follow his leading." Rathmarker grinned. "Why not you, Damian? You fit the criteria for a worldwide antichrist. You can become the god of this world, and I will gladly serve as your prophet."

Gianardo rubbed his forehead and let the weight of his body down on the top of his desk. "I was always impressed that communism, fascism, and Nazism were pseudo-religions. For years, many Americans turned patriotism into a religion of sorts." He snapped his fingers. "Of course. That's exactly what this country needs right now. A strong popular patriotic faith! A United Nations—'We Are the World'—type feeling of unity with me as leader."

"It's what the whole world needs," Rathmarker corrected the president. "You're the person to fill the job. Just stop thinking of yourself as president and get used to the title Caesar."

A smile inched across Damian's face. "What a tremendous thought!" He grinned like a child contemplating Christmas.

"People already see you as the sole leader of the country and the most powerful leader in the world." Jacob pointed to the presidential seal. "In this time of crisis, people will naturally turn to you as the hero, the great man. We must take this tendency on to the next step. They must see you as the incarnated spirit of the nation. From there, it's only a short step for them to focus all of their religious needs on you."

The president clenched his fist. "Exactly! Get me on television surrounded with quasi-religious symbols. I must assume the posture of the ruler of this world."

Jacob laughed. "Fools think modern people aren't religious. The truth is they remain fervently devout; they've just changed their focus. People are looking for something in *this* world to worship, not beyond it."

"And I'm it!" Gianardo boasted. "I can turn those religious explanations upside down and inside out." He walked with new confidence around to the back of his desk. "The first step is to assemble a think tank of advisers to consider and formulate new policy for world domination. We'll start immediately." The president hit the buttons on his telephone. "Get me the chairman of the joint chiefs, the secretary of state, and the treasury secretary! I want the chairman of the Fed in here too." Damian clicked the phone off. "Jacob, I want you to convene the meeting so I won't look self-serving. At the right moment, you will persuade me to accept the course destiny intends."

"I will serve you well, sir."

Damian sat down in his chair and settled back against the leather upholstery. "What do you think Lenin really meant in his poem? 'The prince of darkness sold him the sword'?"

"I believe evil is a personified reality," Rathmarker concluded. "In fact, I'm willing to bet Satan annihilated those trouble-making Christians. We don't have to tell people that's our conclusion. Just ignore their disappearance and cut a deal with the devil."

"But Stalin, Hitler, Mao didn't last. Mao and Stalin died. Hitler committed suicide."

"The times weren't right." Rathmarker shrugged. "For some reason, things are in place now. Think of the greats like Engels, Marx, Himmler, Khrushchev, Idi Amin, as preparing the way for you."

Gianardo pulled at his chin and squinted. "The prince of darkness sold it to me," he mused. "Do you think Lenin meant those words literally?"

"My research confirms a strong satanist link in Lenin's past. Many political leaders talked with the other side as easily as they phoned down the street."

"I want to know how it's done," Gianardo pressed. "Find out how I can get in touch with what you call 'the Evil One.' I'm going to need all the help I can get."

"Consider it done, Mr. President. I will be your prophet, and the Evil One will be your source of worldwide power. A new age is dawning!"

CHAPTER
16

Over the next several days, events moved quickly. Specialists in foreign affairs, international finance, and military strategy streamed through the White House day and night. Pressed in between the marathon planning sessions, the president met with occult practitioners, fortune-tellers, witches, New Agers, clairvoyants, scientologists, and satanists.

The special envoy from Assyria intrigued Gianardo the most. "Sir," the leader of the ancient cult of Zoroastrianism instructed, "are you aware that your name carries the sacred number?"

"I don't understand," the president said.

"The ancient Babylonians assigned a number to every letter in the alphabet. For example, A is equal to six, B to twelve, C to eighteen, and so forth. With this method we were able to assign a special meaning to everyone's name." The gnarled old man grinned a toothy smile. "You, most high one, have a name with a numerical value of 666, the sacred number of the ultimate world emperor. We highly revere such a man."

"Damian Gianardo adds up to 666 using this Babylonian method?" Damian grinned. "666. I am astonished."

The strange little man bowed from the waist. "Yes, it does, therefore, your wish, sir, is my command."

Gianardo slapped him on the back. "My good fellow, we shall yet see what this number means."

The old Assyrian kept bowing as he exited from the room.

Emergency trips and midnight sessions continued into the early hours of the morning. Slowly but steadily, a new national and international policy emerged.

During demonstrations of clairvoyance, ESP, and automatic writing, the president sat spellbound, paying rapt attention to explanations for contacting the devil. Warlocks offered incantations and white witches danced. Repeated incense and spice offerings made the Oval Office smell like frankincense and aromatic gums.

On December 30, the grand scheme was finished and in place. Many politicians and even some cabinet members resigned because of the radical changes: Gianardo's grip on the government was total, exceeding the authority of any president in the history of the country. Even the design of the American flag was changed to show six stars, six stripes, and a special set of six new stars to indicate 666.

As the nation celebrated New Year's Eve, the White House prepared for a very different observance. Aides placed candles around the president's office. Lavers filled with incense sent wispy curls of smoke up toward the ceiling. On the president's desk a skull rested in the center of a red circle. A quill pen, a feather extracted from a raven, waited in front of the bleached, toothless jaw. Knudiaon, the high priest of an ancient Egyptian satanic cult, flew from Cairo the night before for the ceremony. Only Jacob Rathmarker was allowed to watch the president's initiation.

"Notice the amulet around his neck," Rathmarker told the president. "In the center is the ancient Egyptian 'evil eye,' a demonic eye above the pyramid. The image is the seal of the cult."

"Hmmm, sounds like the symbol we Masons use in the lodge meetings." Damian laughed. "Americans have no idea what we slipped in on the back of their dollar bills scores of years ago. Do you realize I am the sixth straight Masonic president? But I am the only one to understand the full meaning of all of the symbolism."

"We must be silent now as we await the priest's coming," Rathmarker remarked. "He told me we must be mentally prepared."

As midnight approached, Gianardo and Rathmarker took their places in two carved chairs placed in the center of the Oval Office. Military guards stood at attention outside the doors. Knudiaon, the senior surviving member of the secret society, entered through a side door used only by the president and his personal staff. He did not acknowledge the two dignitaries waiting for him. His thick black robe could not conceal a hunched back and massive beard. White eyebrows exploded from his forehead like wiry puffs of wool. Knudiaon carried a smoke-stained bowl. The skin on his bony hands was paper thin; the priest's long, unkempt fingernails were yellow and dirty.

With the demeanor of a solitary sphinx lost in the Sahara, Knudiaon walked to the desk and began chanting. After several minutes, he called in English, "Come, Osiris." The black-robed priest walked around the room holding a ceramic dish with a small candle in the middle of some sand. "Come, Isis," he continued. Knudiaon held the hieroglyphics-covered dish above his head while curls of white smoke hung in the air. "Spirits from the land of the dead join us in this hour. Oh, great Lucifer, do not tarry beyond the river of death. Come to us." He lapsed into Egyptian phrases and Arabic words.

Gianardo watched in amazement as the smoke thickened, becoming more like fog, the gathering of a thick mist that took on a life of its own. The temperature in the room dropped. The high priest slowly slumped to his knees, letting the dish of sand slide to the floor and spill over the carpet; the candle bounced and went out. Knudiaon crumpled into a heap as if slain by a hallucinogenic drug.

"It's working!" Gianardo whispered to his vice president. "Just as you said. The master teacher is becoming possessed."

Rathmarker assured him, "The old man is our conduit to the devil. You can trust the prophet."

After a few moments, the priest recovered and stood up, his passive countenance changed. Knudiaon's eyes looked angry and aggressive. "Absolute devotion is demanded!" The priest's voice turned harsh and hard. His face was strangely immobile and void of emotion. "I demand complete fidelity. Are you prepared?"

"Stand up," Rathmarker whispered in the president's ears. "He's ready."

Gianardo rose to his feet, clasping his hands together in front of his coat. He nodded his agreement.

Knudiaon pulled the pointed hood on his black robe down, enveloping his face in shadows. Nothing was visible except his mouth, barely moving in the center of the white beard that dangled down to the base of his neck. The priest reached inside his robe and produced a parchment. He unrolled it and laid it in front of the skull.

Gianardo inched forward with unaccustomed timidity. He took off his coat and handed the jacket to his vice president. The president quickly unfastened a presidential cuff link on his right sleeve and dropped the gold piece in his pocket. Gianardo looked over his shoulder for reassurance. Rathmarker nodded encouragement.

Knudiaon began translating the Sanskrit message written on the parchment immediately below the symbolic pyramid with the evil eye. "My Lord and Master Satan, I acknowledge you as my God and Prince, and promise to serve and obey you while I live. And I renounce the other God and Jesus Christ, the saints, and the church and its sacraments, and I promise to do whatever evil I can. I renounce all the merits of Jesus Christ, and if I fail to serve and adore you, paying homage to you daily, I give you my life as your own. This pact is made on the thirty-first day of December." The old priest stopped and looked Gianardo directly in the eye. His voice dropped nearly an octave lower, rumbling like the sound of chains dragged over stones in a dungeon floor. "Do you intend so?"

"Yes," Damian began hesitantly. "Certainly," he repeated more decisively.

"Give me your hand," the priest demanded.

Damian offered his perspiring palm.

Knudiaon abruptly pulled a jewel-handled dagger from behind the black robe. Before Gianardo could respond, the priest made a surgical slice across his palm; blood instantly filled the president's hand. The old priest laughed diabolically. Gianardo tried to pull away, but the old man held the president's arm with a vice grip.

"The time has come to sign," the priest's cracking voice rumbled. "With your signature, the pact is sealed. Do you agree?"

The president nodded his head mechanically but leaned backward.

Knudiaon picked up the quill in front of the skull. Dipping it in the blood-filled palm, he commanded, "Sign the document!"

The president had to steady his hand against the desk. Blood spilled on the wood and splattered across his shirt sleeve. He breathed deeply but signed with a flourish. Once done, Gianardo straightened and closed his bloody fist.

The old priest smiled slyly. "In the past, the other God has tried to communicate with you through your dreams, but now only the great Evil One will speak to you in your sleep. Should his grace wish to speak with you more directly, Lucifer will have no trouble making contact. Listen to the voices you hear in your head." Knudiaon quickly melted sealing wax with the candle. A blob dropped onto the parchment and Knudiaon plunged his signet ring into the red ooze. "The matter is sealed. You have a new lord. Do not disappoint him. You belong to the devil!" With a flourish the old priest turned and disappeared through the side door.

Damian Gianardo stared at his bleeding hand, unaware blood had already stained his pants and dripped onto his Bruno Magli shoes. He turned to walk away, leaving bloody footprints on the presidential carpet.

■ ■ ■

In accordance with his strict instructions, President Gianardo was not awakened the following morning until late, allowing ample time for dreams to appear. New Year's Day was normally an uneventful time at the White House, but nothing was any longer routine. A week of feverish planning was about to come to full fruition.

Three hours later, Gianardo stepped before the television cameras, opened the file containing his carefully prepared speech, and began at once. "My fellow Americans, we start this new year with grave problems confronting us. I am taking the unusual step of speaking on New Year's Day because I am proposing a new, dramatic path to recovery. I want you to sleep well tonight, knowing your president is about to turn our deficits into assets. Congress has just completed an emergency session that I called two days ago." He stared hard at the camera. "All foreign assets have been frozen. We will hold hundreds of billions of dollars in assets for a period of six months. The nations that agree to become states of the U.S.A. will receive their assets back, while the obstinate will lose their holdings. I would never have done this in the past, but the disappearance of millions of Americans last September has brought on an economic crisis and marks a new, spiritual era. We must do this now to survive."

The president stopped and nodded to the technician. Pictures of European countries filled the screen. Cathedrals and shots of the Vatican emerged. Gianardo waited for a scene of Paris and Notre Dame to appear. "During the past week, Vice President Jacob Rathmarker and I flew secretly to the major capitals of the world with leaders of Congress accompanying us. In secret negotiations, I proposed the creation of a New Roman Empire, resulting in a new world order. Though there was some initial resistance, my explanation of the mutual benefits brought some degree of compliance." Gianardo stopped and smiled wickedly at the screen. "Particularly, if they wanted their moneys back and wanted to avoid nuclear warfare."

Jacob Rathmarker stood in the wings listening. "Masterful stroke," he said to McAbee, his confidential aide. "Because we are the supreme military power in the world, no one can really resist us. Our plan not only eliminates any government debt but instantly makes us the strongest financial nation as well. We've taken a worldwide crisis and turned it into a national asset."

The aide nodded enthusiastically. "But what about the Muslims? Are they really buying in?"

"Even as we speak, we are finalizing negotiations with the consortium that is reconstructing and reorganizing Babylon as the capital of the United Muslim League. Gianardo will link their new Babylonian Empire with our Neo-Roman–American government. As a result, we will have more oil resources than we can ever use. We've got the world by the neck!" The vice president laughed cynically.

"Amazing!" McAbee beamed.

Gianardo cleared his throat and continued. "An international computerized banking system will be located in Rome for our central banking system. While the dollar remains current, I propose an exciting breakthrough. Cash will soon no longer be needed across the empire. Multi-purpose credit cards will offer speedy business transactions. You will receive a universal social security number along with our fellow citizens in Japan, Italy, and Great Britain. With laser technology we can painlessly place a computer chip with the invisible number under the skin of your right hand. The chip could also be placed in the forehead, at the hairline, and no one could ever see it. You wave at a cash register, and the computer will deduct the purchase from your bank account. A completely fair line of credit will be established based on your record of the past three years. A new chapter in economic history is being written. We will finally have a cashless society."

Rathmarker lowered his voice and spoke directly into the aide's ear. "McAbee, universal identification has unlimited possibilities. Total surveillance is just one aspect. We will be able to extend instant control over the worldwide citizenry. Resistance can be crushed in a few hours."

The aide blinked several times. "Why . . . the president . . . will become more like . . . a . . . a . . . world emperor . . ." McAbee's voice trailed off into a whisper.

President Gianardo continued his speech. "As a concession to the United Muslim League, we will be using the ancient Babylonian system for numbering names." Gianardo shared what he had recently learned. "Common denominations by six will be employed, since six is the number for humanity. For example, A would be equal to six; B equals twelve; C equals eighteen; and so forth. Using this system produces a numerical equivalent for my name, Damian Gianardo, of 666. Since I am founding this system, I am asking that all universal social security numbers be preceded by 666, despite the silly superstitions surrounding that number." The president shook his fist in the air. "Let us affirm the power of humanity; 666 is a triple way of asserting the capacities of a human race set free from the old religious superstitions."

Rathmarker's aide turned away from the address. "Can we really get away with freezing the assets of another country?" McAbee grimaced. "A rather bold and, if I may say so, illegal step."

Rathmarker clenched his jaw defiantly. "Who's going to stop us? Congress buckled out of fear and intimidation. The nations of the world will do the same." His eyes flashed. "We have learned the secret of absolute authority, omnipotence, control!" He slapped the aide on the back. "Get on the train, Mac. Gianardo is now the embodiment of sheer power!"

CHAPTER
17

National and international events unfolding over a period of weeks flashed past Michael and Seradim at the pace humans watch the evening news report on television. Each additional episode left Seradim in profound consternation and distress.

"Why doesn't the Almighty stop this nonsense?" Seradim agonized. "I can see where the entire scenario is going."

Michael nodded. "Of course." He pointed at Damian Gianardo. The president was pressing Japanese diplomats to agree to the terms of the treaty his government was imposing on them. The officials looked haggard and tired. "The world has not yet seen a dictator with the mind and finesse of this man. Gianardo's talents and disposition equip him to be both the most winsome and cruelest despot of the entire sweep of history. Moreover, the power of evil is with him."

"Then the Holy One of Israel must intervene!"

"Do not make the same mistake Lucifer made," Michael cautioned. "A host of well-meaning Christians have slipped into the same error, thinking the devil is capable of standing on equal terms with the Lord and posing a genuine threat to God. Lucifer always swings from the end of a rope held by the Holy One."

"A rope?"

"Figure of speech, my friend. Lucifer made the error of thinking it was possible to exist outside the sphere of divine influence." Michael pointed toward the glowing perimeters of heaven in the distance behind them. "Impossible! The Almighty's seeming absence is only the opportunity for His creatures to have the freedom to grow in love. Truth is, the mercy of God is so total and extensive that the Father waits and waits and waits, hoping that His love will be returned to Him. But the day will come when He reels in the rope, and Lucifer will finally realize he has only hung himself by misusing the independence granted from the beginning of eternity."

Using his moral sight, Seradim looked down on the world spinning beneath clouds of moral decadence, and his angelic eyes allowed him to see morality as people view scenery. From the slums of inner cities, smokestacks belched corruption and spilled the black soot of hate across the urban terrain. The junior angel could see millions of aborted babies, rising up toward heaven from bloody graves inside and outside abortion clinics.

"I can't stand it," Seradim cried out. "The pain is more than I can endure."

"Yes. The great surprise both humans and the devil can never grasp is that the Father feels the same pain but to an infinite degree. Lucifer does not value human life and has no capacity for love. When the Holy One finally smashes the devil and his minions, the Father will still feel loss. Amazing grace, indeed!"

The two angels watched Gianardo as humans would view a movie. The president didn't seem to need sleep. Like an aphrodisiac, the lust for power energized him. Gianardo ordered his subordinates around like a chess player moving expendable pawns.

Michael pointed within the president. The angel's moral sensitivity was like an X ray, exposing Gianardo's soul. Michael could see ghostlike spirits moving in, out, and through the president as worms work through a corpse. "His thoughts are not yet completely possessed by the devil, but the demons control him spiritually," Michael explained. "Moreover, evil has permeated the social and political structures around the president so effectively, the man simply functions as an extension of the corrupt world system. Long ago, Gianardo's Italian immigrant parents started worshiping the American way of life. Even though they were originally devout Roman Catholics, "America" became their true idol. Damian thus departed from the faith of his parents and grandparents and became a natural product of the pervasive seduction of his own society. Thinking himself omnipotent, this foolish man has become the ultimate expression of the devil's heart's desire."

"Terrible days are ahead," Seradim concluded.

"Damian Gianardo isn't our charge. We need to help the Feinbergs get ready for the consequences of his decisions. As Jews, the family naturally fears that persecution is coming. Because they are deeply disturbed, the Feinbergs are now spiritually open, and we can help them take the next step. We need to sit in on their meeting with the McCoys. Follow me. We will join them in the Feinbergs' living room. Since Jimmy Harrison began examining his father's writings, he has become amazingly astute about what is going on. Reverend Harrison had a profound grasp of prophecy, and Jimmy has accepted Jesus as Savior as a result of his father's studies. I want you to watch carefully what is happening to Doctor Feinberg; obviously, we can't read Larry's mind, but we can pick up on the spiritual undercurrents."

Larry paced up and down in front of a large oil painting of a castle on the Rhine River. He kept running his hand through his hair as he talked. "I tell you, Joe, we are standing on top of a political San Andreas Fault! The president can wipe any of us out any time he chooses."

"I truly understand." Joe put his arm around Jennifer. "I came to the same conclusion the moment I heard that Gianardo renamed the presidential jet, *The White Horse*. Revelation chapter six says the Antichrist will conquer nations without war, using a bow without arrows, and riding on a symbolic 'white horse.' Once we knew he had assembled a ten-nation confederation in Europe, we could read the handwriting on the wall. That's when we knew how important it was to recognize Jesus as the Messiah."

Jennifer slid forward on the expensive brocade-covered couch. "Here's a sheet listing the prophecies fulfilled in the first coming of the Messiah. On the back is a list of Scriptures yet to be fulfilled." She put the sheet in Larry's hands. "You can see that many of these yet-to-be-completed prophecies are being fulfilled right before our eyes."

Jimmy looked over Larry's shoulder and nodded his head enthusiastically. "Right on the money."

Joe pointed to key verses describing the Antichrist. "The Bible is the only information we have that can make sense out of what we're watching on our televisions."

"We believe the next major event will happen on July 25," Jennifer continued. "If the next phase begins on this day, there will be no question that we are racing toward the Great Tribulation at breakneck speed."

"You are exactly right," Jimmy broke in. "My reading clarifies that July 25 will be the ninth of Av in the traditional Jewish calendar, their next religious holiday."

"Jewish holiday?" Larry frowned. "I've never heard of a summer holiday."

"The Feast of Tishah b'Av," Jimmy confirmed.

"Never heard of it." Larry sounded condescending.

"I have!" Sharon corrected her husband. "I'd forgotten about Tishah b'Av, but my father kept the day. Solomon's Temple was burned by the Babylonians on Av 9 in 587 B.C."

"Really?" Larry's eyes widened.

"Few days in Jewish history have been as significant as this one," Jimmy continued. "My father was big on the meaning of this holiday."

Joe slid to the edge of his chair. "Centuries before the temple fell, the twelve spies sneaked into Canaan and returned in terror on Av 9. The faithlessness of ten of those spies caused another forty years of wandering in the wilderness. Joshua and Caleb were the only two spies who had faith, so God spared their lives."

Jimmy smiled knowingly. "Titus and the Roman legions destroyed the second temple in A.D. 70 on Av 9. A year later the Romans plowed Jerusalem under, and it was on the same day."

"I've been reading Jimmy's books," Ruth joined in. "Because Reverend Harrison underlined so much, it's easy for me to get the high points. Simon Bar-Kochba led the last Jewish uprising against Rome, and his army was destroyed on Av 9, 135. Here, Dad, look for yourself." Ruth handed a book to her father.

Larry turned uncomfortably in his chair. "Are you sure that your information is correct?" he mumbled.

Jimmy opened his Bible on the table. "We've barely scraped the surface. On July 18, 1290, England expelled all its Jews on this same day. France expelled all its Jews in 1306 on Av 9, and later Spain repeated the same injustice. Anyone want to guess what the year was?"

"It was 1492," Ben immediately answered.

"Exactly," Jimmy said. "The year Columbus left Spain, the Spanish Empire expelled eight hundred thousand Jews by August 2 and killed many others. Care to guess what day August 2 coincided with that year on the Jewish calendar?

Larry shook his head. "Av 9."

Jennifer continued, "Our Bible teacher taught us that World War I and Russia's renewed killing of Jews began on August 9, 1914. Want to guess what day that was?"

"I don't need to," Sharon answered. "My great-grandparents were driven from their village in eastern Russia on Av 9."

"And Hitler and his henchmen made their final plans to kill Jews worldwide on Av 9, 1942," Jimmy added. "The gas chambers of Treblinka began the holocaust officially on that fateful day."

"Do you have any idea of the mathematical chance of such a thing occurring?" Joe asked. "As a comptroller and accountant, numbers are my world. I'd guess that the odds are about 1 in 265 to the eighth power. Literally 1 chance in 863 zillion . . . that's 863 with 15 zeros after it!"

Michael nudged his protégé. "Watch Larry's eyes. His defenses against the truth are crumbling. Even though that old psychiatrist doesn't want to admit the fact, Larry likes being in control. Right now, his world is wobbling like a top about to fall over. He can't control anything!"

"He's rubbing his temples and breathing harder," Seradim observed. "Our boy's obviously frightened as well."

Jennifer reached out to Larry. "When we put all the numbers together, the first thing we thought of was your family. Jews haven't fared very well on Av 9. We love you and want to make sure that nothing bad happens this year. We are ready to protect your family from any form of anti-Semitism."

Seradim looked at Michael and exclaimed, "I can sense Larry's response! He is deeply touched. The McCoys' love has broken through his facade."

"Exactly! The spiritual barriers are tumbling quickly." Michael beamed. "Larry Feinberg is very close to accepting the gospel. Our task now is to allow the Holy Spirit to use us in any way possible to finish the job and see Larry enter the kingdom of God."

"What do we do?" Seradim asked.

"Intercede and call for Larry and Sharon to feel the Spirit of God draw them close." Michael retreated within himself and began praying, "Come Holy Spirit . . . come fire divine."

Seradim's voice blended into the plea, "Omnipresent Spirit of God, come and fill Larry's heart. Come now."

Instantly, Michael knew what he should do. "The Spirit of God is directing me to protect our charges. Seradim, look carefully and see what must be done." He stared at the living room scene again. "Something big is about to happen."

"I pride myself on being a scientist," Larry told Joe and Jennifer. "I have to take facts seriously. It's all coming so quickly. I just don't know. I feel like I've been hit by an avalanche. I just can't put it all together this fast. I guess I need some time to think."

Seradim asked, "Why is Larry losing focus, Michael?"

"Look!" Michael pointed on the other side of the living room. Two evil figures emerged through the wall.

"Malafidus and Homelas! They're back!"

"We must act quickly." Michael clenched his fist. "We cannot allow the demons to confuse our friends. Now's the time to blow our cover and take those two head-on. Attack!"

Michael dived into the living room scene in an explosion of spiritual light, blasting the two demons with pure radiance and knocking them back through the walls. "After them!" Michael beckoned Seradim to follow.

The glare momentarily threw the evil pair off balance. Michael locked his mind onto their essence and violently flung them backward. The battle scene shifted away from the space around the Feinbergs' living room, continuing in the eternal void between heaven and earth.

"What's going on?" Homelas called out in confusion. "What's happened?"

"You've just met the God squad," Seradim answered. "Try taking an angel on for size." The junior angel spiritually lunged at Homelas only to tumble off into the emptiness.

"Let's destroy that naive toad." Homelas clawed at the angel. "Get him!"

Malafidus grabbed Seradim from the back, immobilizing him. "Something as puny as you created all this confusion?"

"No," a voice thundered from behind the struggle. "He's got a friend." With a great swipe of his mighty arm, Michael knocked Homelas into space. "You boys are about to get a real taste of godly power." With a burst of the same energy used to begin creation, Michael unleashed the cosmic radiation of the authority of the Word. As the angel spoke, the force of divine speech shattered the demons' ability to think, to respond, to react. In seconds, the pair shot out across the cosmos, light years away from the Feinbergs' house.

"Eventually, they'll find each other again," Michael explained, picking Seradim up. "By then Larry will have come to the right conclusions." Michael laughed at his charge. "They roughed you up a bit. Taking on the two of them at once was no small act of courage . . . but you might be a bit more prudent next time."

Seradim looked sheepish and shrugged apologetically.

"You've got great heart, my friend. Nothing to make amends for in this battle. We kept Larry from being bombarded by doubt. Look." Michael pointed into the living room.

"Thank you." Larry stood up and offered his hand to the McCoys. "I'm sure we'll give this entire matter our undivided attention."

Ben Feinberg turned to Jimmy Harrison. "You've been studying a lot more than the *Blue Book* on used cars lately. A lot more."

"There's much more at stake," Jimmy answered. "Money's one thing. Eternity is another."

"Jimmy, I've badly underestimated you," Larry said. "You have an excellent mind and a very good heart. Let's talk more, son. I want you to help me understand your father's teaching."

Jimmy's eye's watered. "I'd be honored."

"You'll certainly be in our prayers," Jennifer added. "God is obviously at work at the Feinberg house."

CHAPTER
18

During the following weeks, Larry and Sharon diligently studied everything the McCoys gave them. They also talked with Jimmy Harrison. No matter what they read, they remained tentative while waiting for Av 9 to arrive. The Feast of Tishah b'Av would fall on July 25 this year. The Feinbergs sensed the day might be the pivotal event in their lives.

When the day finally arrived, the Feinbergs attempted to follow their normal routine. Larry and Sharon sat down for breakfast as usual. "You're okay?" Larry asked.

"No," Sharon said, breaking a two-decade-old pattern. "I'm not."

Larry really looked at her for the first time that day. "I love you," he said and turned on the TV.

The screen exploded with images of soldiers on horseback riding over rough terrain. The anchorman said, "Last night's report of large-scale movements of Syrian and Russian troops on horseback now makes sense. Continuing economic troubles apparently have some bearing on this unusual approach of horse brigades for combat. At this hour, Russian and Syrian troops are in control of the mountains of Lebanon and are bearing down on the state of Israel."

"It's happening!" Larry leaned toward the television. "Israel's under attack! The war predicted in chapters thirty-eight and thirty-nine of Ezekiel is beginning, just like Jimmy and Joe said it would."

Columns of troops lumbered down a dusty road. "Libya and Iran have dropped paratroopers on Israel," the reporter continued. "Ethiopian soldiers are reported moving toward Jerusalem at this hour." The news broadcast showed images of an Arab despot dressed in women's clothing, making psychotic, fist-shaking statements about Jews worldwide. "Some small nuclear weapons were just fired into Israel," the reporter added, "apparently by artillerymen in the Pisgah mountain range in Jordan, near Petra. Intelligence sources say the missiles were fired from shoulder-held artillery sold by China to Libya. Palestinian terrorists are said to be the mastermind behind the whole Russian invasion. Jordan continues to claim neutrality."

Another reporter appeared on the screen. "The State Department is now releasing its assessment of this attack. The Israeli prime minister has been assassinated. Many have already died in Israel. Hard-liner Russian President Ivan Smirkoff apparently concluded that the current anti-Israeli sentiment would permit a quick strike. Using allies in Iran, Libya, and Ethiopia, Russia evidently has designs on Israel's new oil and gold discoveries, as well as Dead Sea minerals.

"However, world leaders are now expressing their shock. The report of the sudden and unexpected invasion is rocking capitals around the world. The responses point to a serious miscalculation on the part of the invaders. Fear is mounting that Israel will respond with nuclear weapons of its own, since nuclear weapons have already fallen in Israel. We switch you now to a live statement by President Gianardo, who went to Spain two days ago for unexplainable consultations with European leaders."

"Spain!" Sharon gasped. "Oh, no!"

"Fits exactly what Jimmy said." Larry's eyes widened. "He said that Ezekiel predicted that the people of Tarshish, or Spain, would be surprised by the invasion of Israel."

"And Ezekiel said the Russian army will be destroyed by fire and brimstone!" Sharon put both hands to her cheeks. "We have already studied what the reporters are going to tell us."

Larry rushed out of the room and returned with the McCoys' list of Scriptures and a Bible. He quickly turned to Ezekiel. "The Bible says here that Israel will take seven months to bury all the dead Russian and allied soldiers." Larry thumbed the pages. "Let's try this part from the prophet Joel."

Sharon put her finger on the page and started reading. "I will remove far from you the northern army, and will drive him away into a barren and desolate land, with his face toward the eastern sea and his back toward the western sea—"

"That description would fit the Dead Sea and the Mediterranean Sea perfectly," Larry interjected.

"His stench will come up, and his foul odor will rise, because he has done monstrous things," Sharon kept reading.

"All Israel has to do," Larry said as he looked up at the ceiling, "is to nuke them and leave their radioactive bodies to decay if this twenty-six-hundred-year-old prophecy is to be fulfilled."

"And who's the father of that weapon?" Sharon slowly sank down in a kitchen chair. "A Jew! Albert Einstein! Larry everything fits."

"We heard every bit of today's headlines last night. Today is the ninth of Av. Right on schedule."

"What can we do?" Sharon clutched her husband's arm. "We must do something."

Larry searched Sharon's face, his eyes darting back and forth. "I really don't know how . . . but I think we need to pray."

"You start," Sharon pleaded. "I'll just repeat silently whatever you say."

Larry lowered his head into his hands and closed his eyes. *"Shema Israel."* He recited the words he heard at the synagogue as a boy. *"Adonai elohenu Adonai echad.* God of our fathers, Abraham, Isaac, and Jacob, please hear us today. Whoever You are, I believe in You. Forgive my arrogance in ignoring You. I must believe that You intervene in history and that You are sovereign over all things. Whoever You are, please make Yourself known to us."

"Yes," Sharon said softly.

"If Jesus is the Messiah, please show us what to believe. Even if I don't like the truth, I want to see it before my eyes. Help us to know how to help our fellow Jews in Israel and around the world. Please help us find our way out of this confusion. Amen." Larry blinked his eyes but didn't move. Sharon squeezed his hand.

Michael embraced Seradim. "He's done it! We've fulfilled our first purpose. The Feinbergs have crossed the line."

Seradim held his hands up. "Praise God!"

"Listen." Michael looked upward. "Heaven is jubilant."

The rejoicing of the nine angelic choirs flooded the void between time and eternity. Dominions sent to the angels beneath them sang their song of joy. Archangels answered with antiphonal responses of celebration: "The lost has been found!"

■ ■ ■

At the opposite end of the realm dividing heaven and earth, another court assembled. While hordes of demons watched the pair cautiously approaching the seat of all Evil, Homelas and Malafidus inched forward. Blackness hung over the pair like an approaching hailstorm. The awesome silence was as stifling as the eerie calm before a tornado. Homelas and Malafidus looked nervously at the glaring horde. All they saw was frightening contempt.

Lucifer shook his fist. "You have failed," he charged. "We trusted you with the two lives we might have totally destroyed." Fire flashed from his eyes; his fangs were bared. "The children will eventually follow the parents. You let the Feinbergs get away! How dare you!" The devil's rage thundered. "You two fools have failed! Failed!"

Homelas and Malafidus crowded together, looking down, trying to avoid Lucifer's red eyes.

"You know how much I hate Jews! From the very beginning, those worthless God-loving sons of Abraham have been His secret weapon in heaven's battle with me! I have tried relentlessly to destroy Jews for centuries. And you two idiots let an entire family slip through my hands!"

"We were attacked," Malafidus offered timidly. "Just as we were about to intervene, an angel dive-bombed us."

"Not *an* angel," Homelas interrupted. "We were hit by a whole squadron. Must have been several hundred. We were simply outnumbered."

"You couldn't have called for backup?" The devil's voice changed and was now beguilingly sympathetic. "We wouldn't have responded with help?"

"The assault came out of nowhere," Homelas pleaded. "Before we could even consult each other, they got us from behind."

"Poor things," Lucifer cooed. "With four thousand years of training, you two fools couldn't smell an attack coming." The Evil One suddenly screamed, bellowing fire, smoke, and ash. "Angels are always hanging around when humans talk about spiritual things! You completely mindless hunks of snot! There is no excuse for your failure!"

"Mercy!" Malafidus begged. "Mercy!"

Satan arose. "Mercy? Where did you learn that word? I don't have such a useless term in my vocabulary. Been talking to the enemy?" the devil asked condescendingly.

Malafidus covered his head and tried to hide his eyes.

"I don't think you two slime-sucking swamp bottoms deserve to exist. Returning you to hell is too good for you."

"No!" Homelas pleaded. "Hell is too terrifying even to contemplate. Please!" He held up his hands in petition.

"Yes, the lake of fire." Satan pointed to the center of the earth where a lake of molten lava seethed with smoke and fire. Like an enormous volcano, the vast cauldron of fury boiled and bubbled molten brimstone. "A perfect place to roast the likes of you two buffoons."

"A-h-h-h," the pair screamed and wilted in a heap, writhing together in agonizing terror.

"I warn you." The devil pointed at the pair. "If you ever slip up again I'll make you an eternal example." Satan's words belched hate. "You had best rectify this incompetence in some significant way or I will assign you to the abyss."

"Oh, thank you." Malafidus backed away. "Thank you. Yes, we will bring you a trophy of victory. Count on it." The demons kept receding from the devil. "We'll do it quickly."

"It better be good!" Satan roared with a blast of pure malice, blowing the pair completely out of the demonic assembly.

Malafidus looked around the void where they landed. "At least we still exist on the surface of the earth rather than within it!" He could barely communicate. "We survived." The demon cursed. "Man, am I ever glad to be out of there."

Homelas kept shaking but couldn't speak.

"The last time anyone got a dressing down like that was when all those drug-using hippies became Jesus freaks." Malafidus brushed himself off. "A whole legion of demons disappeared from the surface of the earth over that faux pas."

Homelas rubbed his neck and hugged himself to stop the trembling. "I . . . I . . . think . . . we ought to kill someone." He thought for a moment. "Murder would put us back in good graces."

Malafidus nodded slowly. "Excellent idea. Nothing pleases his infernal majesty like a good homicide. Who do you have in mind?"

Homelas thought for a moment. "I know exactly who we should get! They caused this whole mess to happen."

CHAPTER
19

Michael and Seradim watched Ben Feinberg talk to Cindy in front of the UCLA library. Cindy sat on the front steps with her German shepherd guide dog, Sam, at her feet. Ben held the latest newspaper.

"When Israel used atomic weapons on the Russians, one of the prophecies we studied was fulfilled." Ben pointed at the headlines. "The enormous earthquake that followed cracked the earth open and swallowed most of the remainder of the Russian army. It must have been an act of God, along with the fact that the nuclear missiles fired by Libyan artillerymen from the Pisgah mountain range 'accidentally' landed on the Palestinian guerrillas surrounding Jerusalem instead of killing the Jews they were intended to kill."

Michael observed, "Ben is shaken because he understands the spiritual implications of what's happened in the Holy Land. Reality is setting in."

Seradim smiled. "Maybe the son is about to follow in the footsteps of the father. The prophet Ezekiel said this war would show Jews everywhere that the God who loves and delivers Israel is alive and well. Ben is certainly examining the headlines with unusual intensity. Let's get closer."

"Sure. We'll stand next to them. I need to give Ben a special encouragement."

"Ben, we've carefully studied the Scriptures Joe McCoy gave you." Cindy's voice was grave and serious. "Everything is just as the Bible said it would be. We can't ignore the implications."

"I know. I know." Ben folded the paper. "For the first time in my life I've asked God to show me the truth. I don't want to accept what the McCoys have been telling us, but the handwriting sure seems to be on the wall."

"I've been trying to teach my parents." Cindy patted her dog on the head. "They listen, but they are more terrified than anything else. Nothing in their background prepares them to understand. Half the time the news reports frighten them, and my Bible lessons leave Mom and Dad in complete consternation the other half. I feel that nothing is like it was."

"Certainly not for the Russians." Ben rolled his eyes. "And not for my family, either. No one has said it out loud yet, but I think we've already thrown in the towel on the last of our doubts. How can we ignore the meaning of the total defeat of Russia and her allies?"

"Ben." Cindy looked toward the sky as if her sightless eyes seemed to see something she couldn't quite perceive. "I've been trying to pray like the Bible suggests. What I ask, I ask in Jesus' name, with very interesting results."

Ben frowned. "In what way?"

"I have the strangest sense that Someone is there, that I'm being heard. I think it's working."

"I thought the issue is what we believe . . . having the right ideas."

"Maybe it's much more," Cindy pondered. "What if this whole business is about making contact? A personal relationship with Jesus?"

"That's a new wrinkle."

"Here's another one for you." Cindy smiled mischievously. "I've been having these unusual intuitions. Hunches if you like."

"And? . . . And?"

"I think the issue is even bigger than you've thought. I think that God has something very important for you to do in the days ahead."

Ben jerked. "You've got to be kidding."

Cindy's smile faded, and she became very serious. "I can't tell you why, but I feel a strong inner sense of guidance. You have a special task that God wants you to do."

Ben stared. "Cindy, this is getting way too far out for me."

Michael nudged Seradim. "Now's the time for me to give Ben a little encouragement." The angel pointed. "You can read confusion in Ben's face. He's going to need our help to put this moment in the right perspective. I will intervene in the parking lot."

"See you at lunch," Ben called one last time, running toward his car. He mumbled under his breath, "This whole thing gives me the willies. I hope Cindy is not going to get weird on me."

"Now's the right moment," Michael told his colleague. "I'm going to use the same body I put on last time. Watch me give Ben something to think about." Michael stepped out of eternity and into the UCLA parking lot.

"Consider what I said," Cindy hollered after Ben.

He put his key in the car door, acting as if he hadn't heard her.

"Take her seriously," Michael said from behind Ben.

Ben spun around and flattened himself against the car. "Who are you?"

"Michael. I am your friend, Ben." The angel towered above the young man.

"I don't know you." Ben inched back toward the street.

"But I know you. I have known you since the day you were born. Do not be afraid. I bring you good tidings."

"What?" Ben squinted. "What are you talking about?"

"You asked for guidance." Michael stared deeply into Ben's eyes. "Do not be afraid to receive it."

Ben pulled away from the all-revealing stare and started running down the sidewalk. Michael stepped back out of time. When Ben looked over his shoulder, the figure had disappeared, causing Ben to run all the harder for the library.

"Ben?" Cindy was still sitting on the library steps. "Sounds like your footsteps. Back so soon?" Sam watched the approaching figure and barked.

"Cindy," he panted. "I just had the living daylights scared out of me. A big guy . . . a strange man appeared out of nowhere. And then he was gone. Disappeared."

"What are you talking about?"

"The guy said he'd known me all my life. I swear I've never seen him before. Maybe I really am going nuts. He called himself Michael."

"Michael? I know a Michael. Did he have an unusually deep bass voice?"

"Why, yes. Exactly."

"Talk sort of strange?"

"Yes, yes. You've seen him?"

Cindy laughed. "Not hardly. But I have met Michael on a number of occasions. I always thought he was a student. Sort of shows up at very opportune moments."

"Listen, Cindy. This guy is big. Strange. Terrifying."

"Come now, Ben. I've always found him to be extremely considerate."

"You know anything about him?" Ben sounded skeptical.

"Actually nothing. When I've tried to ask questions, he changes the subject. But he's been no problem. Really, Michael has a knack for appearing when I really need help."

"I don't know." Ben kept shaking his head. "Weirdest thing I've seen since the Rapture."

Seradim moved into place next to the couple.

Michael turned to the young angel. "We have to be strategic about making physical appearances. The best time to appear is on the anniversary of the Jewish festivals and feasts. Often, we are especially sent to make a special announcement of God's intentions and plans, but our job is always to encourage people without taking away or destroying their freedom of choice. We help them in their uphill struggles, but we must not remove obstacles from their path that are needed for developing integrity. Moral exercise is imperative for their spiritual development."

"I understand." Seradim nodded. "Endurance helps develop character. And godly character produces unfailing hope."

"Exactly. We want people to come to the place where even suffering doesn't stifle their optimism and capacity to overcome. We must make sure our appearances don't hinder the inner battle that produces victors. That's called 'putting on the full armor of God.'"

Seradim watched Ben return to the parking lot. "You certainly stretched his imagination. Ben's got plenty to think about today!"

"We need to go back to heaven for more training and allow some time to roll by on Earth. Gianardo will soon be creating a security apparatus capable of doing great harm to our wards. By contrast, heaven is also preparing for its own invasion."

"More angels are coming down?"

"No, Elijah and Moses will shortly return to Jerusalem as the big battle in Israel starts to take shape."

"They're not angels?"

Michael shook his head. "No. When people die, they don't turn into angels. We are a completely different species from them. In heaven, people become like us, but they have temporary bodies. After Satan is defeated and time has played out, people will be resurrected to new physical bodies. Understand?"

"Amazing! They'll always be superior to us?"

"Exactly."

"Moses and Elijah?" Seradim pondered and immediately his mind was filled with the knowledge of who the two great biblical heroes were . . . and would be.

"We will help prepare for those great heroes' return to the Mount of Olives on the Feast of Purim. While we work on their project, we'll give Ben a little more time."

■ ■ ■

Throughout the hot summer, the papers and television news reports were filled with stories of radical political change in America and across the world. The new Israeli prime minister was very careful in his public appearances not to offend Gianardo. No one seemed to be able to resist any plan Damian Gianardo proposed. With uncanny skill, the president was always a step ahead of his opposition.

Units of his personal secret surveillance police sprang up in every town.

Seradim's training took him to a new level as he grew to understand the extraordinary appearances coming in the immediate future. As fall approached, the time came for the two angels to get back in touch with Ben and Cindy. Everyone in the Feinberg family was making great spiritual progress . . . except Ben.

As he often did, Ben walked Cindy from her dormitory to the library. "Hope your classes are easy this morning."

"Big day for you!" Cindy beamed.

"Huh?" Ben puzzled.

"Come on," Cindy chided. "You're not paying attention to the calendar. A girl down the hall is Jewish. She said today is Yom Kippur, the Day of Atonement. Your big day for repentance."

"Yom Kippur! I forgot all about it."

"Naughty boy," Cindy teased. "Now you will have to make double confession."

"Wow!" Ben slapped his forehead. "Today is Yom Kippur. All the strange things started happening just over a year ago on Rosh Hashanah. I should have paid more attention to the calendar!"

"Yom Kippur is a time for getting right with God, isn't it?"

"Something like that, Cindy. Unfortunately, my family didn't pay much attention to our traditions."

Michael nudged Seradim. "That's the clue I need. It's time to give Ben a bit more to think about."

"Can I go with you this time?"

"No. I'm all Ben can handle for the moment." Michael stepped into time, standing behind the couple.

"I'm still trying to put everything together," Ben confessed.

"There are times and seasons appointed for all things," Michael spoke over Ben's shoulder.

"What?" Cindy turned toward the voice. Sam looked nonchalantly toward the sound.

"You!" Ben jerked.

"These days are your special times," Michael said.

"Michael?" Cindy asked. "Is that you?" Sam wagged his tail.

"Where did you come from?" Ben stared. "You weren't there a moment ago."

"You are very important people. I am honored to be a comrade."

Cindy reached out and took Michael's hand.

"Look!" Ben trembled. "We haven't done anything to you. What do you want with us?"

"The issue is what I can do *for* you." Michael smiled. "You are part of a great plan, and I will help you execute your part."

"Why do you keep coming and going?" Cindy asked.

"I have special work to do."

"Who do you work for?" Ben held up his hands defensively. "You're an extraterrestrial? A spaceman?"

"I come from the center of reality itself, but I know your world exceedingly well, Ben. I have been watching your people from the beginning."

"My people?"

"Are you Jewish?" Cindy asked.

"No. But I do work for a Jewish carpenter," Michael said. Then he stepped back into eternity.

Cindy's fingers collapsed on themselves. "He's gone."

"My gosh!" Ben choked.

"Where did he go?" Cindy groped around.

"Right before my eyes! Boom!" Ben stared at the empty sidewalk.

"Ben, we're not crazy. This isn't a hallucination. Michael was *here!*"

"Let me sit down . . . for a few minutes. I must get myself together."

CHAPTER
20

Cindy shook Ben's shoulders. "Quit running from the obvious. From reading the Bible I know enough to understand what it means that a 'Jewish carpenter' is Michael's boss."

Ben rubbed his eyes and looked carefully around the UCLA campus. "What are you driving at?"

"In the Bible there is another person named Michael. I don't know if this guy is the same one or what . . . but I do know that the Michael in the Bible was an angel."

"An angel!" Ben sputtered.

"Well." Cindy held up her hands and shrugged her shoulders. "It makes a lot more sense than that spaceman talk."

"An . . . angel?"

"I read one place in the Bible where it said that many people had entertained angels unaware." Cindy sounded defensive. "Why not us?"

Ben stared.

"Working for a Jewish carpenter?" Cindy beamed. "He had to mean Jesus. The whole thing fits together."

Ben ran his fingers through his hair. "Maybe we're both getting caught up in the mass hysteria sweeping the country after all of the strange experiences. Maybe—"

"Stop it," Cindy said firmly. "I'm not crazy, Ben, and neither are you. Maybe my blindness is an asset. I have to depend on far more than my eyes to make sense out of things. I know that we have been talking to a real person regardless of how he comes and goes. Let's be scientific about this encounter. If Michael is for real, he'll be back. And if he is an angel, Michael wants the best for us."

"How in the world can we set up an experiment with an angel?"

"Doesn't Michael seem to show up around Jewish holidays? After all, today is Yom Kippur!"

Ben rubbed his chin and bit his lip. "Seems so," he said reluctantly.

"When's the next special day? Come on, Ben. Think."

"I think," Ben said slowly, "yes, it's the Feast of Tabernacles! I would have to check, but it's probably coming in a week or less."

"Let's have a date that night!" Cindy's voice rang with enthusiasm. "If we're on to something, we ought to be able to make contact with Michael then!"

"If I had told my father about this six months ago, he'd have thought I'd gone nuts! Psychiatrists tend to think spiritual beliefs about God and angels are a psychological crutch. Are they right, Cindy, or are they just spiritually blind and using the massive denial they accuse their patients of? I'm beginning to think the pot is calling the kettle black."

"I won't tell anyone if you don't," Cindy replied. "It's our secret." She reached over and hugged Ben.

■ ■ ■

Several miles away in downtown Los Angeles a contingent of special agents marched up the stairs to the district attorney's office. Brownish smog hung in the air. Cars buzzed by, indifferent to the drama unfolding in front of the halls of justice. Rod Galligher was looking out his second-story window apprehensively, watching the Washington-based investigation crew arrive. He could not see Homelas and Malafidus floating behind the federal officers.

At forty-five, Galligher was relatively young for such a prominent political position. Graying temples imparted dignity and bearing. An ex-Marine, he was known for staying in top physical condition. Galligher was also known for maintaining a no-nonsense posture toward law enforcement. Whatever Rod Galligher did to get elected, he had staunchly maintained his integrity since taking office.

Galligher turned away from the dirty window and spoke to his assistant, Helen Fortier. "Don't like any of it, and I am concerned. We have no choice in the matter, but these agents really bother me. I feel like we're being invaded."

The attractive young woman nodded her head. "I understand." Helen Fortier stood on tiptoe to watch over the attorney's shoulder. "On the phone they sounded more like hit men for the Mafia." Dressed like an ad from *Style* magazine, Helen was both a secretary and a paralegal as well as a good friend. Her black eyes snapped. "Arrogant bunch of jerks." She walked around the desk and plopped down in a desk chair. "Are you ready?"

Galligher clenched his jaw. "Law and order don't seem to mean much to Washington these days. When the attorney general called about this investigation, he brushed aside all questions about due process. I was ordered to follow without question all instructions these men bring with them."

"Real Bad News Bears." Helen Fortier clicked open her briefcase. "I'll try to take careful notes." She laid a small recorder on the table. "We'll keep everything for the record."

"I've got a terrible feeling that I am going to be ordered to take actions that have always been illegal. We want to leave a paper trail."

Helen shrugged. "Certainly, but Damian Gianardo is in complete control these days. I don't think you have much choice anymore."

"No." Galligher pounded on his desk. "We *always* have a choice. The Nuremberg Trials proved that fact. I don't care who these thugs represent, I will not be forced into acquiescing with illegal and immoral directives!"

"It's none of my business, Rod, but I wouldn't try to stand against the tide. People have changed. Everyone's scared to death. The masses don't look at the presidency like citizens did in the past. Gianardo's viewed like a god or superpower. What he says goes . . . without any opposition."

"Not around here while I'm the DA," Galligher snapped.

The door opened, and six men in black suits walked quickly into the inner office. The agents fanned out around the room as if they were taking over. The two demons following them slithered across the room, stopping next to the district attorney and his assistant.

"Agent Adams, representing the president of the United States." The stocky man extended his hand. In his midthirties, Gerald Adams's hair was cropped short, his dark eyes deep-set and hard. "Pleasure to be working with you." He pointed at the men behind him. "Meet agents Miller, Toomey, Pike, Randolph, and Abrams. Each an expert in his field. Computers, forensics, surveillance, research, so forth and so on."

Standing like statues, the men nodded sullenly.

"We must go to work immediately, accessing your entire computer system and particularly all personnel files on police officers. Code names and passwords for all computers are necessary. We need to review psychological profiles to know who will follow instruction without question or reservation."

"Gentlemen," Galligher smiled thinly as he spoke, "we cannot allow public scrutiny of such confidential material. While I understand the priority given your investigation, I must insist we follow the legal procedures of the state of—"

"Excuse me." Agent Adams cut him off. "International legislation now supersedes all state statutes. We are operating on a global level within the framework of the new federation of nations. Nothing is allowed to stand in our way."

"You must understand." Galligher hesitated, biting his lip. "I am responsible for maintaining confidentiality and setting proper standards that—"

Gerald Adams stuck his finger in the DA's face. "You are responsible to do what I tell you! Understand?"

The district attorney's neck and cheeks turned red. "I don't care who you are. I will not have anyone come into the good offices of the people of California and order us around like pawns in some political chess game."

Without answering, Adams brushed past Galligher and strolled behind the DA's desk. Adams raised his eyebrows, a mock frown crossing his lips. "Really?" He dropped down in Galligher's chair. "In about five seconds, I can have you hauled downstairs on a charge of obstruction of justice. If need be, I can take over this entire building with force. I have the armed services of this country at my disposal. Am I communicating?"

Galligher's eyes widened. His jaw dropped.

"I'm not asking permission." Adams leaned over the desk. "I'm giving instructions. Get it?"

Confusing images interrupted Galligher's thinking. A bolt of fear shot down his back. Menacing faces popped into his mind. His usual bold demeanor crumpled. For reasons he couldn't define, the attorney felt weak and incapable.

"Don't toy with me," Adams warned. "I never make idle threats."

Galligher tried to speak but his mouth was dry, his mind addled. Unseen by Rod, Helen, and the federal agents, another conversation was going on in the room.

"I nuked the DA," Homelas boasted to Malafidus. "I touched Galligher's frightening childhood memories of authority figures. He's overpowered. His hard-nosed-attorney front is only a defense against anxieties created by child abuse. Once old Rod's cover is blown, Mr. Tough Guy turns into a quivering four-year-old child again."

"You're next," Malafidus cooed in Helen Fortier's ear. "They are coming to lock you up and throw away the key." The demon bore down. "All this big-time status you've acquired with this high-profile job will vanish in an instant! Why fight the inevitable?"

Agent Adams got up from the district attorney's desk and walked back around to the front. "We will require special assistance." He put his hand on Helen's shoulder. "I'm sure you can expedite matters for us." Gerald Adams smiled salaciously. "Can I depend on you?"

Helen swallowed hard and looked helplessly at the district attorney. "Rod?" her voice was weak and shallow. "What do you suggest?"

Adams picked up the tape recorder lying on the desk. "Rodney would be delighted to have you help me." The agent clicked the machine off. "Any problems there, Rod, old pal?"

Homelas nudged his comrade. "We've picked the right team to get the job done. In short order, we'll be able to reap our revenge. If we play our cards right, we may be able to bag even more scalps than we thought possible."

■ ■ ■

Five days had passed since Ben and Cindy encountered Michael. As the Feast of Tabernacles approached, the words *Jewish carpenter* kept rolling around in Ben's head with disconcerting frequency. When the big night came, the couple settled on a little corner pizza place two blocks from the women's dormitory. As always, Ben and Cindy laughed, kidded, and joked their way through a large pizza and endless refills of soda.

"I guess our little experiment failed," Cindy finally said. "But the evening has still been the best of my life."

Ben did not turn away from Cindy's sightless eyes in the self-conscious way he usually did. Instead he studied Cindy's lovely olive-colored skin and beautifully contoured face.

"You're the most beautiful girl I've ever seen in my life."

Cindy's cheeks turned pink, and she lowered her head.

"I've never known anyone like you." Ben's voice filled with emotion. "I don't want to ever be away from you, Cindy."

"We . . . ah . . . better go." Cindy's voice became softer, lower, more hesitant.

"Don't retreat from me." Ben took her hand.

"Please," Cindy's voice cracked, "don't toy with me. I am a very lonely person, Ben. I've learned to accept the fact, but I can't live with false expectations. It would be too painful."

"Oh, Cindy!" Ben took her hand in both of his. "I would never mislead or use you."

Cindy nodded her head as a tear ran down her cheek.

"You make me very happy." Ben leaned over and kissed her tenderly on her hand. "You can trust me."

"May . . . maybe we should go." Cindy sniffed.

"Yeah," Ben said. "I'm starting to sound like someone on a soap opera."

Laughing, the couple walked out of the restaurant arm-in-arm. Sam trotted along beside Cindy.

Michael turned to Seradim. "Watch carefully. The timing is perfect," Michael concluded. "We'll let them get some distance from the crowd and in an isolated stretch close to the dormitory. Then I'll show up. Let's give our boy a bit more rope."

Ben stopped behind a tree near the door to the dorm. He pulled Cindy back into the shadow and kissed her forcefully.

"You turned out to be my angel tonight, Ben." Cindy ran her hand down the side of his face.

"You really got shortchanged!" Ben kissed her again.

"I've got to give Ben a break," Michael confided. "Let's not completely ruin the moonlight and romance. I'll give them a hint I'm coming." The angel materialized ten feet behind the couple. Sam immediately picked up the sound and barked.

"Someone there?" Cindy called out.

"*Shalom,*" Michael answered.

"It's you!" Ben gasped.

"*Shalom aleichem,*" Michael responded.

"You did come!" Cindy clapped her hands. "I was right. You are an angel!"

"No." Ben shook his head. "I refuse to believe my eyes."

"I want you to meet a friend of mine someday." Michael sounded sincere and serious. "You will enjoy Doubting Thomas. He had a problem similar to yours."

"Why are you here?" Cindy was nearly dancing with glee.

"You're a fraternity prank. I know it!" Ben sounded defensive.

"My Master has a wonderful sense of humor, but I assure you that my reasons for following you are very serious. In fact, it has been my total preoccupation since the day you were conceived."

"If you're really an angel, you should be able to answer questions that no one can know anything about," Ben said critically.

"Sure," Michael answered smugly. "Want to try me?"

"What was my favorite toy as a child?" Ben crossed his arms over his chest.

"You expect me to say a football," Michael said. "You worked hard at convincing everyone you were going to be an athlete because you knew that would please your father. However, your favorite toy was the stuffed bear you secretly slept with until you were well into grade school."

Ben turned white and his mouth fell open. His arms dropped listless at his sides.

"Good question, but not too tough. Cindy, do you have a difficult request for me?"

Cindy thought a moment, obviously enjoying what terrified Ben. "I once had a family keepsake locket that I lost. It was my mother's, and she was very upset when I couldn't find her treasure. It's been years ago, but I would like to have it back. Do you know where it is?"

"Your parents had just started the Golden Dragon, and you helped them put napkins in the holders. You were quite small. Remember?"

Cindy nodded enthusiastically.

"You reached out to find more napkins in the storage cabinet but could not touch anything. When you stretched forward, the necklace fell down inside the cabinet and through a crack in the bottom. If you will move the cabinet, the treasure will be on the floor underneath."

"Wonderful! Wonderful!" Cindy clapped.

"Can you . . . can you read our minds?" Ben's eyes were filled with fear.

"I am your best friend, Ben. You do not have to worry. No, I cannot read your mind. Angels do not do that sort of thing, but we can affect the way you see things. You might say that we nudge you in the right direction."

"Please help us." Cindy said. "We want to believe the right things. We just can't sort it all out. If you work for a Jewish carpenter, then you must know the truth about who Jesus was."

"'Was'?" Michael smiled. "Try 'is.' Ready to find out, Ben?" Ben could only nod.

"His Hebrew name is Yeshua. That's what we call Him in heaven. Angels know that He always existed. When He died on the cross, He had both of you in mind. He has a most special plan for your lives and has sent me to help you find your place in that destiny."

"This is why you have appeared to us?" Ben asked weakly.

"I have important secrets that I cannot yet disclose, but the hour is coming. You will not see me again until Passover next spring, but I will be guiding you toward that time."

"What are we to do now?" Cindy reached out for Michael's hand.

The angel clasped Cindy's palm tenderly. "Keep yourselves pure. Love each other profoundly but chastely. In the days ahead you will need great moral strength."

"Hard time coming?" Ben asked meekly.

"Next year's Passover will be a terrible day for the descendants of Abraham. Cindy, your life will be spent well, and Ben, you shall see the glory of the Lord revealed. Learn now what the love of Yeshua offers, for His love will be your salvation."

Michael held up his hand in a blessing and then was gone.

Ben and Cindy began to weep. They held each other and swayed back and forth as the darkness of night settled over them. Periodically, they said something, but most of the time, they huddled together in silence.

Finally Ben said, "I think I want to pray. I've never really done that . . . I mean in a personal way."

"Me too. You say the words, and I'll follow."

"Jesus . . . Yeshua, we're still very confused, but we must place our faith in You. We want a personal relationship with You, Yeshua, and we also want to believe the right things and get ready for whatever is ahead. Thank You for sending Michael to warn us. I know I've done a lot of selfish things, and I need Your help. Please forgive me where I've messed up in the past . . . today . . . in the future. Thank You for remembering us on Your cross. We now offer You our lives."

After a long silence, Cindy said, "Amen. Thank You, Yeshua."

Michael wept in sheer joy. Seradim lifted his arms toward heaven. The angels immediately tuned in the sounds of eternity. Cherubim and Seraphim were singing in endless praise. "You are God: we praise you. You are the Lord: we acclaim you; You are the eternal Father: All creation worships you." Seradim suddenly joined with the heavenly chorus singing, "Holy, holy, holy Lord, God of power and might.

Heaven and earth are full of Your glory. Thank You for a life saved."

Michael looked toward heaven. He could hear the glorious company of apostles praising God, the noble fellowship of prophets in worship, the white-robed army of martyrs singing. The words of praise thrilled the angel's soul.

He reached out to contact the mind of God. "Come then, Lord, and help all of Your people, bought with the price of Your Own Son's blood, and bring all Your saints to glory everlasting."

CHAPTER
21

The intimidating aura of the White House settled around Agent Gerald Adams like a suffocating blanket of authority. He stood at rigid attention. Secret Service agents and secretaries hurried down the corridors leading to and from the Oval Office. Adams stared at the pictures of the president shaking hands with numerous world dignitaries. Finally the inner door opened and a familiar face beckoned him to enter.

Agent Adams saluted Jacob Rathmarker as the vice president held the door to the Oval Office open for him. Adams marched across the bright blue carpet until he stood in military form in front of the president's desk, waiting acknowledgment. Damian Gianardo stared out the window and did not turn around.

"I've followed your work in Los Angeles," Gianardo spoke without emotion. "Is it true you kept the district attorney behind bars for several days?"

"Yes, sir." Adams answered hesitantly.

"I understand you took command of the police system in the entire L.A. area." Gianardo turned slowly. "And you did so in my name?"

"Yes, sir!" the agent acknowledged slowly.

"They're screaming from Sacramento to Washington, D.C." The president sounded cool, detached. "Congressional leaders complain you and your men have become more powerful than the FBI. Quite a charge." Gianardo turned around, leaned on his desk, and stared coldly at the special agent. "Do you have any reservations about the accuracy of these reports?"

Agent Adams briskly shook his head. "No, sir."

A twisted smile crossed the president's face. He strolled around his desk and extended his hand. "Congratulations, Agent Adams. Well done."

For the first time the stocky security officer relaxed and smiled. "Why, thank you, Mr. President."

"I'm very pleased with your progress. Set a standard for the rest of the country, Adams. Excellent work!"

"I can report that we have secured essential control of the L.A. police department and they will now do as we order them."

Gianardo nodded. "In perilous and unpredictable times we must keep the population under control . . ." He paused as if carefully framing his words. ". . . to protect our people from radical and divisive elements. Understand?"

"Absolutely."

"I am particularly concerned about future opposition arising from religious elements. Fanatics have always been a threat to social stability and cannot be tolerated in the current climate created by these bizarre disappearances."

"I agree completely." Adams kept nodding his head enthusiastically. "We will soon have infiltrated the entire country with agents trained to identify the nut fringe."

Gianardo pursed his lips thoughtfully. "Southern California has long been a hotbed of religious ferment. Jesus freaks, Eastern religions, drug experimenters, suicide cults, heaven knows what else . . . the smog seems to spawn screwball agitators. I consider Christians to be the most dangerous element of all. They have a long history of creating dissent and turmoil. Remember those disruptive abortion protesters?"

"I will make Southern California an illustration to the nation. Young people can be particularly dangerous. We will target the universities and infiltrate on all levels."

"Excellent!" The president pointed at a chair. "Sit down, please."

Adams settled into a leather chair. "Millions of Christians have disappeared during this strange episode some people call the Rapture. I suspect a plot. Perhaps someone figured out a way to transport them, like getting beamed up in an old *Star Trek* movie. And perhaps the absentees are secretly regrouping for an attack on the government."

Gianardo's eyes narrowed. "An insurrection?"

"Be a perfect setup for a self-made pope."

"Hmmm. Very interesting explanation. In fact, the most insightful answer I've had to date explaining this phenomenon. But could this many people really be in hiding? Where could they have disappeared?"

"Multitudes change their identity every day." Adams's countenance took on an air of smug self-assurance and importance. "In medieval times, the pope and his legions controlled many nations. Why not a new strategy for world domination secretly controlled by some leader we've not yet identified?"

The president stared hard. "Stranger things than I would ever guess happen today." Gianardo looked at the picture of himself and the Egyptian satanist priest, Knudiaon, now hanging on his wall. "The freakish and grotesque seem to have become common. Yes, I suspected some such scheme could be behind these disappearances." The president clenched his fist and pounded his palm. "I want these people crushed, wiped out, and I am giving you the personal authority to do what it takes."

"Thank you for your confidence, Mr. President."

Gianardo curled his lip and jutted his chin forward. Standing with his hands on his hips Mussolini-style, he glared at the agent. "Do this right, Adams, and I'll make you the head of a national secret police bureau to rival anything Stalin ever thought possible."

"Yes, sir!" Adams jumped up and extended his hand. "Consider the job done."

Gianardo shook the agent's hand. "I will be carefully following your progress."

■ ■ ■

The leadership of Community Church gathered in the living room of Ed Parker's rambling ranch-style home. Coffee cups and cookies cluttered the large walnut-inlaid coffee table. The overweight accountant listened carefully to Sylvia Springer lecture the group.

"I know the pastor's wife has moved into an apartment of her own, and they are hiding the fact from the public. She has to be running around with some man. Obviously, the good parson cannot control his own home."

"You're certain?" Ed squinted and grimaced.

"I have it on good authority!" Sylvia tossed her frosted hair as her puffy neck turned pink. "How could you doubt my word? I just can't divulge my sources."

Dr. Stanton Young looked wise and knowing. "No one is doubting you, Sylvia. We just need to be sure of the story. Don't want to be misled down any blind alleys."

Dorothy James pointed her bony finger at the chairman of the pastoral relations committee. "I've been talking to people at all levels of the church. When I explain the facts, no one doubts the seriousness of the problem. Ed, we should have gotten rid of Reynolds two years ago when we first talked about it!"

"Yeah. What are we waiting for?" Sylvia reached for another cookie. "We have more than enough support—everyone thinks Reynolds is wrong for the church."

"Not everyone," Parker cautioned. "I received a concerned call from Joe McCoy. He's standing solidly with the pastor and believes we've started a vendetta to get the man. The McCoys could be trouble."

"Well," Dr. Young drawled as he smiled broadly, "we can't win them all. I think the McCoys' influence can be isolated. After all, they are very new to the church. Not really one of us. I've thought for some time they're just a little too pious for Community Church.

Ed scratched his head and smiled nervously. "I'm worried that Reynolds could really upset the applecart with what he's been preaching lately. Since this Rapture thing, the pastor seems to have radically changed what he believes. Keeps talking about how wrong he's been in the past. I get the feeling his wife really moved out because the preacher has gotten too religious for her."

"He's become quite the fundamentalist," Sylvia agreed.

"Fear!" Dr. Young interjected. "Our pastoral leader has succumbed to fear, like so many have done since this strange disappearance of people, and he's started sounding like a Bible-thumping revivalist. I find that behavior to be as offensive as any of the rest of what we suspect might be true."

Ed nodded. "He's got many other frightened people listening to him. If we get some sort of emotionalism going, the hysteria could overturn the control we now have of the church."

Sylvia Springer defiantly crossed her arms over her rotund stomach. "Now is the time to get this business over with. I vote that we immediately sink Pastor Reynolds's boat and find another preacher at once. Delay only works in his favor."

"Hear! Hear!" Dr. Young applauded.

Ed hesitated. "There is one other matter." He pursed his lips. "I had a strange contact from a government official seeking information on Reynolds. I think you should be aware of this situation."

"Really?" Stanton Young raised his eyebrows. "What's that all about?"

"I don't know, but the man asked questions about whether the pastor really supported the government and the president in particular. I didn't know what to say. He insisted I take his phone number and call him if anything suspicious happened."

"Tell him the truth." Sylvia snorted. "The pastor has said some harsh things about the direction the country is going, and last week he questioned Damian Gianardo's religious values. Made me right mad."

Dr. Young chuckled. "Maybe the government can do the job for us. Possibly Reynolds hasn't been paying his taxes."

"Yeah," Dorothy added. "Tell them the McCoys are with the pastor. Let the government haul the whole bunch of them away."

The group laughed and Ed stood up. "More coffee anyone? Got a fresh pot in the kitchen. No one?" He stretched and looked around his luxurious living room. "Well, I think the more realistic approach is to begin taking concrete steps in the next board meeting to officially remove Reynolds. Sylvia, you may want to raise objections to what he said about the president in his last sermon."

"Sure. And I'd like the phone number of that government agent. I want to know more about what's going on."

■ ■ ■

Frank and Jessica Wong hurried around the kitchen of the Golden Dragon, trying to complete the final cleanup before closing for the evening. Frank put the last crates of vegetables back in the cooler. Cindy sat by the chopping block, quietly patting her dog, Sam. She seemed to be waiting for just the right moment to speak.

"Just about done." Frank stopped and wiped the sweat from his brow. "Not much waste tonight. Good for additional profit. We can leave in only a few more minutes."

Jessica looked up from the large battered and blackened pot she was scrubbing. "You are most quiet tonight, daughter. Are you okay?"

"I have something important to tell you," Cindy said quietly, "when you have time to listen."

"Always have time for honorable daughter." Frank pulled up a stool. "You must be learning great things in your university. Have special insight to tell us?"

"Yes. . . ." Cindy hesitated. "But the most important discoveries I've been making lately are . . . religious."

"Religious?" Jessica looked alarmed. "Must be most careful. Religion can be very dangerous." She hung the pot on an overhead rack and stopped in front of Cindy.

"What you learn?" Frank scooted closer.

"I've been giving a great deal of attention to what happened to all those people who disappeared. Ben and I study the Bible, and we now believe God took the true Christians out of the world because a terrible war is coming."

Frank's chin dropped. "Another war?" he gasped. "Good heavens!"

"Not just another war," Cindy explained. "A final, great war to end all wars."

Jessica's eyes widened in horror. "We have run from war all our lives. Go from country to country. This is terrible news."

"But there's so much more . . . and it's good. Actually a new day is coming when peace will cover the entire world and God will set up His king to bring harmony to all the nations."

"Amazing!" Frank shook his head in disbelief. "Where you and Ben hear such things?"

"The complete account is in the Bible. Everything we need to do to be ready for this battle is in the sacred Book."

Jessica wrung her hands. "What you say frightens me. I don't know what to say, daughter."

"Mother, I'm learning marvelous insights into who Jesus is."

"Jesus?" Jessica frowned.

"He's the person Christians follow and was the Messiah the Jews expected. I believe I have found the true way through Him."

"Honorable ancestors believe the Buddha taught the way," Frank answered. "But there is no reason we cannot learn from this Jesus. All religions can teach us something worthwhile."

"Father." Cindy nodded respectfully. "Jesus is much more than a teacher. He is God, and He brings God to us and can lead us into a personal relationship with our Creator."

"O—o—h." Frank's eyes widened in consternation. "Never hear of such a thing as meet God."

"How do you know this idea is true?" Jessica's voice took on a skeptical edge. "Sounds very, very strange to me."

"Ben and I studied the Bible and found it is full of predictions coming true today, right now! The Scriptures describe the events leading up to this great war, and the incidents are happening every day. I just turn on the news and the facts are in my face."

Jessica looked at her husband and scowled disapprovingly. Frank raised his eyebrows in consternation.

"But there is more," Cindy continued. "I know what I am telling you is true because . . ." She stopped, cleared her throat, and took a deep breath. "Because I have been visited by an angel."

"Angel!" Jessica's eyes widened in horror.

"An angel named Michael."

Frank stood up and grabbed his chest. "How you know? You can't see anything."

"Michael's been helping me for a long time, and I didn't know he was an angel until he appeared when I was with Ben. Ben saw him come and then disappear."

"An evil spirit!" Jessica screamed. "My daughter is being visited by demons!"

"Just as happened to us when we go to talk to dead ancestors. We are all doomed!" Frank covered his eyes.

"Stop it!" Cindy pounded the counter. Sam jumped. "I won't tell you any more unless you calm down."

Jessica and Frank huddled together, staring at their child. "You may go to college and read many books, but we know about such matters," Jessica whined. "Chinese people know about terrible reality of demons. Great harm comes from these evil creatures. You are mixed up in frightening business, good daughter."

Cindy took a deep breath. "Please, Mother. Just listen to me. Michael saved me from an attacker and has been the best bodyguard any person could ever have. Believe me, he is no demon."

Frank kept shaking his head. "This Christian business no better than the rest. Daughter now hovers over the brink of disaster. Oh, Buddha, help us!"

" P—l—e—a—s—e." Cindy shook her head in disgust. "I am trying to tell you of the most important discovery anyone can ever make and you're turning this conversation into Halloween time."

"We hear all we can take for one night." Jessica waved her daughter away. "Please no more tonight."

"I can't believe my ears." Cindy slid off the stool and pulled Sam's harness. "Okay. I won't tell you any more, but if a big guy named Michael shows up, don't mess with him. He's dynamite!"

"No more! No more!" Jessica hurried out of the kitchen with Frank scurrying behind.

"Come on, Sam. Let's walk home. You make more sense than they do."

CHAPTER

22

Watching from the other side of time, Michael turned to Seradim. "What have you observed in these scenarios we have been watching?"

"Wickedness and ignorance," he responded instantly. He again conjured up images from inside the Oval Office and Ed Parker's home. "Obviously the Antichrist will manipulate the security agents into hurting and even killing many people. The church committee is going to crucify the pastor. But I am mystified and amazed at how reactionary the Wongs were."

Scenes of Jessica and Frank fleeing the kitchen reappeared. "They are not even hearing their daughter."

"People don't listen well," Michael commented. "Sounds bounce around in their ears, but they seldom focus their attention on what is truly happening around them. Preoccupation causes emotional and spiritual deafness. Emerged in constant noise and stimulation, human beings lose their capacity to tune in the music of nature and the resonance of eternity. They hear only the static of business."

"Tragic."

"Now what should we do, Seradim?"

"We must immediately plunge through the time barrier and straighten these messes out. I suggest we descend on this dangerous little demagogue, Agent Adams, and let him know how the L.A. district attorney felt when Adams dropped him in jail. Next, we clean house in Community Church before these supercilious busybodies hurt a good man. We know the truth about Pastor Reynolds and—"

"Stop there," Michael interrupted. "Why are you getting ready to go to battle?"

"Why?" Seradim looked shocked. "Because that's our job! We have to protect our friends."

"Someone told you to do this?"

The junior angel felt short-circuited. "Well, not exactly."

"You had some suggestion from somewhere to act?"

Seradim was speechless. "Well, no."

Michael bore down. "In some ways, we are very much like humans. Both angels and people have one supreme lesson to learn, and the time has come for you to grasp this basic principle."

Seradim blinked several times. "Am I not called to do the business of God?"

"And what is the business of God?"

Seradim went blank.

"People get into great trouble by assuming they know what God has in mind when they are only doing their own will. Community Church's 'hang-the-preacher club' are quite sure they are about the business of God. Crusaders and inquisitors were no less zealous for the intentions of God as they maimed and murdered their way across Europe."

Seradim shook his head in dismay. "I don't understand."

"Only one thing is needful, friend." Michael consoled his charge. "Obedience. We are called to find the mind of the Father first. Our business is not to do something *for* God; but what God *wants* done. There is a great difference."

The trainee squirmed, searching for some appropriate response.

"Our job isn't to do what we think *might* please the Father. Our responsibility is to listen first so we do *exactly* what the Almighty wills. And humans have the same task, although most go through an entire lifetime and never get the message."

"Obedience?"

"The difference between life and death is in that one simple concept. Disobedience began in Eden, and obedience was completed on Calvary. Lucifer and his followers fell because of rebellion. Eternal life came back to the world because of the submission of Jesus."

"But . . ."

"We must learn how to use our freedom," Michael instructed. "Angels and humans have the same capacity of choice. Our most basic task is to choose what the Father intends."

"But surely He would want us to stop those destructive people at the church."

"Really?" Michael smiled. "The Lord told you so?"

Seradim gestured aimlessly. "No."

"Then you must not presume on what is not given."

"I just don't understand."

"You must learn an important insight into how the will of God operates. Let's look in on how things have gone with Jimmy Harrison as the months and years have gone by. The Rapture and the loss of his parents brought Jimmy to his own crisis of faith, and he turned his life over to the Lord. Take a look."

Seradim watched as scenes from Jimmy's life flowed past like a VCR on fast speed. He watched Jimmy plod away at the car lot in Laguna Niguel, selling everything in sight. Jimmy quickly acquired 10 percent of the business and was doing well while he prospered spiritually. Seradim smiled, observing Jimmy's relationship with Ruth deepen into true and meaningful devotion.

Michael pointed to the scene. "There are laws of psychology, sociology, society, relationships, and human dynamics at work. Jimmy labors; he prospers. The young man turns to God; God turns to him. You are seeing the order God placed in the universe working."

"Yes," Seradim answered without fully comprehending.

"We don't interfere with God-ordained principles. We work in accord with the Creator's purposes. Angels respect what the Almighty started in the beginning."

"I think I understand."

Michael pointed through the veil of time. "Let's go down and watch what is happening." Seconds later the two angels were inside a Southern California restaurant.

Jimmy and Ruth were finishing a romantic Valentine's Day supper at the five-star Five Crowns restaurant in Corona del Mar. Cindy and Ben had joined them. The Tudor-style restaurant was elegant with its stucco-covered walls decorated with English coats of arms and hunting trumpets.

Cindy ran her sensitive fingers over the fine linen tablecloth. "We know that God is going to take care of us," she said quietly. "No matter what . . ."

"Things have completely changed." Ben passed the thick-sliced homemade bread around again. "In the past, I wouldn't have given much consideration to anything more serious than my next want. Now we're caught up in a great adventure. I know bad stuff is out there, but I feel alive and part of something very exhilarating. Sure, we have some very formidable enemies, but we're on the side that's ultimately going to win . . . although the Bible says that vast numbers of believers will die during the Great Tribulation."

"We have Michael watching over us." Cindy cut into her petite filet.

The senior angel turned to his charge. "Yes, we're watching," Michael said, "but we must not keep humans from the sovereign will of God or the natural consequences of their decisions. Our job is to fight off the demons when it is appropriate, but we must never take away the autonomy that is vital to human development."

Seradim rubbed his chin, pondering the scene carefully. "Why not?"

"People grow by overcoming obstacles. Struggle perfects their faith and character. If we remove barriers or make the struggle easier, we ultimately diminish what humans can become. Remember the attack on Pastor Reynolds? We can't pull people like the pastor out of the fire without cheating them of an important opportunity to become stronger."

Seradim nodded slowly. "So, I can't fight their battles for them?"

"Not the ones they must face to develop endurance, patience, additional strength, and the capacity to love."

Ben looked at his sister as he spoke. "Our lives used to be flat and overindulged. We were spoiled rich kids, but that's behind us. I wouldn't go back to the old days for anything."

"Me too!" Jimmy agreed. "I just didn't realize how important my father's ministry was. He was in the real battle every day of his life."

Michael nudged his charge. "See! Jimmy and Ben are getting the picture. They have become different people through turmoil."

Ruth reached out for Jimmy's hand. "I don't know how much time we have left together." Her voice was low and intense. "Who knows what tomorrow will bring? We have to make the most of every second."

"Yes," Jimmy said soberly. "I'm afraid you're right. Our great adventure is going to be filled with drastic uncertainties."

"I think we need to take advantage of this very moment," Ruth insisted. "I have the perfect idea for finishing the evening. What better time to get married than Valentine's Day?"

Jimmy started to laugh, but something in Ruth's decisiveness checked him. "You're not kidding."

"No, I'm not. Jimmy, I want to marry you tonight."

Ben and Cindy almost stopped breathing.

"To . . . tonight?" Jimmy stuttered.

"Why not? We love each other, and that's all that matters."

"But I thought you'd want a big wedding . . . the white dress . . . the walk down the aisle." Jimmy kept blinking his eyes.

"In a short while we may be dying." Ruth's voice became almost a whisper. "I don't want to face that moment alone. More important, I want us to be together through every step of the way into eternity. I say let's go for it tonight!"

"But . . . how?" Jimmy was uncharacteristically befuddled. "Where?"

"Mexico!" Cindy and Ruth said at the same time.

"Sure!" Ben clapped. "Mexico is only an hour and a half from here. For a couple of bucks anything's possible there. We could leave right now and have you married before midnight."

"Midnight?" Jimmy swallowed hard and then beamed. "Why not?"

"Let's go!" Ruth stood up. "I'm ready to become Mrs. Jimmy Harrison on Valentine's Day."

Seradim began slowly nodding. "Love wouldn't be possible without having free choice, would it? This scene couldn't have happened without the couple having the unencumbered ability to make their own decisions."

"You've got it, Seradim. Our job now is to protect the couples on their way to Tijuana. The world is filled with improbabilities—unexpected, random events. Accidents happen. We can help them over these intrusions so their own choices can blossom and come to full flower. But we must use discernment in recognizing what is the appropriate action at any moment."

Seradim and Michael gently ascended out of the restaurant and hovered above the couples' car as it sped south on Interstate 5 toward the Mexican border. The young angel turned to his mentor.

"How can I make sure I'm reading the signals right?"

"Always turn to the mind of God. Tune in His purposes. Only then will you know you are acting in obedience and not presumption."

"But don't the purposes of God override human decisions?"

"The purposes of God are final and ultimate. Only in the mystery of the mind of the Almighty are His plans fully comprehensible. One of the reasons we are here is to make sure the Evil One can't frustrate God's plan for Ben, Cindy, Ruth, and Jimmy. We must fight to keep the demons from interfering in those arrangements."

"I understand much better."

"Human existence is a complex interaction between the laws of the universe, random chance events, and the final purposes of God," Michael explained. "Our job is to help the process work and keep the devil's army from creating chaos. Lucifer never liked playing by the rules."

The angels watched the wedding and the return trip. The newlyweds were dropped off at Jimmy's apartment, and Ben took Cindy back to her dorm.

"What do you think is ahead for us?" Ben asked as he pulled in front of the dorm.

Cindy felt the window of the door as if rubbing a magic looking glass. "I don't know." She seemed to be peering out into the black night. "The angel said . . ." She stopped.

"I guess we can't get married." Ben was clearly pained. "I don't understand it. Michael seemed to be clear that we were to maintain a certain proper distance."

"Perhaps we are to develop a perfect love for each other." Cindy turned toward Ben. "Maybe in heaven . . ."

"I don't want to wait for heaven." Ben groaned. "I want now. I envy Jimmy tonight. Cindy, you'd be heaven enough for me."

"We must trust God to know best." Cindy leaned against Ben. "You have something important to do in the days ahead, and we must not do anything that could spoil your purpose."

Michael beamed. "Cindy has caught the vision. Only by allowing them the freedom to slip could we give Ben and Cindy the opportunity to develop such maturity. Let's follow Ben home."

By the time Ben returned to his room it was three o'clock. In spite of near exhaustion, he lay on the bed praying. "What is it You want from me?" he finally cried out. "I don't understand." Releasing the last grasp of frustration, Ben fell into a deep sleep.

Michael and Seradim listened intensely to both his silent and spoken prayers. "You will know soon enough," Michael answered. "Soon enough."

As the two angels left, the senior angel instructed his charge. "The couples are reaching out for the Father's highest purposes. They will not be disappointed! When we fall on the will of God, all trains arrive on schedule."

CHAPTER
23

Jennifer watched her children glare at her from across the den. It was late, she was tired, and now exasperated. Jennifer caught her breath and tried another approach. "Your father and I are not trying to cram anything down your throats. We appreciate the pressure your friends are putting on you, but these matters are very serious. The government is investigating Christians. We could be in deep trouble very quickly. We need your cooperation."

Erica crossed her arms over her chest and rolled her eyes contemptuously. "O-o-o, James Bond stuff. Give me a break. R-e-a-l-ly!"

Family strife attracted the demons like the scent of fresh meat brought to wolves. Homelas and Malafidus immediately descended through the McCoys' roof and slipped through the walls. One demon inched next to Joe Jr. and the other cuddled close to Erica. Each of the apparitions began slowly breathing into the ears of the children.

Joe Jr. smirked at his mother. "What a pain! Everything was fine until you started going to that stupid church and turned into religious wombat freakos. Next, we got embroiled in all the stupid fighting with these church people who have the maturity of a bunch of monkeys in a zoo. Now, we have to pray before we eat. Pray before we sleep. Pray before we think. Bor—i—n—g."

"Stop it!" Jennifer bit her lip, trying not to explode. "You are two over-indulged, spoiled brats who can't see any farther than the latest MTV slice of immorality. I'm tired of your self-centered preoccupation with nothing more significant than the designer label on your clothes."

Homelas nudged Malafidus. "Olé! Mom's about to pop! If we can keep the pressure up, maybe we can create a real screaming fight. Let's really rattle Miss Pious in front of the kids."

"Gosh," Erica choked. "I've never heard you talk like *that* before."

"Yes, and that's part of the problem," Jennifer shot back. "I've let the two of you grow up as nothing more than a pale reflection of this spineless society. Now your father and I are paying the price."

Erica hesitantly looked at her brother and shrugged. "It's just that I think we have the right to choose our own religion and—"

"You don't have a religion," her mother interrupted. "And since when did you start choosing the important things in your life? You don't decide whether or not you're going to school or to a doctor when you're sick. So don't tell me about whether or not you're going to church."

Homelas flinched. "Stop the religion talk if you can. Head it off! We've got to keep a wedge between the children and the parents. It's essential this conversation turn nasty."

"You've got to admit there's a problem." Joe Jr. came off the couch shaking his finger like an attorney on cross examination. "The leaders of that stupid Community Church are after the preacher like a pack of wild dogs, and they're saying bad stuff about you and Dad. Why should we go some place we're not welcome?"

Jennifer took another deep breath. "I'm trying to tell you children how serious the issues are. It isn't a matter of going to this or that church. Evil has been unleashed in the world, and terrible things are ahead. Do you understand?"

Joe Jr. rolled his shoulders indifferently. "Sorry, Mom. Just can't see the problem. All this bizarre political stuff going on in Washington doesn't interest me any more than this squabble over the preacher and his wife. Count me out."

Erica stared at the floor. "It's getting late, Mom. I've still got some homework to finish, and I'm tired." She edged toward the door.

Malafidus sent a message to Joe Jr. "Cut out of here while the getting is good. Move on while your mother's not looking."

Jennifer rubbed her forehead and stared at her daughter. "Time is running out," she implored.

"That's exactly my point." Erica slipped into the hall and hurried for the stairs. "I'm going to bed."

When Jennifer turned back, Joe Jr. had disappeared down the hall. She sank into the overstuffed chair and buried her face in her hands.

"Excellent!" Malafidus applauded. "She not only has been defeated, but she feels the loss. Look at the pain in her face."

"Heavenly Father, help me." Jennifer's prayer rose from the depth of her soul. "Please help me to know how to witness to my children and offer them the new life we've found."

Jennifer prayed for nearly twenty minutes until she was finally interrupted by Joe Jr.'s return to the den. Avoiding her, he sat down in front of the large-screen TV and switched it on.

"I want to watch TV." He kept hitting the clicker. "You don't have to say anything. I won't even get near the MTV channel. At least not as long as you're here." He laughed at his little joke.

To Joe's amazement, every channel was preempted by a special news bulletin from Jerusalem, where it was already morning. The excited voices of announcers were explaining an amazing phenomenon that was occurring. The broadcasts kept repeating news clips of clouds boiling and swirling above the Mount of Olives. Two figures descended slowly out of the clouds toward the earth.

Joe's mouth dropped. "Is this science fiction," he finally stammered, "or is this for real?"

Jennifer blinked and moved closer to the TV. Brilliant light flooded the terrain as the two figures moved over the ground as if they were floating. The news anchor explained that the two figures kept changing languages, speaking flawless Russian, Arabic, Chinese, English, and Spanish.

"Man!" Joe Jr. cheered and shook his arms. "What a cool program."

Jennifer slowly rose to her feet. "I . . . I . . . I . . . know what's happening. Good grief. I read about this prediction in the Bible. It is the Jewish festival called Purim, and sacrifices will cease in Israel if Jimmy Harrison's predictions are right."

Joe turned around to his mother and frowned. "Come on, Mom. Please give it a rest. This is TV."

"Those two men are . . . are . . . Moses and Elijah. I just know it."

Joe laughed. "Mom, you're as big a weirdo as those two guys in long robes."

The CNN correspondent was visibly shaking. His assistant aimed his TV camera at the two giants. "In an early morning meeting on this day of Purim," the reporter announced, "Gianardo ordered Israel to halt animal sacrifices, and now this unbelievable duo from who knows where is descending from the sky. Are they space aliens? Are they two of the people who were beamed up two years ago?"

The larger of the two figures pointed his finger directly into the TV camera. His deep-set black eyes looked as if they could pierce steel. "Hear me!" he said in perfect English. "We have come that you might hear the final witness of the Holy One of Israel. Listen well, lest your own words become testimony against you. The hour of accounting is at hand!"

A correspondent inched forward holding a microphone at arm's length as if to protect himself. "Who . . . who might we . . . ah . . . be . . . ah . . . talking with?"

"Moses!" the huge man roared, his voice sounding as if it might shake the mountain. "I have come with my heavenly colleague. Behold, Elijah the Tishbite!"

The correspondent fell backward, and the two figures moved past him down the hill.

"It *is* Moses!" Jennifer's hand came to her mouth. "Just like the Bible predicted. Moses and Elijah have returned."

Joe's smile faded and bewilderment crossed his face. He stared at his mother. Terror filled his eyes.

Malafidus reached for Homelas. "What . . . what's . . . happening?"

The demon put his hands to his ears. "By the fires of hell itself! I've heard such a thing was predicted." Homelas retreated from the television set.

"We've got to get out of here," Malafidus choked. "Got to get to headquarters and find out what's going on."

"The Jews are always the source of the trouble," Homelas whined. "Someone should have nuked Jerusalem long ago. Nothing but trouble ever comes out of there."

The two demons disappeared into the blackness.

■ ■ ■

Very early the next morning, after phone calls from the McCoys and calls to Jimmy and Ruth, Larry and Sharon Feinberg replayed their video recording of the day's events in Jerusalem for the fifth time. Sharon stared at the Bible in her lap. "The whole event is right here." She put her finger in the book of Revelation. "We have watched eternal history in the making today."

"Jimmy is right in his conclusion," Larry answered. "We must leave this country and go to Israel before Passover if Jimmy's predictions are right. Bozrah is going to be the only divinely protected city of refuge for the Jewish people. As a Jew and a doctor, I have no choice but to be there to help our own."

Sharon nodded. "Ancient Bozrah is known as Petra now, and it's the place prepared for us in the wilderness, mentioned in Revelation and Isaiah and Obadiah. Jesus even alluded to it indirectly in Matthew 24."

"If we are anywhere else in the world after the Antichrist desecrates the temple, as Daniel warned, then we'll be

killed," Larry added. "Especially Jewish believers in Jesus."
He consulted the map in his Bible. "Petra is in Jordan, sixty
or seventy miles southeast of Jerusalem. We'll have to act
like tourists. Pack our necessities and get there before
Passover. Jimmy says Passover is when the worst Jewish holocaust in history will start and then Yeshua will return 1,260
days later."

Sharon looked around their luxurious home. "Hard to
leave all this behind."

"We had relatives in Europe before the Holocaust who
had the same choice," Larry concluded sadly. "Those who
decided not to leave paid for their reluctance with their
lives."

"Jimmy and Ruth will go with us, but I know Ben will stay
here and try to help the students he works with. He won't
leave Cindy and her family behind."

Larry shook his head. "I felt great pain when Jennifer
and Joe said they must stay because their kids are sucked
into the ideas Gianardo and his associates are putting out.
We must pray constantly for the conversion of those young
people."

Sharon took her husband's hands. "Events are going to
move very fast. We can expect Gianardo to seize all remaining power. Many will die."

A long silence fell between them. Only the sound of the
ticking of the hall clock filled the room.

"Everything we've held dear in this place will soon be
gone," Sharon finally spoke.

"We will be wanderers on the face of the earth once
again."

"Our people always have been." Tears ran down Sharon's
cheeks. She slipped to her knees in front of the couch.
Looking toward the ceiling, she prayed fervently. *"Shema*

Israel Adonai elahonu echad." Tears filled her eyes. *"Echad ela-honu gadol Adonenu kadosh shmo."*

"Maranatha," Larry answered. "Come quickly, Lord Jesus."

CHAPTER
24

As did the McCoys, Frank and Jessica Wong began each day by tuning in the events unfolding in Jerusalem. They watched the cameras panning the two white-bearded prophets. Crowds lined up to stare at the scene in front of the Western Wall where Moses and Elijah were sitting.

They found it nearly impossible to grasp what was occurring in this scene, which both intrigued and terrified them. Cindy tried to explain, but her parents inevitably were left confused and mystified.

"We have nowhere left to run." Frank winced. "How can we hide from such strange events?"

Jessica nodded frantically. "The world has gone crazy. People filled with madness. I fear for Cindy. She and Ben stand too close to the fire."

"I just don't understand who these two men really are. I can't comprehend their religion. Very strange."

The screen blurred and the scene shifted. The words *Fast-Breaking News Alert* covered the screen. An announcer declared, "An important series of statements is anticipated momentarily from the vice president of the United States and the prime minister of Israel." A picture of the hastily rebuilt Temple in Jerusalem appeared. Surrounded by troops, Gianardo and Rathmarker stood in front of the reconstructed edifice on the Temple Mount.

As the announcer continued, the president walked around the sacred precincts of the Temple as if there were no boundaries or limitations to visitors. The high priest followed Gianardo, frantically trying to wave him away. A microphone had been set up just outside the Holy of Holies. The presidential seal was being attached as the announcer said the prime minister of Israel was ready to make a statement.

The prime minister shuffled to the microphone and began reading from a crumpled sheet of paper. "The New Roman Empire called the Knesset into session this morning and demanded that control of all nuclear capacity be turned over to them. Failure to comply would bring immediate attack upon our country. We had no choice but to comply and have now done so. Mr. Gianardo has also demanded that we recognize him as the supreme ruling power in the world. Failure to do so would invite disaster. The president of the New Roman Empire obviously does have supreme authority." The old man stepped backward, staring at the ground.

In a hushed voice, the announcer said, "Vice President Jacob Rathmarker will now make a response."

Rathmarker moved quickly to the microphone. "Thank you, Mr. Prime Minister. We are gathered at this place as a matter of principle. Clearly, the New Roman Empire is uniting the globe in order to create a more just and decent world. We are the last hope for a peaceful order. The empire will insist on nonaggression even at the price of going to war in order to stop killing. However, global order demands recognition of our authority at every level. History records that religion has been a constant source of strife and conflict. As you know, immoral animal sacrifices were stopped a month ago. Today, on your Passover, we are going to put an end to further religious discord."

Rathmarker whirled around and jerked a section of the huge curtain open, letting outside light flood into the holiest place. The priest screamed and the Israeli prime minister dropped to his knees, but Rathmarker marched into the center of the sacred chamber, deliberately knocking aside a golden plate of incense. Calmly, the vice president returned to the microphone.

"No longer will Damian Gianardo be known as president. As of this moment, his title shall be world emperor, and I will be prime minister of the New Roman Empire. Our authority extends over matters of state *and* religion. As it is treason to resist the secular office, so shall it be sedition to oppose our religious authority. We will not allow anyone in the religious community to stand in the way of global peace. Those two impostors by the Western Wall who call themselves Moses and Elijah will submit to our rule or face the same penalty." Rathmarker stopped and glared at the Israeli prime minister. "No longer will religious charlatanism be tolerated in any form!"

An ominous quiet fell over the crowd. No one moved. People stared in terrified awe.

Rathmarker declared, "Today, I will place a life-size statue of Emperor Gianardo in the center of the Holy of Holies so no one forgets where ultimate control and authority lie."

Frank Wong turned to Jessica. "Honorable wife, do you understand? Did he say they kill the two holy men?"

Jessica shook her head. "Apparently, Mr. President now take over all religion. Very frightening."

"Reporters and priests seem very upset that president now walk around inside most holy room." Frank pulled closer to the screen. "Gianardo run everything now . . . everywhere. Such a man is greatly to be feared."

■ ■ ■

At that moment Michael and Seradim stood among the throngs of Guardians observing the same event. Behind them stood the Thrones. These angels, who conveyed the juridical power of God, standing in rapt attention, scrutinized Gianardo walking into the Holy of Holies. Anger seethed from the depths of their beings. Above the hosts of angels the Dominions and Virtues hovered, poised to attack. From out of the center of heaven, Gabriel led the archangels in a flurry of activity while the Principalities prepared for war in Jerusalem.

"Not yet," the Divine Voice rumbled from the very center of the essence of light itself. "Hold steady until the full measure of evil is fulfilled. The hour is close at hand, and the bowls of wrath will be poured out on those who kill My chosen ones; but the time is not yet."

Michael and Seradim instantly received their special instructions and knew what to do. The resonance of the voice of God continued to ring through their beings long after the content of His message was received.

Michael turned to his charge. "Ready?"

Seradim's countenance became intense. "I have learned much of waiting for the divine timing. Yes, I will be obedient to that which the Father speaks, and I am prepared to follow His word to the end."

"Then we are ready to return. We must visit Ben and Cindy immediately. We have a message to deliver. They are watching TV in the Feinbergs' living room."

Seradim paused. "Why would Ben and Cindy receive such special delivery when other people hear nothing?"

"In the economy of God," Michael explained, "special leaders are singled out for unique tasks. At those moments, the Father gives them specific and distinct direction. The Virgin Mary was instructed about the future. Saul was given the insight that would allow him to become the apostle Paul. Now the time has come to inform Ben and Cindy about their future assignments."

The angels instantly thought themselves through the time barrier and shot like heavenly rockets into the Feinberg home, settling just behind the couch where Ben and Cindy were talking. Michael slipped into human form and stepped toward them.

Sam looked up and barked.

"Someone's here!" Cindy jumped.

"Be not afraid." Michael's voice was hushed.

Ben leaped up from the couch. "Michael! You're here!"

"Yes." Michael walked in front of them. "The moment has arrived for me to give you complete instructions. Events are moving quickly. The next three and a half years will seem like both an eternity and a flash of time. Some days will feel totally unbearable, but in retrospect they will be a blur. Ben, I want you to know beyond any doubt that you can and will survive. Long ago you were chosen for these assignments because we knew that your family had the capacity and the ability to endure during these last times."

"My family?"

"The Feinbergs are from the tribe of Levi. Even though you have largely ignored your heritage, you come from the priestly lineage. You carry a godly capacity to stand before the heavenly Father on behalf of others. Once again your family will fulfill their call."

"We're not prepared for such a thing. . . ."

"To the contrary! Who has a better analytic mind than you, Ben? You're the family chess master. Your ability to strategize will serve your survival needs quite well, and we will protect you."

"But my parents?"

"The Holy Spirit is currently drawing multitudes of Jews to Petra–Bozrah where they are already safe. Many will need medical attention, but far more will be so traumatized by the catastrophes unfolding around them that their emotional care will be paramount. The members of your family are extremely well equipped for the work. The hand of God will protect the area, and no one will be able to hurt them there."

Cindy slowly raised her hand. "You said 'survive.' Sounds like Ben's going to be a general in a war. That's scary."

"Sit down, children. Listen well."

Ben picked up a pencil and a pad.

"Gianardo has committed the ancient sin of Babel, thinking he can stand tall enough to shoot an arrow into the heart of God. Even as we speak, secret security squads are already beginning to kill millions of Jews, especially Jews who believe in Jesus as predicted in Revelation chapter 12 two thousand years ago. Nothing is left to restrain this man's arrogance."

"What can we possibly do?" Cindy shook her head. "A blind Oriental girl and a Messianic Jew aren't going to make much difference."

"Yes, you will. Cindy, you are going to become a key helper in our counterintelligence operation. In some instances, you will automatically know what to do. At other times, I will direct you to the people you are to contact. You will be bringing hope and insight during these final days. The first point of contact will be your fellow students at UCLA."

"Amazing," Ben exclaimed.

"We know you have a heart for the task. Ben, you are one of the 144,000 chosen ones mentioned in the book of Revelation. No one can harm you in any way. Others will be killed, including believing Jews, but not you. Cindy, however, has no guarantees."

"Please tell us everything you can," Cindy pleaded. "We'll need all the insight you have for us."

"First, I want you, Ben, to move your operation to a more secluded place. I will lead you beyond Los Angeles to an obscure house in the country, which will become your center of ministry. Next, you need to share all of this information with the McCoys. They will assist you in your outreach."

Ben nodded but shot a worried look at Cindy. "We have shortwave contact with my parents in Petra–Bozrah. I can't wait to share your instructions with them."

"You must be very cautious, Ben. As soon as Gianardo's secret police are fully functional, they will have the capacity to monitor all radio contact."

For the next few minutes Ben and Cindy discussed with Michael the implications of his directions. The full scope of their involvement and the danger became more apparent as each detail fell into place. Finally Cindy asked, "What can we expect next?" She reached for Ben's hand.

"We saw the white horse of the Apocalypse when Giannardo seized world power after the Rapture. Russia's defeat last Av 9 in Israel was the red horse of the Apocalypse. The widespread famines throughout the lands of Africa and Russia and her allies was the black horse of Revelation chapter six.

"And now the pale horse of the Apocalypse, Death, has begun to ride, my children. War, famine, plagues, and wild animals will be used as vehicles of judgment. The alarm is being sounded, and none will be able to say that they were not warned. You will see great consternation everywhere. Twenty-five percent of the world population will die in the next few months, but fear not. The Lord Yeshua is with you to the very end of the age. I always stand in the shadows."

■ ■ ■

Across the city, the McCoys were engrossed in the special news program. As the last words of the emperor's speech faded, Joe turned the TV set off. "Now, children, do you see the truth? This is exactly what your mother and I have been saying would happen."

"Great guess, Dad." Joe Jr. shrugged. "But I had a hunch that religion was the next thing Gianardo would go for. After all, he's already picked up most of the chips."

Jennifer shook her hands at the ceiling. "Children! This is a life-and-death matter. Don't you understand what's ahead?"

"Sure," Joe Jr. said forcefully. "I'd shelve all that religion talk you've been having with the Feinbergs. You could get all of us into a lot of trouble."

"Please, Mom," Erica begged, "get rid of those Bibles. One of my friends might see them and think that Joe and I approve of what you're doing."

"Children," their father begged with tears in his eyes, "you've got to change your minds. We're not only trying to avoid trouble. Our eternal destiny is at stake. Don't you understand?"

CHAPTER
25

Special Agent Gerald Adams looked around the dimly lit room at the strike force assembled in the commandeered Los Angeles district attorney's office. He knew each man fit the psychological profile of a sociopath. Suffering did not touch this crew; they could inflict pain without the slightest tinge of remorse. The agents were his kind of guys.

"We suspect treasonous activity throughout this entire area," Adams lectured the group. "A number of religious groups and churches are under surveillance. In fact, we have operatives in some local congregations already. However, we must infiltrate more churches, clubs, and college campuses until we have an ironclad grip on the entire state of California. Understand?"

Affirmation rippled across the room.

"We are also monitoring all radio signals and computer-generated transmissions—any form of international contact. By tracing these communiqués back to their origins, we'll be able to pinpoint the location of any troublemakers. Once we've got 'em in sight, we'll hit 'em hard."

A man in the back raised his hand. "Robert Schultz, sir. Just transferred in from Atlanta, Georgia. When we locate culprits, how long do we wait for due process? Are search warrants still necessary?"

Adams shook his head. "We're special forces, envoys of the president of the United States and world emperor." He chuckled. "Almost above and beyond the law. Seriously, let's not push our luck and hit some uninvolved citizen by mistake. Creates a backlash. But when we're on to the real thing, strike first and ask questions later."

"And if there's resistance?"

"Mr. Schultz, in the case of hard-core religious fanatics, we can also claim they attacked us first. Shoot 'em. We can control the press. Gianardo wants a high body count on the subversives."

The agents smiled at each other knowingly.

"We've been looking for this sort of climate for years," Adams continued. "An environment in which we can do our job without having to contend with meddling lawyers and bleeding heart judges. Let's do it right."

■ ■ ■

Ben and Cindy's student ministry on the UCLA campus proved to be extraordinarily successful. Explosive conditions around the world and political tyranny in the United States created a natural backlash among many intelligent students. Affiliating with Christians was a convenient way to oppose the government. Along the way, many of the students discovered the truth about Jesus. Student rebellion turned into personal conversions.

But the rebellion of the McCoy children continued no matter how hard the parents tried. Circumstances, however, were changing.

Adams's men showed up at Newport Union Harbor High School. In Erica McCoy's class, students were piling into their chairs and completely ignoring the teacher's attempts to call the class to order. Mary Higbie, Erica's arch rival, sat next to her. Erica kept talking to a boy beside her in order to ignore Mary.

"Please!" The teacher pounded on the desk. "We have a special speaker. I need your attention for an important announcement."

The students continued talking as if nothing had been said. Erica flipped a paper wad at a boy several rows over.

From the other side of time, Michael beckoned for Seradim to follow him. "Erica is going to need our encouragement. This could be an opportune moment for us to touch her life. Let's go."

The two angels settled on each side of the teenager. Michael instructed Seradim, "Concentrate on how much Erica's parents care for her."

"Stop it!" The teacher slammed a book on her desk. The boom echoed across the room. "What do I have to do to get your attention? Kill someone?" Students jeered and applauded the suggestion but quieted down.

"We have a representative of the office of education. Now listen carefully to what he's got to say. Please welcome Mr. Robert Schultz."

"Recognize him?" Michael asked.

"That's one of Adams's special agents!" Seradim declared. "He must be a plant in the education department."

The tall, lean man walked to the center of the room with an indifferent swagger. His voice was cold and hard. "I'm here to talk about abuse. As you know, the educational system takes all forms of abuse very seriously. Anyone who reports sexual, physical, or emotional abuse will receive immediate care and protection. We simply will not allow parents to take advantage of their children."

"Yippee!" A youth in the back row yelled. "Can you come out and work my old man over? He's been short on my allowance lately."

The class roared.

Schultz walked down the row until he stood in front of the teen. Suddenly the undercover agent lifted the boy completely out of his chair. "You have something to report?"

The astonished student's mouth dropped as he silently shook his head no.

"If you have nothing intelligent to say, then don't interrupt." Schultz let the student drop back into the chair. His notebook went flying off the desk.

"We're not out here playing games." Schultz continued walking through the desks. "Abuse is serious business, and we take it seriously."

The room was completely silent.

"Today we have identified a new form of abuse . . . religious abuse. Understand?"

No one spoke.

Michael breathed heavily on Erica. "Listen, child. Listen to the man's words. Notice what's really happening in this room. Listen to his threats."

Schultz leaned over the desk and stared at the kids on the front row. "The leader of our country is now the supreme authority on all religious matters. Noncompliance can be very deadly business. We will not allow rampant misrepresentation of religious truth to be disseminated through our society. Should your parents fail to comply, they could be putting you in jeopardy. Such action would constitute abuse."

"I don't understand." Erica held up her hand. "Please give me an example."

"If your parents try to force on you religious ideas that are not approved by Emperor Gianardo," Schultz spoke slowly, "or if they teach you that any power exceeds that of our leader, then you are being put in an abusive situation."

"Do Christian ideas count?" Erica asked hesitantly.

"If Christian principles are used to avoid obedience to the empire's rules, then they are immoral and illegal. We are increasingly suspect of Bibles. Let us know if anyone pushes biblical beliefs on you. That would be religious abuse. Good question, young lady."

Erica smiled back pleasantly, but her eyes were fixed wide open. As the man continued talking, Erica began scribbling violently on the notebook on her desk.

"Listen to your heart, Erica." Seradim concentrated intensely. "Tune in to your best self."

Erica did not even realize that Schultz had finished and sat down until Mary spoke softly in her ear.

"Didn't you say your parents are always putting fanatical stuff on you?"

Erica looked in horror at the smug grin on Mary's face. "Sure," Erica fumbled. "You know we all complain about our parents at home, but I didn't mean anything like this guy was describing."

"You said they were always studying the Bible," Mary insisted.

"Yes, but they read lots of porn too," Erica lied. "Just broad readers."

Mary smirked and looked the other way.

"Listen, Erica," Michael continued. "Listen carefully. Your life depends on it."

Erica stared at the blackboard as if in a trance. When the teacher sent reading material down the aisles, she mechanically put her handout inside her notebook but her expression did not change.

"What do you suspect she's thinking?" Seradim asked his companion.

"I don't know. I often wish we could read their minds. The best we can do is offer suggestions. Of course, demons can't get inside their minds either."

"We've got to do something," Seradim protested.

"A human soul cannot be forced, even spiritually," Michael explained. "The best we can do is to inspire a person."

Seradim pondered their dilemma. "What can I put into her thinking?"

"Push all the teenage garbage aside," Michael instructed. "What do you think is at the bottom of this tension between Erica and her parents?"

Seradim puzzled. "Rebellion?"

"Rebellion against what?"

The angel's face brightened. "Against how much she feels bound to her mother . . . because she loves her!"

"Touch that center of love. Jennifer McCoy has always been a very loving mother."

Seradim reached to where God's love resonated at the center of his being. An image rolled up in his mind. A young mother was stooping over her newborn child. The room was poor, meager, but the devotion in the woman's eyes was profound and constant. He saw the Virgin Mary holding the baby Jesus.

Michael tuned in on the scene and felt the mystery of incarnate divine love, enfleshed in and expressed through the child. The prototype, the archetype of all parental devotion, radiated its own aura of profound solicitude.

The two angels kept projecting the image of the Virgin's joy and devotion. Erica's distant stare focused. A gentle smile crossed her face. A tear ran down her cheek.

Shortly after Erica's scare at school, Ben had a scare of his own at a rented house. While sending a radio transmission to his parents in Petra–Bozrah, Adams's forces had uncovered and identified his late-night radio signal and honed in on the house. Providentially, Ben saw a shadow outside the window and immediately stashed the transmitter. When the police broke through the doors, he was able to sneak out through the kitchen and cut through the backyard. He escaped with only a few scratches, but the incident had been too close for comfort.

As he related his tale to Joe and Jennifer McCoy and some of the students at the McCoys' home, Cindy offered to stay behind at UCLA to minister to students there.

"I don't know" Ben hesitated. "I don't like the exposure."

"You sure don't need to be wandering around down there," one of the guys replied. "A quick computer check of your family background would reveal that your parents left with passports for Israel. They'd nail you in a minute."

"In addition, you may have accidentally left some clues back at our old meeting house," another student reasoned.

"I suppose so," Ben mused. "But Michael assured me I'd be safe. I'm just nervous about Cindy being pursued. Only my two very good eyes and the grace of God saved me the other night! I know Michael promised that no one could hurt me, but I'm still human. I get scared sometimes."

"We'll take good care of Cindy," the student assured Ben.

"Let's join hands and commit the plan to the Lord." Joe McCoy reached out for a tall black student and a Hispanic student next to him. "We need to pray for protection for us, our families, and all of our contacts."

After the heartfelt prayers had ended, the group prepared to disperse into the summer night. Some left by the back door while others waited before going down the front driveway so they would not appear to have been meeting. After all the other guests had gone, Ben, Cindy, and her dog, Sam, left.

"Drive carefully," Jennifer called after them. "Your lives are precious."

Ben and Cindy talked all the way back to the campus until they finally pulled in front of Cindy's dorm. Sam sat up in the backseat.

"The work is really going well." Ben smiled. "I'm amazed at how many students you have been able to reach. People seem to be especially attracted to your honesty."

"Perhaps my blindness is an asset, like Michael said. I'm easy to trust."

"Maybe so. I've also been amazed at the response from the people Michael sent me to contact. The results have been equally exciting. They were obviously ready for the gospel."

"I worry that the university will try to track you down."

"No, I'm just a person who dropped out of school for medical reasons." Ben opened the car door for Cindy. "I think my tracks are well covered. I don't see how they could possibly locate me unless I let myself get caught like I nearly did last night."

"Don't let that ever happen again!" Cindy mockingly scolded. "You're better at getting me around than my dog. You'd be hard to replace!"

They kissed each other good night, and Ben hurried back to his apartment.

CHAPTER
26

Are you getting a feel for the battle?" Michael asked his charge.

"Amazing the difference a little practice makes," Seradim concluded. "In the beginning, I thought just having a few facts and the commission from on High was enough to be ready for the war. Obviously, I missed the mark rather badly. One certainly has to know the terrain."

"Since we stepped out of history, the enemy's fury has broken loose. In a power bluff, Gianardo set off a round of atomic exchanges with the Chinese. To his dismay, he discovered they had a much larger nuclear capacity than Gianardo dreamed possible. The world is in a terrible state, and things will get much worse. The power-mad dictator has unleashed great suffering on the innocent as well as the guilty. We have a few more tasks to do, and then I want you to handle a situation on your own."

Seradim smiled broadly. "I hope I'm ready."

"You're getting there. We need to go back and check in with Ben. Big Jewish commemorative day coming up. Time to give him an important message. Ready?"

Seradim agreed and they were immediately transported to Ben's house. Without a sound they slipped through the wall of time and into his room. After turning on the automatic coffeemaker, Michael sat down in a bedroom chair and waited for Ben to wake up. Soon he stirred and reached for the clock.

"Good morning, Ben."

The alarm clock hit the floor. Ben sat straight up in bed. "Who is it?" he shouted.

"I thought you'd recognize my voice by now."

"Don't you ever knock?" Ben looked disgusted. "You scared me silly."

"I apologize. I just wanted to get the morning started right for you. Important day, you know."

Ben frowned and reached down to pick up the alarm clock. "Why?"

"It is July 22nd. The Fast of Tammuz."

"Already?" Ben blinked. "How did it get here so fast?" He got out of bed and put his pants on. "Let me get a shirt. No telling what's next."

"Actually, nothing you can see today, Ben. Pour yourself a cup of coffee and I will explain."

"Coffee?" Ben stared uncomprehending at the coffee steaming in the pot.

"Today a new phase of the Tribulation begins. The Lord Jesus will break the fifth seal that John wrote about in the Revelation. The saints who have died so far during the persecutions have been kept under the heavenly altar. Today their cries to be avenged will be heard, and the next period of woes begins."

"So, we start again." Ben drank a sip of coffee and sat down at the kitchen table. "The police got very close the other night, Michael. I was really terrified."

"Yes, I know. Perhaps I should clarify some things about your situation. There is no place in the world that is completely protected except the Bozrah–Petra area. Even there, people are still subject to the normal bodily processes like heart attacks, strokes, or injuries. Here in California you are living in a genuine war zone. You must start now to get ready for what is ahead, and I want you to let your parents know about the next catastrophe. You must also understand what the atomic exchange has done to the world."

"We really *did* get hit? Can't trust the news reports anymore."

"Indeed. Skin diseases will multiply like a plague. You must wash your body often and carefully. Wear long-sleeved clothing and a hat. Expect problems. Crops will fail and food will be in short supply. Animals will go on savage rampages. Wild dogs will roam the streets. Take no chances."

"No kidding!"

"The nuclear explosions have produced large amounts of nitrogen oxides, which are quickly depleting the ozone layer. Nuclear fireballs have set many fires around the world. Hundreds of tons of smoke and soot have been released from the burning cities. The nuclear winter is coming, which will drop temperatures by an average of thirty degrees."

Ben took another long drink of coffee. "What will the results look like when it hits people . . . us?"

"People will feel nauseated and tired, and many will vomit. Then they will feel better for a while, but they will be developing fewer and fewer white blood cells, antibodies, and platelets. Infections will be hard to fight, and many people will lose their hair. Others will suffer severe weight loss and struggle with internal bleeding. Skin lesions and cancers will be quite common. The degree of injury will depend on how long people are exposed to concentrated radiation."

"And these effects will increase as the days go by?"

"Unfortunately, yes."

Ben set the cup down and looked out the window. "It's going to be a long summer. And what can we expect at the end of the period?"

"In about a month . . . on Tuesday, August 12 . . . Av 9 comes around again. At sunrise in Jerusalem, the sixth seal will be broken, and the most violent upheaval the world has ever known will shake the very foundations of creation."

"And I am to tell my parents everything you have said?"

"Yes. They must be prepared for the bad condition people seeking refuge will be in. You must be in a safe location when the earthquakes come, for nothing of this magnitude has ever befallen the globe."

"I'll get to the transmitter as soon as I can. By the way, Michael, any help you can give me along the way will be appreciated. Something simple would do fine . . . like a warning that the bad guys are coming."

"Fear not, Ben. Great is your reward in heaven."

■ ■ ■

As Michael had promised, he led Ben and his crew to a farm near the little town of Lancaster. As the summer progressed, the effects of the Chinese atomic attack caused by Gianardo's power grab became increasingly clear. Communication across the United States was in total chaos. Government problems mounted and citizens were captured by their fears. The world seemed paralyzed to respond. Only

Damian Gianardo appeared to have any sense of where events were leading.

The retreat at Lancaster quickly became a haven and escape for the youth in Ben's movement. The McCoys became the communication link between Cindy's UCLA ministry and the farm, and they kept the troops in food. The small living room was usually filled with college students laughing, teasing, praying, and devouring food. One day in August, Ben and Cindy gathered their team for an afternoon discussion.

"We've got the transmitter wired up," a student named Deborah told Ben. "I think we've found a good place to keep it protected when the big quake comes."

Deborah pointed upstairs. "We've got all the electronic equipment inside a metal box, and it's surrounded with foam rubber padding. If the house falls in, the equipment will make it."

"What a job you've done!" Ben beamed. "How can I ever thank you?"

"Thank us?" the group echoed.

"How can we ever thank you?" George, a Jewish student, answered. "You and Cindy have brought life itself to us. Without you, we would all be hopelessly entangled in the lies and destruction devouring the world. You have been our lifeline to eternal survival."

"We are just grateful that God chose to use us." Ben reached out and grabbed Cindy's hand. "The truth is that anyone who really desires to know the true God will find the way even if an angel has to be dispatched. We owe a great debt to our friend Michael. Actually, we found each of you because Michael directed us."

George pointed to several students. "We Jews came to the Lord through your witness, Ben. No matter what lies ahead we will live and die with the supreme satisfaction that we found what our ancestors prayed for. God has surely fulfilled our deepest longings and greatest hopes."

"And we've become great friends," Ben added. "I've found a friendship among you that I've never known before." He stopped and the room became very quiet.

Cindy squeezed his hand. "Why don't we try the radio out?" She broke the awkward silence. "Let's call Petra."

"Terrific idea." Deborah stood up. "We can show you our handiwork. Let's go upstairs."

The group fell in behind her and piled up the steps. Deborah led them to a sparsely furnished room with only a table and chair in one corner. At the bottom of one wall was a large metal grate covering the heating duct.

"Watch this!" Deborah dropped to one knee and pulled the cover off. She slid a metal box out of the wall. "Rather clever, I'd say." She opened the top and lifted the transmitter out. "We're ready to talk to the world."

"We've made a new hookup." George put a small speaker on the table and plugged in the wires. "You won't have to use a headset and we can hear."

"Excellent." Ben carefully fine-tuned the dials. "Calling the Woman in the Desert," he repeated several times. Static crackled over the speaker and humming filled the room. "Come in, Woman in the Desert."

"Hello . . . hello . . ." The voice sounded low, far away but familiar.

"Jimmy? Jimmy? Is that you?"

"Hey, Ben." Static broke in. "It's me. The old used-car salesman."

The group cheered. "You've got an audience here," Ben explained. "The whole gang of believers is with me."

"Can't sell you any cars today," Jimmy's voice crackled. "But I've got a couple of low-mileage camels with lots of tread left."

"Save us a couple. How's the family? Ruth? Mom?"

"Of course, it's night here in Petra, and Mom has turned in. Ruth is out at the hospital. Ought to be here shortly. Been a busy, hard day, but everyone's healthy. People just keep showing up. The pronouncements by Moses and Elijah are having their effect. More and more are believing."

"People in bad shape?"

"Yeah," Jimmy drawled with his Texas accent. "The world's falling apart and so are the people. Ruth and I work from sunup to sundown, but we love every minute of it. Wouldn't have missed this trip for the world."

"Ready for the earthquake?"

"We think so, but we're not sure what God's special protection will mean. We can only go by the quake earlier in the summer. We expect to feel the effects but not suffer damage. We are far more worried about you. Southern California is not a great place to be for a really big one."

"I know, I know," Ben sighed. "The whole group will be out here with us when it comes. At least we'll be away from L.A., where the big catastrophes will happen. We think we're prepared."

"We'll be praying for you."

"Better sign off," Ben concluded. "Don't want to stay on too long in case we've got any eavesdroppers. So long until the next visit."

"Peace!" Static filled the speaker, and Ben switched the set off. Everyone applauded.

"It worked!" Isaiah Murphy shouted. "We're beating the system!"

Someone clapped. "More lemonade for a toast," George demanded. The entourage rushed for the door and stampeded down the stairs.

"Cindy . . ." Jennifer McCoy stopped at the door. "Could I ask you for a favor?"

"Of course."

"We can't bring the children out here." Jennifer's face suddenly looked drawn and sober. "We would only endanger the whole mission. We will have to stay behind with them from now on."

"Oh, no!" Cindy protested.

"No. Joe and I have already discussed the matter. They could easily betray us because of their flippant attitude. Erica's improved some, but she has a long way to go. We will try to take them to another safe place. But I was hoping that you might at least witness to Erica before next Tuesday. It's almost our last hope."

Cindy's brow furrowed. "You know that I would do anything in the world for you and certainly to help the children. But . . . it . . . seems only the people that Michael directs us to or those who seek our help respond. And he warned that when we go beyond those boundaries we could be in serious jeopardy. I just wouldn't want to raise any false hopes. . . . But you are my dearest friends."

"Sure, I understand. I guess Joe and I are getting desperate."

Cindy hugged her friend. "I'll see her tomorrow if you'll set it up. Don't give it another thought."

"Well," Jennifer hedged, "maybe we ought not."

"Tomorrow," Cindy insisted. "I'll pray and do my best."

■ ■ ■

The next afternoon Jennifer drove Cindy to the McCoys' house. As she led Cindy up the walk, Jennifer explained, "Erica and a group of girls are working on cheerleading yells. They should be going home shortly. I'll let you know when I think Erica's friends are gone. There's quite a bunch of them."

"Why have your children been so resistant?"

"Painful question." Jennifer opened the front door. "I anguish over that issue, and I'm not sure I fully understand the answer yet. Joe and I were good parents even though we were gone a great deal of the time when Joe Jr. and Erica were small. We couldn't support a Southern California lifestyle on one salary. I guess today you'd label our children as affluent latchkey kids. Perhaps the lack of contact developed their tendency to give more credence to their friends. That's sure the way they are now."

Cindy felt for a chair. "Just pray that I can get through to her today." Sam lay down at her feet.

"I'm going to take you outside to the backyard and let you sit by the gate. A couple of comfortable chairs are there. When the squad leaves, I'll send Erica out with a glass of lemonade."

Noise echoed from fence to fence as the girls yelled, danced, and waved pompoms. Cindy sat in her obscure corner listening and praying silently. Sam watched the scene intently. After about twenty minutes the rehearsal ended, and the laughing voices drifted away.

Erica's familiar voice jolted Cindy out of her prayer. "Mother said to bring you this drink."

"Erica!" Cindy turned toward the sound. "Sit down. I haven't talked to you in weeks."

"Well . . ." Erica was hesitant and distant. "I have to leave with my friends. We're meeting some guys for pizza. I really can't stay."

Cindy felt the cold glass touch her hand. "Erica, we might never have the opportunity to speak together again. I've got to say several things to you. The hand of God is moving very quickly."

"Please," Erica begged, "we shouldn't be talking about religious stuff. I know you're sincere, but you and my parents are playing with fire."

Cindy set the glass down and took the teenager's hand. "In a few days the earth is going to be nearly shaken out of orbit. We're all going to slosh around like terrified fish in a bowl. Most of what you see around you will collapse."

"Look." Erica's voice was hushed. "I'm sure you believe these things, but some of these kids would turn us in to the authorities just for laughs. I have enough trouble making sure my parents' Bibles are well hidden when the girls are over here."

"I understand . . ." Cindy looked down. "I really *do* understand, but your eternal destiny is at stake. Even if something terrible happened to me, I would do everything I could to tell you about Jesus."

"You're a very good person, Cindy. Kind. Giving. I've watched you when you've been here with Ben. But the world doesn't have a place for people like you anymore, and I have to go on living with some of these creeps who call themselves my friends. I must leave religion alone for the good of everybody."

"Erica, no one has much time left. The days are numbered. In a very short while your friends and their opinions won't matter. They *will not* be here. But God has a plan for your life for today and for all of eternity."

Erica chewed her lip. "After next week, I'll listen. I've got to catch up with the gang now. But I'll talk more if you'll just wait until then."

"I'm going to be praying for you. I'll ask God to keep you through what's coming on Tuesday. There is no power on earth greater than the Lord Jesus."

Suddenly the back gate swung open. Mary Higbie stepped in and stared at both of them. "I wondered where the God talk was coming from."

"M . . . Mary! You . . . you've been listening!" Erica stammered.

"I came back to find you. The girls are waiting. I just happened to come in the back way."

"Mary?" Cindy asked uncomprehendingly.

"You Christian freaks!" Mary sneered at Cindy.

"I don't understand," Cindy answered vaguely. "Who are you?"

"Really weird conversation, Erica." Mary smirked. "I thought your family was straight. Next thing we know you'll be leading cheers for Jesus." The girl spun on her heels and ran toward the car waiting in the driveway.

"Mary!" Erica darted after her. "Mary! Stop it!" Her voice trailed away as she chased her old nemesis. "Please. Don't make something out of nothing."

Cindy heard the door slam and the car drive away. The backyard seemed intensely silent. "Michael warned me," she said to herself. "He cautioned me about just such a danger."

CHAPTER
27

How's it going to happen?" Seradim asked.

"Let me show you. We have the capacity to look right through things," Michael answered. "You must learn to use inner sight and see through mountains and continents. It is possible to read earthquakes." Michael beckoned his charge to follow. "Concentrate on seeing beneath the surface of the earth."

Seradim struggled but slowly began to sense the strata of the earth.

"About sixty miles below the surface of the earth is the Eurasian Plate's base. The continents rest on these gigantic masses. If the Scotia Plate below South America and the Caribbean Plate move at the same time, the earth will shake like a bowl of jelly."

Seradim nodded. "Yes. Frightening for the humans."

"One man has figured it out, but no one is listening to him. Terbor L. Esiw knows the result of such movement would also push the Somali Plate off the coast of Africa and the Philippine Plate into a slide. Never has the world known the shaking that would follow such a collision. The Creator will use this shift to fulfill prophecy."

Seradim watched in rapt fascination. "Of course, the San Andreas fault would split open," he concluded. "Structures in California would tumble like a stack of children's building blocks."

"Gianardo is too big of an egomaniac to allow Esiw to warn the world. Disaster awaits for multitudes of people."

Seradim pondered. "Are the Principalities and Archangels prepared?"

"Of course. The human race has been given ample warnings, but they have ignored them. The heavenly Father is merciful beyond comprehension. When he finally acts, no one can say they were not offered every opportunity to choose the right and better course."

"The time has come," Seradim concluded. "I am ready."

The two angels turned toward the center of heaven. Angels swirled in magnificent arches around the throne of God. The hosts of heaven kept singing in angelic response, "Worthy art Thou to take the scroll and to open the seals." Michael and Seradim watched the Lamb of God, who was holding the scroll as the angels sang, "For You were slain and by Your blood did ransom humanity for God." Myriads of angels, numbering thousands of thousands kept repeating, "Worthy is the Lamb who was slain, to receive power and wealth and wisdom and might and honor and glory and blessing!"

The impulse to worship swept Michael and Seradim into the mighty response of the chorus, "To the Lamb be blessing and honor and glory and might for ever and ever." The four living creatures bowing before the throne of God began repeating, "Amen, Amen, Amen. . . ." The elders fell down in silent worship. The Lamb reached out and broke the sixth seal, and all heaven paused in awe.

Michael and Seradim turned toward Earth. As the sun rose over Jerusalem, a deafening rumble began rising from the ground. Like a rug shaking on a clothesline, the terrain of the entire globe began moving. Gigantic luminous flashes exploded in the sky, and meteorites plunged toward the earth. Huge clouds of black smoke moved across the globe.

Michael and Seradim watched in awe as the tremors roared and shook every continent. Slowly the planet returned to a state of stability as the ground stopped shifting. Wherever the two angels looked, skyscrapers had toppled and buildings were broken like matchboxes.

"We must return." Michael pointed toward California. "I have my assignment, and you have yours."

"I . . . I . . . do?" Seradim fumbled. "Yes. . . . But what is it?"

"You are to visit Frank and Jessica Wong. Help them get a grip on themselves and understand what to do next. Stay in tune with the will of the Father."

"Am I ready?" Seradim's eyes widened.

Michael chuckled. "Quite so."

Once the angels penetrated the time barrier, they descended in different directions over California. Seradim beamed in on Lake Forest, and Michael sped toward Lancaster. Michael found the students gathering up their blankets and trying to pull themselves together after the "great shake."

The time was right to appear physically and speak to the entire group. Once more Michael stepped into human history at a point about ten feet from the front porch of the farmhouse.

"Peace be unto you!"

"Michael!" Ben spun around. "We knew you'd be here!"

"I can see him!" Deborah exclaimed. "I'm actually see-ing an angel!"

"It's really him," George pointed. "I can't believe my eyes."

"Today I come to all of you as a sign of favor. Behold, you have found a special place in the sight of God. Rejoice! For as this world passes away, you chose the better portion that is eternal."

"Michael, tell us what has happened." Ben took Cindy by the hand and led her forward. Sam strained on the har-ness behind her. "Petra . . . is everyone okay?"

"God's hand has more than protected. Your family and friends have endured very well, even as their enemies were being swallowed by the earth."

"Praise the Lord!" Ben shouted.

"What about the rest of the globe?" Deborah walked for-ward cautiously.

"Do not fear. Come close and listen."

The students huddled around the farmhouse steps.

"Many people will be ready to receive your witness now. I will send each of you to those who are hungry for hope. Yet be prepared for danger to increase! The times are becoming more desperate with every judgment."

"What's happened to California?" a student ventured.

"Judgment has engulfed San Francisco. Their wicked-ness has been called into accountability. The city is no more."

"L.A.?" George held up his hand.

"The city is in flames, and many sections have been lev-eled. Yet other portions in Orange County stand. Railways, overpasses, and bridges have buckled before the glance of the Lord."

"And our people?" Cindy asked. "The Christians? And my parents who are not Christians?"

"Your own parents are alive and well, my child. When you see them next, you will find new receptiveness to your message. But the last sixteen weeks have taken a great toll. Believers all over the world have become martyrs. Hundreds of thousands of Israelis who embraced Yeshua as Messiah have already paid with their lives. Those who have fled the persecutions of Gianardo compose a new diaspora. Petra–Bozrah has become a haven for these people of the truth."

"What are we to do now?" Ben asked.

"I will talk with each one of you separately. I have many assignments for you to fulfill in the coming months. You will find that the time flies as you complete your mission. Yet for the world, each day will seem an eternity of agony. As the end of this period approaches, you will know what to expect next. Watch the skies, for the next great judgment will come from above. Now come and receive your divine appointments."

The students lined up and Michael began giving instructions.

■ ■ ■

"Help! Help!" Frank Wong screamed at the top of his voice. "Wife is trapped. Please, someone come!" He turned to every corner of the smashed kitchen, looking for assistance. No one was there.

Patrons of the Golden Dragon pushed pieces of the roof aside and struggled to crawl out of the wrecked restaurant. Dust still hung heavy in the air and pieces of the walls kept dropping in. But no one paid any attention to the cries for help coming from the kitchen.

Frank yanked pieces of ceiling tile aside, but his effort was futile. The chopping block had fallen on top of Jessica, and he could not budge the heavy wooden table. She kept moaning until she lost consciousness.

Frank frantically rubbed her hand and wept. Her lips were turning blue. "Cannot live without wife. Oh, Jessica, don't leave me."

The door to the kitchen fell from its hinges. The massive plate glass in front of the restaurant was scattered in a thousand shards. Frank looked out and could see huge cracks in the parking lot. Some cars had fallen into the ground. Voices cried for help everywhere. People walked about in a daze, disconnected from the calls for help.

"O God of Cindy," Frank cried and held his hands up to the cracked ceiling. "If you help with honorable wife, we will give you our lives. As you protect our daughter, please, please, help us."

Seradim stepped into time a few feet behind Frank. "Let me serve you," he said simply.

Frank whirled around. "Where you come from?" He stared at the six-foot, red-haired young man of decidedly athletic proportions. "You not here just minute ago."

"We must get your wife out quickly," Seradim said. His blue eyes flashed.

"Table too big for three or four men," Frank lamented.

"Perhaps not." Seradim put his hands underneath the edge of the toppled table and lifted. He slowly set the chopping block back on its legs.

Frank gasped. "Such strength not possible!"

"She could barely breathe." Seradim bent over Jessica. "We must put more air back in her." He gave quick powerful blasts of air in her mouth. With his hands on her shoulders, Seradim concentrated. "Yes, her leg is fractured and will need to be in a cast for a while," he concluded, "but as soon as she gets enough oxygen circulating, she will be fine."

The old man stared. "Who are you?" he asked in awe.

"Your friend."

"Where did you come from?"

"From your prayer."

Jessica moaned and then opened her eyes. "I hurt. What happened?"

Frank reached out as if to touch Seradim but couldn't quite bring himself to do so. "My prayer?" He wept as he spoke.

"A terrible earthquake has shaken the whole world. You must understand this is a sign. God is calling the entire globe to turn to Him. The time has come for you to believe."

Jessica grabbed Seradim's forearm. "I was dying," she muttered. "Suffocating."

"Please, your name," Frank ventured.

"Seradim."

Frank shook his head. "Never hear of such a name."

"You saved me." Jessica looked into the deep blue eyes. "If you not come, I soon die."

"Life awaits you, Jessica. Do not be afraid to receive the One who gives you the life you cannot lose."

"Where can I find this life?" Jessica squeezed his arm. "Please?"

"Listen to your daughter. Cindy can tell you."

"You know Cindy?" Frank puzzled.

"Believe what she tells you." Seradim stood up and walked to the doorway. "I must go now."

"How you know Cindy?" Frank called after him.

"I'm a friend of Michael's," Seradim answered and then disappeared into the shambles of the once proud restaurant.

CHAPTER

28

Sitting behind the former district attorney's desk, Gerald Adams studied the five special agents standing in front of him. Each man seemed poised for action, trustworthy of his complete confidence. Adams turned in his chair and looked out the window. Buildings were in shambles. Cars were still barely able to make their way down the cracked and debris-strewn streets. An ugly gray smog hung over the city.

"The word from the top," Adams said, "is that more disasters may be on the way." He tried to sound detached and unemotional. "We have been warned to expect a possible collision with some sort of asteroid capable of great damage. After the nuclear explosions and earthquake, people are rather unstable. No telling what another catastrophe might create."

Adams turned back to face the agents. They looked straight ahead and did not flinch.

"Frightened people get superstitious, crazy. Think they're seeing ghosts, angels, God, who knows what else. We've got to keep a lid on the religion thing. Gianardo believes a rampant religious revival is one of our major threats to national stability." Adams rocked back in his chair. "I'm concerned about what these college kids are doing. I don't like the tenor of what's being distributed on campuses. We think there's an organized ring working the streets. Any progress on what you're finding south of L.A., Schultz?"

Robert Schultz smiled. "I've made significant inroads and infiltrated all of the target churches. Yes, a number of adults are a part of a well-coordinated system. They have transmitters and international connections. But we're on to them."

"Good," Adams acknowledged coldly. "Same with the rest of you boys?"

The group nodded.

"Sir, I am about to interrogate a leader in one of the churches," Schultz said. "I have a lead on a group that may be one of our government's prime enemies. We have come close to catching their leaders and believe we are about to zero in on one of the major organizers."

"Really?" Adams raised his eyebrows. "I'd like to observe."

"Interrogation's going on right now." Schultz pointed toward the hall. "Come on down."

The group followed Schultz into the hall and down the corridor. At the far end, behind an unmarked door, three agents surrounded a heavy-set man seated in the center of the room. The agents circled their frightened prey, firing questions at him from all sides. The man's tie hung loose below his unbuttoned collar. Large damp spots dotted his shirt.

"I'll take over from here," Schultz instructed his men as Adams and the other four agents joined the interrogation. "I believe you're Mr. Ed Parker with the Community Church?"

Parker mopped his forehead with his handkerchief. "I don't understand why I'm here." He looked nervously around the room. "I've always been a good law-abiding citizen." His pudgy neck had turned red, his face flushed in pink blotches. "Honest. I'm only involved with that church because it's good for business."

"You're a shaker and a mover with the church, aren't you, Ed old boy?" Schultz paced in front of him.

"I'm just a member." Ed shrugged and dabbed at his neck.

"We understand you're a committee chairman. Local big shot." Schultz suddenly got two inches from Parker's face. "Helped can the pastor. Ran him off."

"Look." Ed bit his lip. "We felt the pastor's sermons were . . . well . . . just not what we should be hearing. That's not illegal."

"Not at all!" Schultz patted Ed on the back. "We couldn't agree more with what you did. The preacher was polluting the people."

The heavily perspiring man swallowed hard. "Really? You mean it?"

"Certainly, you helped get your church in line with the leadership of our exalted national and international leader. Excellent move." Schultz smiled and winked at Ed.

Parker heaved and exhaled. He mopped his forehead again. "Then . . . then why am I here?"

"We need information on some other people in that church." Schultz picked up a file from the agent originally interrogating Parker. "We'd like to know what you know about Joe and Jennifer McCoy."

"Them!" Ed rubbed his mouth. "Well, I'll tell you whatever you'd like to know. I'm no friend of the McCoys. No sirree. Those people are trouble."

"Yes." Schultz smiled broadly. "I understand they resisted the effort to remove the pastor."

"Caused me lots of problems." Ed raised his eyebrows. "Created deep divisions in our church. We're still trying to get rid of the McCoys."

"Maybe we can help you, Ed." Schultz sat on the edge of the table and smiled down at the overweight committee chairman. "Think these people would oppose the government by organizing subversives?"

Ed blinked several times uncomprehendingly. He looked carefully around the room at the sullen, staring faces. "You're saying the McCoys are in on an antigovernment plot?"

"I'm asking if you think they have the kind of fundamentalist faith that would make them capable of espionage?"

Ed's eyes widened. "Listen. I got nothing to do with those folks. They're screwball types. Real pious goody-goody phonies. Yeah, I can believe they'd be trouble."

"Then we want you to help us accumulate data on them." Schultz bore down. "We want to know about their influence on young people. We want you to keep tabs on what they're doing with people in their circle of influence. Can you do that?"

Ed's head bobbed up and down enthusiastically. "Whatever you say. I'm just a good law-abiding citizen. Never breaking any of the—"

"Good, Mr. Parker." Schultz ingratiatingly patted him on the back. "My associates will have some specific instructions for you. We will be in direct touch with you from time to time. Thanks for the assistance."

Adams and the other four agents followed Schultz out into the hall. Gerald Adams carefully measured the man in front of him. He liked everything he saw in Schultz.

"Excellent work. Shouldn't be long until you zero in on these McCoys, Robert."

"Got 'em in the crosshairs right now, boss."

Two other figures had observed the entire procedure. Lurking unseen in the shadows, Malafidus and Homelas carefully followed the conversations and inquisition.

"Do the police need any help?" Homelas pondered.

"Not when they've got a pansy like Ed on the hook. The McCoys' kids belong to us, and Ed's church buddies won't hesitate to do the parents in. I think we'll get this one wrapped up quickly and soon be back in the good graces of the front office."

"I don't want them to slip through our hands," Homelas fretted. "We're all spread too thin right now."

"No problem, I tell you. The government is taking care of the McCoys for us."

■ ■ ■

The atomic explosions and earthquake had changed the McCoys' house. Although their home fared better than most, windows were cracked and several had to be boarded up because of the shortage of glass. Water rationing made it impossible to care for the grass and plants. The heat turned everything an ugly brown. Barkley, the family dog, died. Death hung in the air.

Jennifer closed the door behind her when she entered her daughter's bedroom. Erica was stretched out on the bed, looking out the second-story window at the street below.

"Mind if I come in?" Jennifer asked.

Erica shook her head without looking up. "Our beautiful neighborhood looks like a war zone."

Jennifer sat down on the bed. "Grim, isn't it?"

Erica turned toward her mother. "I'm terribly afraid. I try to keep up appearances, but the truth is my friends are just about as disgusting as this neighborhood. The whole world seems trapped in some kind of monstrous evil plot." She suddenly sat up and threw her arms around Jennifer's neck. "Oh, Mother. I'm most afraid for you. Security police are floating around our school all the time. They ask questions about our family. What is going to become of us?" Erica began to sob.

"I know it's very hard for you to understand, but we must go on as if everything is normal." Jennifer hugged her daughter and then gently pushed her back so she could look straight into her eyes. "Erica, you must grow up very quickly and grasp what an important mission your father and I are involved in. Cindy Wong was trying to tell you the same thing. Even though you can't yet accept the idea, God has called us to work for Him. We are part of an eternal plan. Dear, God has a plan for your life as well."

Erica drew her legs up next to her chest in a tight ball. She buried her face in her knees; her hair fell around the side of her jeans. "I don't know what to believe anymore, Mother. But I am sure most of what I hear at school isn't right. I can't trust the people I know. There is nowhere to turn . . . except . . . to what you say . . . to what you believe."

Jennifer closed her eyes for a moment and inhaled deeply. A prayer raced through her mind. *Please, Lord, help me. Help me seize this moment.*

Instantly, Michael and Seradim were invisibly present. "I'll make sure we have no intrusions." Seradim began circling the mother and daughter. "No demonic influence is going to deter this moment!"

Michael moved next to Jennifer and put his hand on her head. "Come, Holy Spirit," the angel implored. "Come and inspire. Come and fill."

"Erica," Jennifer's voice was low and intense, "I can't force anything on you and wouldn't if I could. Only you can decide if you want to give yourself to the ugliness you see everywhere or whether you will entrust your soul to the beauty that only God can give. But, Jennifer, you *do* have control over what's inside you. If you invite Jesus to come into your life, it won't make any difference what anyone else says or thinks."

Erica suddenly grabbed her mother and held her tight. "But how do I do that? How does it happen?"

Jennifer whispered in her daughter's ear. "The Jews call Him Yeshua; we call Him Jesus. He's the key. He's here to help you find your way to God. All you have to do is ask Him to forgive your sins and come into your heart for an eternal relationship."

Michael called to Seradim. "Pray! She's almost there! This is the moment we've been waiting . . ." He stopped. Coming toward them from heaven was a glorious light, moving as if swept forward by gentle winds of subtle power. In the center of the brilliant splendor, the descending figure moved with one hand lifted as if in a benediction. Michael covered his face. The Light engulfed the angels with wondrous warmth. "He has come. . . . He has come!" Michael exclaimed. The angel fell prostrate before the pulsating luster of the all-encompassing resplendence.

Erica closed her eyes tightly. "Please, Jesus. Help me find out how to know You. I want to give You my life before someone in this crazy world takes it away from me. I surrender myself to You. Please forgive me for all my sins and enter my life."

Michael instantly sensed the Light had broken through their side of eternity and engulfed Erica's soul. The darkness inside her mind and spirit dissolved like a sunrise after a stormy night. The angel could see the spiritual transformation unfolding within the teenager.

Erica began to weep.

Jennifer stroked her head and prayed aloud, "Thank you, Lord. Oh, thank you."

As the brilliance receded, Michael heard words thunder through him. "The angel of the Lord encamps around those who fear Him, and He delivers them. Well done, faithful servant." The incandescent figure lifted heavenward.

"Something is very different," Erica whispered in her mother's ear. "I can feel something different inside me."

"Yes, dear. That's how it was with me. 'To as many as receive Him,' He gives the power, the capacity to become children of God."

Erica sat back and beamed. She pointed at her heart. "It's a new beginning! No matter how bad it is out there, in here, I'm starting over!"

CHAPTER
29

During the following months, the secret police interrogated the McCoy children several times. Joe and Jennifer suspected there was a leak in their Bible study group, but no one could be sure. The children were making significant spiritual breakthroughs, but Joe Jr. had not yet trusted Jesus and was terrified whenever the police cornered him. Each time the interrogators were professional and polite. Their questions were vague and their demeanor nonthreatening. Mostly the investigators asked about Erica and her friends, and the possibility that Joe and Jennifer were pushing religious ideas on the kids.

Although Seradim and Michael remained invisible most of the time, they did not cease to watch over Ben and Cindy, and on several occasions Michael had to intervene. Seradim spent more and more time watching over the Wongs and encouraging them. Frank and Jessica listened to Cindy with new intensity.

In late March the secret police nearly cornered Ben and one of his friends in a UCLA dorm that had survived the

great earthquake. Michael saw the police preparing to surround the building. Ben and George were in a sophomore's
room sharing the gospel. They did not have much time to
spare, so Michael materialized in the hallway and knocked
on the young man's door.

"Can I help you?" the puzzled student said as he opened
the door. "You're not the one I thought was coming."

"I believe there is a Mr. Ben Feinberg here."

"Yeah, sure." The sophomore answered uncomprehendingly.

"Michael?" Ben asked from across the room.

"Sounds like Michael," George chimed in.

"Yes. Some urgent business has just come up," Michael
stated matter-of-factly.

"What?" Ben bounded across the room. "What in the
world are you doing here?"

"We must run," Michael whispered. "Time is short, very
short." He frowned.

Ben stared for a moment and blinked uncomprehendingly. Suddenly he understood. He grabbed his friend's
arm. "Hey, we'll try to be back tomorrow." He jerked George
past the startled student. "See you then." Ben pulled George
into the hall and shut the door behind them.

"Michael! What are you doing here?"

"Police are closing in on the building. The student you
have been talking to is a plant. The security agents will be
here any minute."

"What can we do?" George looked panic-stricken.

"We're on the second floor!" Ben looked desperately up
and down the hall.

The student's door flew open, and the sophomore ran
down the hall toward the stairs at the opposite end.

"Quick! Ben . . . George . . . into the student's room. Lock the door and turn out the light. Get on the ledge outside his window. Give the police time to get in, and then drop into the bushes and run for it. I will be your decoy inside the dorm."

Ben and George slammed the door behind them, and Michael opened a janitor's closet and grabbed a broom. In less than thirty seconds the police were charging up the stairs and moving onto the floor.

"Stop!" the lead cop shouted. "Who are you?"

"Just cleaning up."

"Three men were here. Where did they go?"

"Three men?"

"Two college students and a big guy! About your size."

"Oh, I'm just cleaning up the mess they left."

"Let's check up the stairs at the other end."

The first wave of police disappeared, running up the exit stairs to the third floor.

"I'd recognize the other guy." The sophomore's voice was loud and nervous as he bounded up the stairs with the second detachment of police. "Sort of a strange-looking man."

Michael stepped into the little janitor's closet and back into eternity as the secret police ran up and down the halls.

"Where'd the janitor go?" The leader of the first group came back downstairs.

"What janitor?" one of the second group asked.

"The man sweeping the floor."

"The janitors aren't here at night," the sophomore interjected.

The security officer glared at the college student. "Don't mess with me. I'm not blind. I want to know where the janitor we talked to went." The man swung the closet door open and looked inside. "If this is a college prank . . ." He jerked the sophomore forward by the shirt.

"Hey, I don't know what you guys are talking about. I'm on your side, remember?"

"There's no one here," a policeman who returned from the top floor reported. "This thing smells like a little joke pulled on us by the boys' dorm."

"Where's the janitor?" the policeman growled in the sophomore's face. "We'll teach you to trifle with national security personnel."

"No . . . no . . . no." The student flattened against the wall. "Really, there were people here pushing religion on me. Honest. HONEST . . ."

"Try this room." One of the policemen reached for the door. "It's locked."

"Can't be." The student fumbled for his keys. He swung the door open. Curtains were blowing gently in the evening breeze.

The policeman ran to the window. "There they go!" He pointed across the campus. "Two guys are running into those trees."

Michael left the student to face the secret police's accusations and followed Ben and George to make sure they returned safely to the farm. Ben had made the mistake of going to a student who seemed open to the gospel, but he was not someone Michael had assigned for contact. Although he meant the best, Ben's mistake could have been deadly, at least for his friend George. Ben was quite ready to follow the rules in the future.

Their subsequent conversation allowed Michael the opportunity to warn of the approaching Doran asteroid, which would be the first sounding of God's trumpets of judgment. Michael prepared Ben for the Whiton asteroid and comet Wormwood as the divine adjudication fell on the earth. His charges were well prepared for the next catastrophe.

■ ■ ■

Weeks later the Doran asteroid flashed its bright red tail in the predawn skies across the world, and after NASA fired a nuclear missile at the asteroid, millions of burning rock particles scattered over the earth's stratosphere. Alaska shook when the remaining central chunk burned its way into a small coastal island. In the following days, the night skies were a constant display of showers of exploding and falling stars, but their frequency lessened. By June most of the unusual night displays had subsided and people were back indoors. The sun was setting much later, and both the public's fear and fascination were passing.

Erica McCoy took the bold step of inviting her closest friends to listen to her parents explain what was happening in the world. The group of five girls gathered outside around the McCoys' swimming pool.

Joe pointed to the sky. "I'm not trying to frighten you, but these strange occurrences are warnings God is giving the world. We still have another asteroid and a comet headed toward the earth. Unless we repent, a great price will be paid."

Erica's best friend, Melissa, interrupted. "My science teacher says the odds have just caught up with the earth. Sooner or later we were bound to get hit by something big anyway."

"Sure." Joe walked back and forth in front of the group, holding his Bible. "But the real issue is timing. Think. How many things are happening right now that fit the Bible's timetable for the final days of history? And why are so many happening on Jewish holy days? Is it really a coincidence? How can Moses and Elijah predict the precise times and dates so far in advance if God isn't telling them?"

Another classmate, named Paula, said, "My parents don't want us to speak about the possibilities at home. But I hear them talking when they think we are asleep. Mom and Dad went to church when they were children and know what you are teaching us is right."

"None of us would be here," Melissa added, "if Erica hadn't sworn us to secrecy. I know we're in danger, but I want to know the facts."

"My sister and I really rebelled against our parents for a long time," Joe Jr. said, "but the earthquake changed our minds. My parents told us for weeks that it was coming. It's taken me a while to say it out loud, but I know now that what the Bible says about Jesus is the truth, and I've put my faith in Him."

"We have a special Bible study group for parents," Jennifer McCoy said. "We help people like Paula's parents. I think your mothers and fathers would be more open than you think. The police system works by fear. Once you refuse to be intimidated, they've lost their hold over you.

"Girls, that's our story." Jennifer joined her husband and son in front of the group. "Our family has gone from being another Southern California wreck to a real unit that stands together. Sure, it's scary, but I wouldn't give anything for the joy that has been restored to us. Even if we were hauled in tomorrow, we have the joy of knowing that we will face eternity together."

"You probably have questions you'd like to ask," Joe added. "Erica, Joe, Jennifer, and I will be here for any response you have. If you don't have any questions, then grab a cola and we'll break up in a bit."

While the girls talked with the McCoys, three cars pulled up down the street. Plainclothes security police quietly shut the doors. A teenager got out of the last car and pointed to the McCoys' residence.

"How do you know they are there?" Robert Schultz asked.

"Because they didn't invite me," Mary Higbie answered indignantly.

"These are the people you told me about several months ago?"

The teenager smiled cynically. "I've overheard a number of conversations in the McCoys' backyard when the Chinese girl was pushing Christianity. I've seen Bibles lying around their house."

"And you'll testify to these facts?"

"Absolutely," Mary said defiantly.

"Got that on tape?" The leader turned to the man behind him.

"Every word of it. Fits exactly with the reports we have from Ed Parker."

"What?" Mary looked puzzled.

"We don't want you to back out," the man in charge grumbled. "We've been waiting quite a while to make a big bust, and we're going to hit these people hard. Your testimony makes it stick."

"Hit hard?" Mary retreated. "I just want them arrested. Humiliated like Erica treats me . . . but nothing more."

The police drew their weapons and began inserting the bullet clips. "This isn't some kind of game, kid." The agent began pointing in different directions and his men moved quickly. "We're going to make a real example of these fanatics."

"Well, sure," Mary said nervously. "But I don't want anyone to *really* get hurt."

"Hurt?" The security agent laughed. "Pain is our business. Let's get 'em, boys!"

Suddenly the men dispersed into the trees and shrubs. The first carload of agents charged the front door. One lone agent held Mary tightly by the arm. "Stay put. We want you to identify the suspects."

For a couple of minutes Mary and the security officer stood under a tree. They could hear distant shouts. Then an agent came out the front door and motioned for them to come in. They hurried through the house and out into the backyard. The teenagers were huddled together on the ground with police circling them and pointing their guns. Joe and Jennifer and their children stood together. Police aimed guns at them too.

"Identify the traitors," Schultz ordered Mary who stood at his side.

"Mary!" the girls echoed. "How could you?"

"Really," the terrified teen muttered, "I think I've made a mistake. . . . Yes. . . . This is all a big mistake."

"Identify the McCoys!" the agent demanded. "We already have your accusations on tape."

"I didn't mean for this to happen." Mary tried to pull away.

"Identify them!" the man exploded.

Mary pointed a trembling finger at the McCoys.

"Get the women first." A policeman grabbed Erica's wrist while another man reached for Jennifer.

Joe suddenly pushed the first man backward so forcefully that he fell in the shrubs. Pulling Erica and Jennifer with him, Joe darted toward the side gate. "Run!" he yelled to Joe Jr.

A policeman charged out of the shadows and swung the butt end of his Uzi into Joe's face, sending him sprawling in the grass. Two other agents rushed Erica and her mother. One man wrapped his arm around Jennifer's neck in a stranglehold. The other man hit Erica in the stomach with his fist. She doubled up with an agonizing groan.

"Get 'em over here." Schultz pointed toward the edge of the swimming pool. "Line 'em up."

The security agents dragged Joe through the grass and dropped him on the swimming pool tile. Erica was pushed down by his side. A big man held Joe Jr. by the edge of the water while another agent pushed Jennifer next to her family. The teenagers began screaming.

"Shut them up!" The man in charge motioned to the other police. "We don't need a bunch of crazy girls!"

"Please stop!" Mary pleaded. "I didn't want any of this."

"Shut up!" the policeman in charge yelled. "Or they'll get it right now!" Immediately the girls became silent.

"The man assaulted me." The agent with the Uzi kicked Joe's hand aside. "I should have shot him then. Let me finish them off now."

"We don't know about the status of the girls," another agent interjected. "Are they witnesses or victims?"

Schultz walked over to the terrified teenagers. "Do you believe what the McCoys were preaching here tonight? Are their ideas representative of your convictions?"

"No! No!" the girls whimpered and pleaded. "No! Never!"

"Okay," the leader snarled. "They're victims. Get their names, addresses, and parents' names, and then let them go. Photograph 'em as well as this backyard."

"And our criminals here?" The policeman pointed his Uzi at Joe's stirring figure on the ground. He tried to sit up but couldn't stabilize himself. Blood was running out of Joe's mouth, and his lips were extremely swollen.

"He tried to escape. So did the girl and her mother."

"You won't get away with this!" Joe Jr. strained against the man holding him. "God will judge you for what you are doing to us."

"You know our orders," the agent in charge grumbled. "Get these teenagers out of here and then shoot the family."

CHAPTER

30

The secret police herded the McCoy family together on the grass bordering their swimming pool. Erica fell backward on top of her father's limp form; he struggled to speak but still could not clear his mind. Trembling, Jennifer hugged her son tightly. Joe Jr. clutched at his mother's waist and hid his eyes.

Schultz nodded and the agents cocked their weapons. The clicking sound of bullets sliding into metal chambers echoed into the black night.

Seradim wrung his hands in agitation. "We can't just watch. We have to *do* something."

Michael looked knowingly at his charge but said nothing.

"Yes. Yes. I know we haven't received orders from on High yet, but . . ."

"But?"

"They are going to kill the McCoys, Michael!"

Michael knelt down beside Joe and put his hand on the father's shoulder. The angel looked up into Erica's terrified eyes as if she could see him through the veil of time.

"Can't we do anything?" Seradim implored.

"Now comes your final lesson, my friend." Pathos inched its way across Michael's sad smile. "We have to recognize the final boundaries in any intervention. It is not given to us to stop the course nor block the path that human free will takes. The Father will not allow us to circumvent the devastation that sin and human rebellion bring."

Seradim reached out to stroke Erica's hair even though she could not feel his hand. "This poor child is horrified. I must find some way to comfort her."

"Lend her your spiritual strength," Michael advised. "Send love, but you must not keep her from this crossroads. This is Erica's moment of truth."

Seradim looked helplessly around the dark backyard. Agents stood poised with their loaded guns pointed at the family. The teenage girls' whimpering could still be heard in the front yard.

"Some things can never be fully grasped or comprehended either by us or by humans," Michael said. "Terrible events will come to pass and still be part of a plan yet to be seen. What the heavenly Father does not intend, He still uses."

The angels listened to Schultz instructing his agents on what to do with the bodies after the execution.

Seradim cringed and gnashed his teeth.

"You have come a long way, my friend," Michael concluded. "You have struggled and persevered when observing the suffering of the innocent. Nothing in this world is more powerful than suffering love that will not retreat in the face of brokenness."

"They will suffer." Seradim reached out for Joe Jr. as if he could shield him from the unrelenting path of the bullet. "I want . . . to . . . keep him from this moment."

"We always want to do the impossible," Michael reflected. "Yes, even after all of these centuries I still want to rip through the veil of time and smash these evil men. But I can't. I must not. I am first and last only a servant of the Most High. Not even we who stand so close to the throne can always understand the destiny of humans, but the sovereign intentions of God *will* prevail."

"But their pain?" Seradim protested.

"At this moment fear is like a noose around each of their necks, but their actual pain will be but an instant, and then the agony is over forever. Death is more merciful than it appears."

Seradim shook his head in consternation and looked away. "I don't think I can watch it happen."

Michael looked into the faces of the children. Joe Jr. cowered next to his mother like a whipped puppy. Erica buried her face in her father's chest. Joe was still having a hard time maintaining consciousness.

Schultz's men raised their weapons. Shots rang out in a rapid drumbeat. Shells flew in every direction, bouncing on the cement around the swimming pool. For a moment Agent Schultz looked at the bodies, then blanched and turned away.

■ ■ ■

"Where . . . where am I?" Joe Jr. reached out for something to hold on to.

"Mother?" Erica blinked several times. "Dad? Are you here?"

"Joe?" Jennifer looked around. "Joe?"

"My head doesn't hurt anymore." Joe rubbed his eyes. "There was that terrible noise, and then my head stopped throbbing."

"Everything looks so different," Joe Jr. gasped. "I feel like I'm almost floating."

"We're all here!" Jennifer exclaimed. "A moment ago we were over . . ." She turned and looked at the bodies behind her. "Oh, my goodness how horrible!" Jennifer looked away. "Who are those poor people?"

Erica shook her head. "Everything is so different. I remember being terrified and then . . ."

"I seem to have stepped through an invisible barrier," Joe said. "Like I closed one door and then walked through a gate."

Erica looked at her father. "Dad! The blood's all gone from your face. Your lip isn't swollen anymore."

"I can see the swimming pool." Joe Jr. pointed. "But I can't quite reach it. How strange. The backyard seems to have turned into a mural."

"I can't get over how quickly my pain disappeared." Joe kept feeling his face where the agent struck him with a weapon.

"Excuse me." Michael stepped from behind the family. "Let me help you."

"Michael!" Joe exclaimed. "We haven't seen you since your appearance at the farm at Lancaster."

"What are you doing here?" Jennifer asked.

"Is he the angel you told us about?" Joe Jr. asked in awe.

"Please meet my colleague, Seradim." Michael beckoned for the other angel to join him.

"Wow!" Erica beamed. "Two of 'em."

"Michael," Jennifer begged. "We must help those poor people on the ground. They've been badly hurt."

"We did." Michael smiled. "Now we must turn our attention elsewhere."

"We can't leave them," Jennifer urged.

"We already have," Michael answered. "I would suggest that none of you look back again. Actually, those people were you, your family."

"What?" Jennifer muttered.

"Seradim and I have come to welcome you to eternity. Your old bodies have been left behind, and you are now ready to receive your reward."

"We're dead?" Erica's eyes widened.

"No," Michael smiled. "For the first time, you are truly alive."

"This is heaven?" Joe Jr. probed. "No wonder Mom and Dad and Erica and I all look the same age now."

"We've come to take you to heaven," Michael answered.

Jennifer turned and looked at her home. "Strange. Seems so close and yet, yet, like a place from long ago."

"I am so glad to be out of that mess!" Erica beamed. "What a terrible time we had the last few months. What a bunch of traitors and crooks."

Joe Jr. looked up toward the stars in bewilderment. "We're going up there?"

"Well, yes and no." Michael laughed. "We're actually going to take you to another place beyond the stars. You'll quickly see that the world was a constantly deteriorating, changing scene. Now, we're going to take you to the place where everything is permanent."

"And you are martyrs," Seradim added. "Very special guests in the House of the Lord."

"Martyrs?" Erica puzzled.

"That's right!" Joe snapped his fingers. "They were about to kill us because we are Christians."

"As a matter of fact," Michael hesitated a moment. "They did kill you."

"Strange." Joe sounded perplexed. "I don't remember . . ."

"Happened awfully fast," Seradim added.

"Really, the perceived pain of death is one of the devil's tricks," Michael explained. "Christians usually fail to realize both how easy the crossing is and how instantly the struggles of the world are left behind."

"And now we are beyond time?" Jennifer asked in amazement.

"Exactly," Michael explained. "You'll notice you didn't bring any watches with you."

"Far out!" Erica shouted.

"Wait a minute," Joe Jr. said. "How did we get here so easy?"

Michael put his hand on the boy's shoulder. "Young man, you actually passed from death unto life a number of weeks ago."

"Huh? What do you mean?"

"Do you remember when you decided your folks were right? That their religious convictions were true?"

"Yes," the boy said slowly.

"Then what happened?"

"Well." Joe Jr. paused to remember. "I knew their faith was right and so I accepted Jesus like they had taught me."

"At that moment you were ready for eternity."

"I don't remember anything being all that different."

Michael laughed. "That's the problem with the earth. You seldom can see what is actually happening in eternity. Nevertheless, at the moment you invited Jesus into your life you passed from death to life. Your heart stopping was only a technicality."

"Is it that way for everybody?" Erica asked.

"Oh, no," Michael answered. "If people are spiritually dead, then when physical death comes they are swallowed in the terrifying blackness of hell. Their experience is quite the opposite of yours."

"I see," Erica said solemnly. "For the first time I am truly sorry for Mary Higbie. She must be dying in her guilt right now."

"Well put," Michael agreed. "At this moment Mary is one of the loneliest people in the world . . . and that's a form of death."

"But that's behind you now," Seradim chimed in. "The Lord Jesus is waiting to greet you personally and thank you for all you did."

"Us?" Joe choked.

"Yes," Michael answered. "To be absent from the body is to be present with the Lord."

"Your life's made quite an impact," Seradim congratulated the family. "You've come a very long way from that New Year's morning when you decided it was time to take your spiritual needs seriously."

"What do we do in heaven?" Erica asked.

"You will come into the fullness of everything you had hoped to be." Michael pointed upward. "We will first get you ready to return in the great victory march of the reappearing King of kings. You will experience this preparation as only a short span, but during this period a significant amount of time will pass on Earth, wrapping up all history. Your friends the Feinbergs and Jimmy Harrison will live through the final tribulation and then you'll see them again, but some of your friends may also become martyrs and join you here."

"Follow me," Seradim beckoned. "You now are capable of a new mode of travel. We think ourselves places. Just think about flying with us and you will ascend quite naturally."

"I can do it!" Joe Jr. exclaimed. "Look at me! I'm really flying!"

The family rose upward with the angels, ascending above the housetops and beyond the flashing lights in the street in front of their house.

"This is far out, absolutely awesome," Erica squealed. "Way beyond the other side of cool!"

"Far out?" Michael laughed. "You're on your way 'far up.'" The undertakers will bury your old bodies, but Seradim and I are your 'uppertakers,' and we're quite pleased to take you to your new eternal home."

Seradim pointed ahead. "The time has come to cross the veil and leave this place behind."

"I don't see anything," Joe puzzled.

"You will grasp where this crossing is only once you've been on the other side," Michael explained. "Ready?"

The angels and the family shot through the great barrier. Instantly brilliant splendor engulfed them in a blaze of glory.

"What's that sound?" Erica choked.

Around, above, below, and beyond the family, countless multitudes of angels applauded. The reverberation was more like the harmony of a great symphony that produced not music, but a choral hymn attuned to the deepest yearnings of the soul.

"The angelic hosts are saying thank you. Your reputation precedes you." Michael beamed.

From the center of the Great Throne emerged an eminent shimmer of brilliance that shone with colors never seen by the human eye. A singular orb of glorious light advanced toward the McCoys. Both one and indivisible from the original Light and yet separate and distinct, the circle of luminous splendor descended toward the family. The closer the Shekinah glory came, the more discernible was the Figure in the center.

Joe pointed but could not speak. Jennifer grabbed his hand, and the children huddled close, staring in total amazement.

The exalted figure held one scarred hand in the air in a magnificent sign of benediction, and the other hand He extended to the family. The McCoys sank to their knees, overpowered and stupefied.

Thunder rolled across heaven and lightning flashed from the center of the Throne of Glory. The Voice from within the circle of light said simply, "Well done, good and faithful servants. Enter into your Master's glory. Welcome home."

CHAPTER
31

"Time to go back," Michael told Seradim. "We have much more to do before the end comes."

The other angel nodded. "I'll see how quickly I can help the Wongs cross the line. I want to be part of another homecoming."

"Makes everything worthwhile, doesn't it?"

Seradim sighed. "I will never forget what I saw happen in that backyard. I know who is behind such terror and tragedy. I am poised to find our enemies and do battle."

"You are ready. I must meet with Ben and the students and let them know what has happened."

Once more Michael stepped into history at about the same place on the porch that he had materialized on his last visit to the Lancaster farmhouse. The group of young people continued looking at the sky for several minutes, not realizing that he was present.

"I'm going to find out what the radio reports." George turned toward the house. "Look!" he pointed. "It's Michael!"

"Peace to you on this night of consternation."

"Michael!" Cindy turned toward the house. "I knew you'd be here soon. Tell us what is happening."

"Sit down and listen carefully."

The students quickly assembled around the porch steps.

"First, let me tell you about the condition of the world. The fires of the past months have seriously defoliated most of the forests. Reduced rainfall and rising temperatures last spring hampered crops. Fresh water is diminishing. You must be aware that the decreasing food supply will result in increased violence. Soon guns will be worth more than gold. People will kill for water."

"What's happening to the population?" Cindy asked.

"AIDS and drought have decimated the continent of Africa. Zimbabwe is nearly deserted. In Kenya the soil is baked clay. Drought has spread from the Cape of South Africa to Cairo. Starvation has taken a great toll."

"And South America?" a Hispanic student asked.

"El Niño winds have caused drought from South America to Australia. Except for Israel and Petra, the whole world is experiencing the full judgment for corrupting the atmosphere. The hand of God has been heavy while He waits patiently for the nations to turn to Yeshua as Messiah. However, in Israel and Petra, the land is being prepared for His return and rule."

"What's happening here?" Ben asked. "What is going on in Southern California?"

"You can feel the effects here tonight. Although air pollution has blocked one-third of the sunlight and moonlight, nothing is stopping the increase of ultraviolet radiation. Not only skin cancer but incidences of terrible cataracts are increasing. Respiratory illness is rampant. What is occurring in the skies is the fourth trumpet of judgment.

"Each of you has been affected in ways that have already begun to take their toll, even though you may not feel them. It is important that I pray for you and relieve the harmful effects. As our Lord did, I am going to lay hands on you that you may be healed of what has accumulated in your systems. Kneel and let me walk among you."

The students bowed on the ground. Some lay prostrate on the grass with their faces in their hands. Michael slowly moved among them, touching them on their heads prayerfully as the power of the Holy Spirit cleansed and renewed their eyes, revitalized their respiratory systems, and healed their skin lesions. The darkness of the night continued to be broken by thousands of intermediate bursts of meteoric explosions of light.

"Now, let me share with you the heavy words that I must bring for this hour."

The students gathered once more around the steps. "In the days ahead, the final woes will be visited on those who have rebelled and been disobedient. The Evil One prowls the earth; he knows that his final hour is at hand, but he is too obstinate to face the implications. You must understand that he is not alive and well but wounded and dying. His final weapon appears to be death, but it is not so. He can use only fear and anxiety to deceive you. Death will come, but you must not be dismayed. Dying is only part of the natural process that continues to work in this world. For the unbeliever, death is terror; but for you, it must be seen as the final means of transformation."

"Why are you giving us this instruction?" Ben interrupted. "Sounds rather ominous."

"You must remember that faithfulness does not exempt you from the consequences of life on this planet."

"Some of us are facing death?" George asked hesitantly.

"All of you have the potential to fall at any time, except Ben, who is one of the 144,000 and is absolutely protected."

"Michael, what are you suggesting?" Ben asked. "What lies ahead?"

"Remember, martyrdom is the mark of ultimate victory . . . not defeat."

"The McCoys!" Cindy gasped. "You're trying to tell us that something has happened to our friends."

The group became deathly quiet. Ben blinked apprehensively and reached for Cindy's hand.

"Yes. The McCoys have entered into their reward. Let your loss be tempered by the knowledge that they went as a family and now stand together before the throne of God. The faith and patience of the parents ultimately resulted in both children trusting Yeshua."

Cindy's often stoic features froze in place. Ben bit his lip and closed his eyes. Two of the students gathered around Ben and Cindy, putting their hands on their shoulders.

"They were faithful to the end. . . ." Cindy's voice broke uncharacteristically, and she began to weep.

"Such good people," Ben muttered. "Was . . . was the end terrible?"

"Swift and without lingering pain. The McCoy family left this troubled world together."

"We must hold some sort of memorial service for them." Ben pointed to a large oak tree next to the house. "The area beneath that tree would make a nice burial plot. We can't actually bury them, of course, but we could honor our friends with a memorial there."

"Yes," Deborah agreed. "Let's make crosses out of the old lumber behind the house. We can write their names on the crosses and stick them in the ground like grave markers."

Without anything more being said, the students started preparing a special site under the thick branches of the spreading oak. Some of the youths piled up rocks while others tied two-by-fours together with pieces of rope. Deborah wrote the McCoys' names with an indelible marker she found in her backpack. Soon the four crosses stuck out of the heap of rocks. After the students gathered around them, Ben began reading from the fourteenth chapter of John's Gospel: "'Let not your heart be troubled; you believe in God, believe also in Me. In My Father's house are many mansions; if it were not so, I would have told you. I go to prepare a place for you.'" Ben stopped and looked at the little group circled around the four crosses. "Would anyone like to say something?"

Deborah spoke softly. "Without Cindy's testimony, Erica would have perished in her sin. We don't have a choice about living or dying, but we make a decision about where we go. Cindy made that difference in Erica's life."

Silence settled over the group. Finally, Ben read again, "'I am the way, the truth, and the life. No one comes to the Father except through Me." He closed the Bible and the group started singing in hushed, broken tones. "Amazing grace! How sweet the sound that saved a wretch like me. . . ."

Their strong young voices filled the night air as they sang louder with each succeeding verse. Their hymn faded, and they stood quietly beneath the great oak tree, watching the thousands of meteors explode in the black sky.

To his surprise, Michael wept as he stepped back across the barrier of heaven and earth. As he moved away from the scene, his tears increased. Images of more friends dying filled his mind—the death of Ruth Feinberg and her unborn child in Bozrah. He looked back at the students, especially at Ben, and clenched his fist. *The end is coming,* he thought to himself. *And I will be ready to strike a blow like nothing Evil has ever known!*

CHAPTER

32

Wincing in horror, Michael and Seradim stood at the other side of time and watched the nuclear exchange between Damian Gianardo and the Chinese prime minister tear the world apart. Even though the angels knew what was coming, their pain was still overwhelming. Innocent children were consumed by the same firestorm that devoured the wicked. By the time the two egomaniacs stopped, the world was in shambles, cities destroyed, and food sources contaminated. One-third of the remaining global population was wiped out. Suffering was vast and widespread.

"How much more can the world endure?" Seradim lamented.

"Time is growing very short indeed." Michael looked out toward the horizon where the sun was setting. "The final war is just ahead. Only a few pieces of the puzzle remain to be fitted into place. Our time is almost at hand."

Seradim looked intensely at the world beneath them. "The Chinese government gave Gianardo more than he dreamed possible. Obviously, he seriously miscalculated.

Even at this moment he is trying to shift all the blame for his aggressive and impulsive behavior on the Chinese people." Seradim looked carefully at Southern California. "I see Gianardo has started a counterattack on his own citizens. Anyone of Oriental descent is his target tonight. Look." The angel pointed toward Lake Forest. "The Wongs are in harm's way."

Michael studied three government vehicles speeding down Highway 5 from Los Angeles. The black automobiles turned off the freeway onto the exit ramp into the Lake Forest area. Within minutes the three undercover agents' cars pulled up in front of the Golden Dragon.

Michael pointed at the city. "Yes, Adams's men are arriving at the Wongs' restaurant even as we speak."

"May be my last and best opportunity to help Frank and Jessica," Seradim pondered. "This time I'm going to take a rather unique approach. Please forgive me, but time is too short for explanations."

"You've got to move fast. Adams and Schultz are almost at the door."

At that moment Cindy Wong was sitting on a stool in the back of the family restaurant, listening to her father read the newspaper aloud. Her mother continued to stir a boiling kettle on the stove, preparing for their evening customers.

"Say here that emperor make peace with Chinese premier three days after nuclear disaster. Now that one week pass, it clear that in addition to many millions who die, millions more injured." Frank put the paper down and shook his head. "Craziness. Gianardo is madman."

"The emperor's losing his grip," Cindy added. "We would never have seen such a story one year ago. He can't censor the press any longer."

"Empire is collapsing!" Jessica shook her finger in the air. "The evil man not stand forever."

The kitchen's swinging doors flew open, and a large man barged in. "Please follow me without saying a word," he commanded.

"Who are you?" Cindy's father dropped his paper.

"We must move quickly. Go out the back door now. Do not make a sound."

Jessica reached for a large chopping knife. "You not rob us tonight!"

"We only have seconds to leave before the security police arrest you."

Before Cindy could speak, the man pulled her off the stool and headed for the rear door. "Follow us," he demanded. "Secret police are coming in the front door this very minute."

"Hurry," Cindy yelled. "Trust him."

The Wongs ran silently behind their daughter and the stranger. The group darted down the alley behind the shopping center. Near the back fence line, the large man pushed a piece of the broken fence apart, and the Wongs slipped through.

"What happening?" Frank puffed.

"Get across the street!" The stranger took Cindy's hand and waded into the traffic, winding his way among the cars waiting for the stoplight to change. Only after they turned into the first street that ran into a residential area did he stop.

"Michael!" Cindy exploded. "What in the world are you doing? I recognized your voice in the restaurant. That's why I did just what you said."

"Michael?" the parents echoed.

"Listen carefully," the angel said. "The government is rounding up all Chinese-American citizens tonight. You must hide for several days. Within forty-eight hours confusion and chaos will be so great that the emperor's decision will have to be rescinded, and the government will be forced to release all prisoners. However, the police will be double-checking to find any Christians who might have been caught in the sweep. Cindy, they have your picture on file."

"Oh, Michael! You saved me again."

"We have no time to talk. Listen to what I want you to tell the students you are discipling. We have less than a year left. The Antichrist will become more desperate as his empire disintegrates. His inability to defeat China will result in other nations, such as Russia, the Ukraine, and the United Muslim League, defying his authority. He will be even more reckless and dangerous. If the police had taken you tonight, you would have been dead before morning."

Jessica grabbed her daughter. "Help us!"

"Quiet! Just listen to me. After the next couple of days pass, there will be a period of relative quiet. Governmental leaders will be so involved in trying to handle the disasters in the various nuked cities of the empire, they will leave the Christians and the Chinese alone."

"Cindy tell us about you, Mr. Angel." Frank's voice quivered. "We also meet another angel once. It difficult to believe . . . but we have heard your name often. We are old . . . foolish. But must believe in your Jesus now . . . tonight . . . this moment."

The shrill whining of sirens split the brisk night air. Police cars could be heard closing in from opposite directions. "They are arresting your Chinese employees right now, but do not worry. In three days they will be back to work. Catching Cindy would have been the deathblow to all of you."

Frank bowed up and down in the Oriental manner. "Mr. Michael, when workers come back, I tell them to believe in Jesus. I tell them angels never stop doing His work. Yes, we tell them we believe. They should believe too."

"Cindy, even though it is some distance away, you and your parents must get to the McCoys' house. No one has been there for months. The police will not be expecting anyone to hide in that place because of its reputation for harboring disloyal citizens. The back door is unlocked, and there are still canned goods in the pantry."

"Ben will be terrified," she pleaded. "I must let him know that we are okay."

"I will appear at the farmhouse after I leave you. Do not worry. I will put Ben's mind at peace. Now go!"

"We believe. We believe," Frank kept saying over his shoulder as the family scurried down the street.

Michael abruptly stepped into time and stood next to Seradim. Together they watched the Wongs disappear into one of the dark side streets. "Very clever," Michael said. "You took the form and voice I always use when appearing to Cindy. We look and sound like twins."

"Wasn't enough time left to chance her not following my instructions without questions. No point in explaining the switch. Might have further confused the Wongs. Praise God they have found the truth."

"You've truly learned to be a Guardian, my friend. You're ready to be a frontline solider in the final conflict."

Seradim smiled broadly. "Thank you. I already know who my targets will be."

■ ■ ■

As time passed, Seradim's predictions proved to be correct, and Gianardo backed down on his oppression of

Chinese citizens of the New Roman Empire. By early spring, the Wong family had closed the restaurant and moved into Ben's ministry headquarters, away from the roving gangs that had become an even greater threat than Gianardo's secret police. Frightened, hungry people roamed the streets like packs of wild animals. Anarchy and chaos reigned throughout California and across the nation.

Homelas and Malafidus were frantically responding to an unending array of opportunities. Easy marks distracted them from their old projects. Renewed confidence and expectation of final and total victory motivated all the legions of demons to work with frenzied fervor.

"Another new assignment!" Homelas shouted to his cohort. "Just came in. Killing the McCoys got us promoted. We've been attached to one of the new young generals in Gianardo's inner circle. We're getting near the heart of world control."

"Excellent!" Malafidus concentrated a moment, retrieving the complete files on their new target, General Calvin Browning. "Yes! Browning's a nuclear attack expert. He'll offer superb opportunities for action. Let's go."

When the demons descended on Washington, General Browning had just sat down at a small table next to four other military leaders in the center of a maximum security chamber. This room in the National Security Building was totally sequestered and free of possible electronic eavesdropping, but nothing could keep Homelas, Malafidus, and their comrades out. The two demons settled on each side of the young officer. Looking around the room, they acknowledged the other demons working the briefing.

Gianardo walked in and shut the door behind him, and the five generals immediately stood. "I am now surrounded by old fools and reactionary idiots," he mumbled to himself. The emperor flung a number of files down on the table and motioned for the group to sit down. "My New Roman Empire is being assaulted by the last vestiges of resistance to my complete control. We must now be ready to crush the enemy without fear of disobedience or resistance from within our own government."

Homelas and Malafidus could see the totally pervasive extent of Gianardo's degeneracy. Cruel conniving was etched in his being; deceit and malice in his eyes.

"Notice how his soul is yellowing," Malafidus said to the swarm of demons that hovered around the emperor. "You boys are doing an excellent job."

"Got the arrogant old fool under total control," Belial, the leader of the pack, shot back. "We've totally captured his imagination and dreams. We control his every intention."

Gianardo cleared his throat. "Your time of opportunity has come. General Smith thinks that I am not aware of his attempts to thwart me. We must be ready to stop his men at a moment's notice. When the final strike against the Chinese and the United Muslim League comes, each of you must be prepared to assassinate anyone who stands in our way. You may have only one shot. You must not miss."

"You can count on us." Browning saluted.

Malafidus concentrated on touching the burning ambition simmering at the center of Browning's heart and mind. He gently massaged the young man's sense of self-importance.

"When this period is past," Gianardo said with complete confidence, "you will not only be commanders in this empire but the first military leaders of the entire globe. I congratulate you on a very intelligent decision to stand by me."

A greenish ethereal fog emanated from the demonic swarm. The haze rolled out over the table and settled around the generals.

Gianardo pushed a file toward each person. "I have already appointed each of you to a new position that will take effect at the moment we strike. Askins will head security. Browning, you'll have the nuclear strike command. Jackson, I have selected you to coordinate all ground and attack forces. I want Imler to oversee domestic coordination of all legislative activities. Salino will handle the final details of surrender after we have humiliated our international enemies."

General Jackson smiled broadly. "We are your servants as together we write the history of the beginning of the third millennium. What can I do at this time?"

"Watch him," Malafidus whispered in Browning's ear. "Jackson's trying to upstage you. Don't let him get an edge with Gianardo."

The emperor–president pointed beyond the walls. "I want you to create a system that will circumvent the nuclear detonation device in this building. It must be portable since we will be taking it to Rome with us in a few months. We will reassemble our command post there. No one must be aware of what you have done except an expert that I will assign to you. Terbor Esiw will know what to do. He is the secret creator behind this effort."

"Speak up now!" Malafidus shouted in Browning's face. "Take the initiative."

General Browning immediately asked, "Who else is aware of this plan?"

"No one. You will note that the instructions are in my own handwriting. When we meet, you will tell your staff personnel that I have appointed you to an ad hoc task force preparing plans for the rebuilding of this country. Any other questions?"

"Can the world survive another war?" Imler probed. "I'm sure that you have covered this option."

"A world with less population will be much easier to manage." Gianardo smiled. "Yes, long ago I recognized the need to reduce population to a level that would be more controllable. In the future we will not have to worry with negative public response or the failure of any form of compliance. I will have completely united religion, politics, and all forms of philosophical thought. Gentlemen, we will be gods!"

Browning applauded loudly and the rest of the generals followed. He smiled ingratiatingly at the emperor, who appeared quite pleased at the young general's responses.

As the military leaders dispersed, several of the hovering demons lingered behind. Belial joined them. "Our infernal leader is pleased," the highest ranking demon confided. "Never have we had such unassailable control over the world. These presumptuous warmongers are mere pawns in our hands."

"When do we get to kill them off?" Malafidus asked. "Anyone know?"

Belial answered, "The indicators are clear that these fools will continue to precipitate worldwide crises. We think some can be nudged into killing each other, just as Gianardo is planning the assassination of General Smith. There will be more carnage than even our appetites can handle."

Homelas looked knowingly at Malafidus. "We've knocked off families, children, leaders for the other side. What a season of hope it's been."

"Headquarters keeps a running total of our assassinations," Belial hissed. "Don't worry, boys, they'll know when you suck your young general down into the blackness of the pit."

C H A P T E R
33

Standing at the edge of heaven, Michael and Seradim scrutinized Earth's final months as history spun out of control.

Gianardo became obsessed with establishing Rome as the geographic center for his reign. He took over the papal palace and chased the new pope out of the country. He halted all worship in St. Peter's Basilica. Periodically Gianardo strolled into the chancel and sat on the high altar, proclaiming himself omnipotent. Ironically, his so-called "total power" was not sufficient to stop the continuing disintegration of the United States.

In late August the emperor summoned the five young generals now controlling all military operations to the Sistine Chapel. Full-scale maps, drawings, and plans were laid out on long tables beneath the ceiling that was Michelangelo's greatest accomplishment. The junta planned their final battle strategy.

Near the end of the meeting, Gianardo placed his finger on a point on one of the maps. "I have personally planned every detail of what lies ahead." He thumped the map of Israel. "We are going to land on the beaches near the ancient city of Megiddo. I want to prepare for a drive down the Valley of Jezreel, called by some Armageddon. We will cut the country into two sections."

Browning leaned over and stared at the map. "Armageddon? Why there? In fact, why in the world are we going to Israel of all places?"

"Two reasons," the emperor snapped. "For some unexplainable cause, the Israelis are the only people who have escaped the ecological damage visited on the world by my enemies. They have the only real estate left where we can hope to escape the effects of pollution and radiation. We will govern from Jerusalem until the rest of the world cools off. In addition, their capital has religious significance. In the future, Jerusalem will be a more suitable place for my throne."

Browning stared at the map, the consequences of the action racing through his mind. *We are no match for the Chinese army,* he thought, *particularly since the Japanese and the Muslims have joined them. We will eventually have no recourse but to use atomic weapons. Then Israel will no longer be free of radiation effects. We are courting total global disaster.*

While Browning reflected, Gianardo explained exactly how he wanted the landing handled. The emperor abruptly turned and stared at the young man. "Some problem with my plan, General? You disagree?"

Every eye in the room trained on Browning. He shook his head; the blood drained from his face. He slowly slid down into his chair at the table. *Our days are truly numbered! We can never survive this assault.*

Gianardo's once brilliant ploys were now so paranoid that each new idea was more exaggerated and bizarre than the last. Because no one was left to moderate or restrain him, any balanced perspective was lost.

A month later a helicopter lowered the emperor down in front of the Western Wall in the old city of Jerusalem.

With television cameras offering the world a picture of his every movement, Gianardo marched to the spot where Moses and Elijah had been sitting unharmed for three and a half years, passing the judgments of God and foiling many attempts to kill them. Gianardo angrily confronted the two biblical giants, but they calmly stared at him.

"I have the power of life and death in my hands." The emperor's voice was menacing. "You nuisances have been allowed to stay only because of my choosing. Do you understand that in a moment I can dispatch you back into the mist from which you came?"

Across the plaza no one moved.

"Now let the world see who laughs last!" Gianardo screamed. He turned to a soldier behind him and jerked the man's pistol from his holster. The emperor cocked the gun and ran directly in front of the prophets. "Let every eye see who has the power." He fired rapidly, toppling Moses and Elijah from their thrones. Complete silence descended on the holy site. Disbelief and dismay covered people's faces.

Gianardo turned to the stunned multitude. His voice split the silence. "I am the most powerful force in the world," the emperor screamed. "Do you understand? I have exposed these frauds. I have done what even Pharaoh of Egypt could not accomplish." No one moved.

"The world thought some abstract idea called God was the power of life and death. I alone am this power. I am the supreme one! Throw away your superstitions! I decree these bodies be left in the city that the world may watch. No one touch them! Watch them rot!"

When no one moved, Gianardo threw the gun down and stomped back toward the steps. Soldiers fell in around him. The square emptied as his helicopter disappeared. Yet silence hung like an impenetrable fog over the temple mount.

■ ■ ■

For three days the two great leaders lay face down on the platform next to their thrones, jagged holes ripped open in the back of their robes where the bullets exited. No one dared to touch their bodies.

On the fourth day the sun broke over the mountaintops around Jerusalem. Light bathed the plaza in front of the Western Wall in a blaze of arid sunlight. Moses slowly got to his feet and Elijah reached for the arm of his chair, pulling himself up. The two prophets silently surveyed the strange scene before them; a ring of fully armed troops slept at their feet.

Moses thumped his staff on the wooden platform. The hollow sound echoed menacingly across the square. A soldier looked up and blinked. A second raised his head. Another leaped to his feet. "They're alive again!" He scrambled for his gun. "Look!"

"Call the CO!" another soldier in the back called.

"Do not fear us." Moses waved them back. "Rather fear him who would steal your soul. The time is short. Repent now, for the era draws to a close."

Clouds began boiling in the sky, just as they had on the day of their appearing. Moses and Elijah quickly retraced their steps up the Kidron Valley toward the Mount of Olives. The ground began shaking violently, and roaring noises filled Jerusalem.

On top of the mount at the site of Jesus' ascension, the two prophets disappeared gradually, ascending very slowly in sight of many in a swirl of cloud covering.

Within seconds the earth rocked even more violently and every building in Jerusalem rumbled. Crevasses opened across streets and entire buildings fell in. Seven thousand of Gianardo's men disappeared as the earth kept shifting, swallowing them alive. Throughout the rest of the day, aftershocks rocked not only the city but people across the world. Damian Gianardo was increasingly discredited because of the impact of the television pictures of the resurrection and ascension of Moses and Elijah—pictures which had been seen around the globe.

In the late afternoon General Calvin Browning barged into the emperor's office. "I have an update on how the troop landing is progressing. We believe that our units are moving at top speed to secure the entire area near the entrance to the Jezreel Valley." The building shook. He paused to catch his breath.

Although there had been no signs of a storm, a bolt of lightning flashed across the sky. A great explosion of light filled the room, followed by a deafening roar. Gianardo and Browning rushed to the window. A large tree across the street was now a smoldering, splintered stump. Streaks of lightning popped and crackled through the air. People outside dived for shelter in the nearest building.

"The earth is coming apart," Browning sputtered. The building shook again, and across the street large rocks bounced as another earthquake began. The general's eyes widened. "Everything is coming unglued."

"Get a grip on yourself, Browning! The environment's messed up from the pollution and A-bomb attacks. Don't go nuts on me."

A file cabinet toppled over and Gianardo's desk began sliding toward the opposite wall. The general lost his footing and nearly fell. Staggering like a drunk, he tried to reach the door. "I'll try to get some kind of report to you later." Browning ran, not even attempting to close the door behind him. He stumbled down the hall and staggered into a corner where he slumped, curling up in a ball.

"We've lost our control over him," Malafidus swore. "I didn't think he would crack."

"Headquarters will be livid if we don't reel him back in." Homelas groaned. "We've got to get inside his head."

Browning placed his hands to his ears and began whimpering. He pulled his knees tightly against his face.

"Fear has gone from being our tool to a barrier." Malafidus circled the general. "Oh, no, the idiot's starting to pray!"

"Dear God," whimpered Browning. "What have I done? It's all true, isn't it? This is Your doing. Is it too late . . . too late for me?"

Belial emerged through the wall. "What's going on here?" He stared at the general on the floor. "Not him!" the demon roared. "Don't tell me he's capitulated!"

Malafidus and Homelas exchanged nervous glances.

"We're working on the problem," Homelas answered. "Go on back to Gianardo. Everything will be okay in a moment."

Browning uncurled himself and kneeled, bowing his head down to the floor. "Sweet Jesus, only now do I see my father was right about You. I don't want to die . . . not without You."

The senior ranking demon inched toward Browning, listening intensely. "I swear! The man really is praying. Stop him!" Belial screamed. "He could contaminate the entire place."

The building shook again and big sections of the ceiling fell down. A support beam split and crashed. A piece of the paneling fell on Browning's head. The general slumped, blood running down his face.

"He's still alive!" Belial shrieked. "Better he die than repent of his sin! Fools! Idiots! Incompetents! I don't want Lucifer to know I was even in the vicinity!" The demon disappeared instantly.

"He'll turn us in!" Homelas grabbed his head. "Belial will show no mercy."

Malafidus listened intensely. "I can hear . . . yes . . . at this moment . . . that old devil *is* reporting us. . . . No . . . no . . ."

"What will they do to us?" Homelas agonized. "They won't let this failure stand." He stumbled backward and fell through the wall out into the streets.

Lightning fired through the sky in great streaks of brilliant fire. Thunder roared in deafening answer. Bowls of wrath were being poured out everywhere.

CHAPTER
34

The final call went out. From across the expanse of the cosmos, the hordes of evil swarmed into the center of darkness. Like vultures landing on dead tree limbs, demons gathered for the assault. The legions of malice turned their undivided attention to the very heart of Perdition where cold emptiness reigned supreme. Homelas and Malafidus slipped into the back of the pack, trying to be obscure although nothing could be hidden in the realm beyond time.

Quiet settled. The silence of death permeated the assembly. No one moved, waiting for something not yet formed but surely coming like an eclipse at high noon. Satan waited in a grand pause as before the closing movement of the last symphony. After relishing the supreme moment of fulfillment, the Evil One appeared as the axis in their midst.

A clamor of awe arose like vapor from a steamer. Though Satan had appeared in many disguises, never had the multitude beheld their leader in such glory, sparkling like the brightest of stars. Ugliness was replaced by the magnetic aura of power and majesty.

Satan looked astonishingly like Damian Gianardo, suave and debonair. Yet, the eyes were dark and foreboding as if they contained the collected wisdom of the centuries, awful and frightening in their comprehensive insight. The Evil One slowly crossed his arms and genuinely smiled for the first time since the beginning of creation.

"I stand on the verge of total victory," he pronounced. "I battled to gain undisputed control of this realm because I always knew the power of the Creator was not omnipotent. Now I have proven myself correct."

The assembly writhed in delight and roared in endless waves of exhilaration until Lucifer again raised his hand. Silence was instantaneous.

"I have tried many approaches," Satan lectured. "In ancient times I offered humans the forms of Osiris and Isis of Egypt, Marduk of Babylon, and Molech of the Canaanites. Yes, they worshiped me in many shapes and guises . . . for a time . . . but our Nemesis would not stop. First this and then that. Sacrifices, prayers, prophets, and worst of all the angels." Satan paused and glared. "But for every one of His attempts I had a counterattack." He thought for a moment. "The offering of political domination, authority, strength was unparalleled. Power was always the best aphrodisiac. Caesar made a much better god than any alternative a fertility cult ever manufactured."

Homelas meditated carefully, offering Malafidus as gentle and quiet a thought as he was capable of extending. "I don't think Belial was able to do us in. Things are going to be okay."

Malafidus squinted out of the corner of his eye and shook his head despondently.

"Of course, the Christians' dying savior was a serious problem," Satan muttered. "His descent into death hurt. Confused people. Made Easter propaganda." The devil snorted. "Took away our best weapon," his voice trailed away for a moment.

"But we didn't stop!" Satan screamed. "We offered humans such awesome portions of pleasure that death's sting was swallowed by sheer mindless distractions. From Monte Carlo to Las Vegas, from the boardrooms of America to the power brokers of the Arab world, we made them forget any other world existed by polishing the veneer we laid over this one to an intoxicating luster!" Satan ground his fist into his palm.

"We offered them the lamb with the voice of a dragon." His voice dropped almost to a whisper. "Purposeless religion that was nothing but soothing, meaningless words." Satan ranted. "Words, words, words flowing endlessly like sewage to a cesspool. The false prophets were always our best allies!"

"We won!" a demon screamed. Again the hordes of hell broke into buoyant celebration. "You prevailed!" they screamed.

"We've made it." Homelas leered as he spun around his friend. "All is forgiven. We've prevailed!"

"The final battle is at hand," Satan intruded. "My pawn, Gianardo, thinks himself the supreme religious personage of the age. As soon as he is dead, I will fill the vacuum once and for all. The world will be united in their capacity to embrace my full disclosure. The Creator will retreat from further intrusion, and my kingdom will be established. The time has come to prepare for the final battle. Assemble yourselves!"

The unruly mob instantly formed into rank-and-file order, shaping into a multidimensional sphere, filling height, depth, breadth, and space with Satan at the center. Homelas and Malafidus settled into the reassembled Attack Command with Responsibility for Power Centers in the United States.

"As dawn breaks in their world," Lucifer continued his instruction, "armies will collide. When angelic interference occurs, attack with a vengeance! Be fearless. Your assignment is to create a bloodbath, drenching them up to their armpits. Feed on their fears and banquet on their anger. Tease them with power and terrify them with death. When it's done, I want a valley full of corpses to offer to the heavens! Let the Creator try and tell this world that death no longer reigns!"

No demon moved, each standing in rigid attention.

"The world is united for the first time in human history as one entity. Communications, electronics, and mass transportation provided the tools that the most ambitious dictators could only dream and hope for. I will show this race of contemptible idiots what *we* can do with their toys. Onward to Armageddon!"

The horde abruptly glided forward toward the great barrier into time. At that moment, only Malafidus and Homelas heard the same message simultaneously.

"Do you think I am not aware of the failure of you two incompetent, blundering oafs?"

The countenance dominating the two demon's awareness changed. Loathing and sordidness were etched in the lines of his face. The visage became a singular entity, blotting out everything else in their minds.

"Reward?" Satan's voice kept increasing. "When this day is done, you two are through forever. You are to stay out of the battle!" His command rang like explosions of fire. "Why should I reward you with the joy of observing death and disfigurement? You have one final assignment left."

The remainder of the devil's instructions rocked through them with a roar that blinded and destroyed all capacity for response. The two demons dropped from their ranks and floundered on the edge before tumbling into time, trying to regain composure.

■ ■ ■

Well before dawn, the eastern side of the Jezreel Valley exploded with staggering bursts of fire. Phosphoric pieces of smoldering debris sailed through the night. From out of the blackness, countless hordes of demons swarmed on, over, down, and around the battlefield. As day broke, waves of airplanes dumped endless forays of bombs while the sky filled with fighter jets locked in mortal combat. By ten o'clock, the fallout and dust were so thick that it was difficult to breathe even miles away along the coast.

The Chinese counterattacked with a simple strategy. Waves of human beings were hurled into the fray. Bodies were quickly strewn over the area like tree limbs after a tornado. Demons attacked again and again in an endless feeding frenzy. By late afternoon, the eastern slope and the terrain down the Armageddon Valley were completely filled with dead bodies of the Chinese and their allies. Gianardo's losses were even more staggering.

Malafidus and Homelas stood alone above the fray, isolated from the struggle. The two demons could only observe, nothing more.

"When do we know to begin our final task?" Homelas asked.

Malafidus hung his head. "I suppose some demon will let us know . . . at some point . . . maybe *he* will speak . . ."

"He did say 'final,' didn't he?"

"I think so." Malafidus's voice trailed away. "The shouting was so loud I didn't catch everything. At least we are to escort a load of these victims to the Pit and . . . then go in with them." He wrung his hands.

"Will we ever come out again?" Homelas's voice was barely a gasp. "What do you think?"

"I've never heard of anyone returning." Malafidus choked.

■ ■ ■

In his quarters in the concrete command bunker far beneath Megiddo, General Browning struggled to function. His head was tightly bandaged, but the pain of depression was a far more formidable distraction. By the time Gianardo summoned him and the four other generals to his bunker, Browning had found the resolve to do what he must.

The field command general quickly reviewed the losses and gains of the battle. Another general gave a five-minute summary of the current world situation. The news was devastating. Browning said nothing and stared at the floor. Silence settled over the room.

"What do you think?" Gianardo asked his grim-faced assembly, huddling together in his Megiddo communications center. "Where are we on this Friday night, September 28? If memory serves me right, tomorrow's the big Jewish Feast of Trumpets. Anyone requesting leave for the holidays?"

No one smiled at the feeble joke. Finally, Browning spoke up, "I have always prided myself on being a soldier, not a butcher. Never have I witnessed what happened out there today. Surely the carnage exceeds the worst ever seen by the human race."

The emperor dismissed the general's comments by not acknowledging them. Gianardo changed the subject and quickly detailed his final scheme to outflank the Chinese by proposing peace and then releasing a final nuclear attack while the opposition was preparing for a cease-fire.

"You offer peace while planing to totally destroy the Chinese and their allies!" Rathmarker declared proudly. "Very clever. This will be the war to end all wars. World dominion with no opposition will finally be ours."

"Brilliant, is it not?" Gianardo smirked. "This is not the time to retreat."

"You are quite right." General Browning slowly rose to his feet, a look of determination and, strangely, peace on his face. "This is not the time to back off." He walked out of the room alone, the weight of his past finally lifted from his shoulders.

CHAPTER
35

The blackness of that night exceeded anything previously known on Earth. The moon and stars were completely obliterated by smoke. Life was systematically being snuffed out. As dawn approached, an awesome stillness hovered over Jerusalem. The exhausted emperor and Rathmarker huddled together, ready to respond to any surprise move by the Chinese and their allies. Vultures hovered overhead, anticipating the feast of their lives.

At that exact moment the sun started to rise, the clouds over the Holy City broke, and a great shaft of light shot through the sky like a beacon in a stormy night. The spear of illumination cut through the murky smog and shot out toward the ends of the globe. To their utter surprise, the citizens of Jerusalem awoke to wonderful morning light streaming into their windows. They rubbed their eyes in amazement at the shimmering daybreak no one had seen for several years. Out in the streets, people looked awestruck toward the sky. The glorious aurora did not blind their eyes but felt soothing and healing. To their astonishment, the continuing glow seemed to swallow the smoke and pollution, imparting a renewed clarity to the sky.

Homelas and Malafidus stared incredulously at the brilliant light cutting through the smoke over the battlefield. The sunlight penetrated their own darkness with a glow of an uncanny dazzlement.

Malafidus blinked and put his arm over his eyes. "What . . . What's happening out there?"

"I . . . I . . . don't know." Homelas closed his eyes. "Headquarters didn't say anything about . . . blackness was supposed to prevail . . . death would reign. I thought the war was over."

"Bad intelligence, guys." A voice spoke from behind the demons.

"What?" Malafidus turned around.

"Who are you?" Homelas gawked at the awesome figure.

"Part of the God squad, remember?"

A look of recognition passed over the demons' faces, quickly replaced by looks of fear.

"Been following you boys around for several years," Seradim answered, towering above the evil creatures. "Cleaning up your messes."

"A-h-h-h," Malafidus shrieked. "They've turned us over to an angel to destroy us!"

"No! No!" Homelas begged. "We know you can obliterate us with a single blaze of celestial light. By all the devils in hell, we have no hope." He tried to hide his face.

Seradim held up his fist as if to smash the demons in a single blow. He looked intently into their cowering faces, dreading their imminent assignment to hell. From his face luminous radiance emanated outward in all directions. Incandescent love made the angel appear as a singular spotlight of splendor. Cleansing light wrapped around the two demons and traveled out across the endless expansion of eternity.

"Has the Master of Evil ever offered you any promise of joy . . . genuine joy?" Seradim said gently.

The two demons huddled together, shaking their heads, refusing to look up.

"You don't deserve grace . . . but then again no one ever does. Look straight at me!" Seradim commanded. "Open your eyes."

The demons retreated.

"Even now you would reject Him who is the Light, the Truth, the Way?"

"I think it's a trap!" Homelas balked defiantly. "A test to see if we'll cross over. The real angels were defeated in the battle. This one isn't for real." He pointed at Seradim. "The boss has come again disguised as an angel of light."

"Do I really look like Satan?" Seradim radiated the brilliance of divine love.

"The devil's seduced the best of 'em." Homelas remained recalcitrant. "I'm not about to throw in the towel after fighting against namby-pamby, bleeding-heart goodness for so many centuries. I'm standing with the front office. Even in the Pit, our side still holds the final power. Evil is stronger than goodness." Homelas cupped his hand to his mouth. "Hear me, Lucifer! Even if I flunk this last test, I know you'll bring me back from the depths. We're going to win in the end."

"Yes," Malafidus said resolutely. "This time we're not going to fail the test. We've been given another opportunity to redeem ourselves." The demon turned and looked at the expanding illumination lingering above the Mount of Olives. "I don't know what's going on, but I'm betting our boss has an alternative strategy at work."

"We're not fooled!" Homelas screamed. "The war is over and we've won!"

"No, warfare is not finished," Seradim answered gently but firmly. "The last battle has just begun."

At that moment a brilliant explosion of resplendence shot out from the Mount of Olives. The Source of the light broke through the clouds on a great white horse. Wearing a golden crown and holding a sharp sickle, the risen and exalted Yeshua once more rode into human history, this time as Lord of the Third Millennium. Across the dazzling white robe of the Messiah was emblazoned in Hebrew, "King of kings and Lord of lords."

His appearance sent shock waves backward into and across eternity. Like the force of an enormous invisible explosion, the imperishable winds of immortality swept over the three figures. Homelas and Malafidus were hurled backward into the receding darkness, disappearing in the expansive blackness and then pushed into the gigantic black hole at the end of all existence. Their screams echoed until endless silence swallowed them as they plunged down into the Pit.

Legions of angels swooped from the heavens onto the Armageddon battlefield, descending with unrelenting purity of cleansing light. The Seraphim choirs from highest heaven echoed their song above the last encounter. The Thrones released the full force of the judgments of God. Dominions issued instructions for attack and counterattack. Evil retreated in scattered disarray. The mouth of hell opened, and demons fell into the Pit. The Powers were relentless in their pursuit.

■ ■ ■

On the other side of the world, pitch black darkness was torn apart by the light. Brightness filled the room where Ben and the Wongs were sleeping. The moment each person was bathed in the light, the sallow color of their skin damaged by the environmental pollution, turned to a pink healthy glow.

"For goodness' sake!" Frank Wong looked around the room in bewilderment. "What happen?"

"He's returned." Ben's dry raspy voice was barely audible. "The Lord has returned! Today is a Feast of Trumpet's Day we will remember for eternity."

"We're saved," one of the students gasped. "We're going to survive."

"Praise Him!" Deborah raised her hands toward the ceiling. "Praise God! Praise Yeshua, His Son!"

The night had turned into a glorious sunrise. The usual murky gray sky changed to a brilliant blue. Even the trees and plants were visibly energized and revitalized. "Oh, thank You, Lord!" Ben ran to the window. "The whole of creation is coming into its own!"

"So *that's* you, Ben!" a small delicate voice said from behind him.

Ben turned. "What? Cindy?"

"You do have a beautiful face!"

"What are you saying?"

"I can see you, Ben. For the first time in my life, I can see."

At that moment Archangels and others in the heavenly ranks broke forth out of the stream of light covering Jerusalem. The heavenly hosts processed into the world, passing on both sides of the Messiah on His white horse. Vast multitudes flew forth over the face of the earth as the exalted Yeshua sat suspended in the air. A mighty chorus proclaimed together, "The kingdoms of this world have become the kingdoms of the Lord and of His Christ. And He shall reign forever and ever!"

When the Messiah's horse touched the place of His original ascension nearly two thousand years before, the Mount of Olives broke apart. A great quake split the earth to its center, and the shock wave reverberated to every fault line across the globe, opening a path from the Dead Sea through the Mount of Olives to the Mediterranean. Lightning flashed across the world, and the skies were filled with a staggering aerial display of color and energy.

■ ■ ■

Anticipating the Return at sunrise, Jimmy Harrison and Larry and Sharon Feinberg climbed to the top of the highest mountain in the area well before dawn. At their refuge in Petra–Bozrah, they had helped many thousands of Jews survive the continuing disasters. The physical and emotional toll had been enormous, especially the struggle to adjust to Ruth's death during childbirth the previous year. All trace of weariness was gone now as they waited in eager expectation for this glorious daybreak.

Below them in the valley, groups of Jimmy's students were kneeling in silent prayer even before the all-encompassing beam of light first shot across the sky. As the procession of angels began passing overhead, the new believers covered their faces. They knew from Scripture that whenever the Battle of Armageddon was won by Yeshua, He would personally come to Bozrah to gather His brothers and sisters and lead them through the East Gate of Jerusalem to begin the forty-five-day transition into the third millennium A.D.

Jimmy fell with his face to the ground. Larry and Sharon huddled together with their heads bowed. A great chorus of overpowering singing and heavenly praise encouraged them to look again to the sky. They watched awestruck as millions of angels appeared in the clouds. An ever-increasing army of martyrs and saints followed, spreading out in all directions. Many in the cavalcade paraded above them, sweeping closer and closer to the ground as they passed by. The group approached Bozrah–Petra.

White-robed saints waved to the citizens of Bozrah as if they knew them and were reunited with old friends they had been observing for a long time. In turn, the people began waving back. The Jews stood, clapped, held their hands to heaven, shouted, and prayed. They danced and waved to the hosts overhead, weeping for joy.

Jimmy Harrison stood mesmerized by the sound. He closed his eyes as his ears drank in the blissful music that exceeded any strain he had ever heard. "Jimmy." Sharon shook his arm. "Two people are waving at you. They are trying to get your attention."

"Jimmy! Jimmy!" Sharon began sobbing uncontrollably. "To your left. Look! In the white robe . . . it's Ruth!"

Open-mouthed, crying, Jimmy reached up on his tiptoes for the sky. The dark-haired beauty in the white robe extended her hand as she slowly descended.

"Ruth! Ruth!" Jimmy called. "It's really you!" The McCoys and Ruth steadily moved toward the trio standing on the mountaintop with their hands lifted as high as they could reach.

"A young man is holding on to Ruth's hand." Larry pointed to his daughter. "Jimmy! He must be one of your ancestors. He looks so much like you."

Jimmy found it nearly impossible to see through his tears. He danced from one foot to the other, waving, holding his arms outstretched. "Ruth . . . Mom . . . Dad . . . Joe and Jennifer . . . Erica and Joe Jr. . . . . we're here. . . . We've waited so long."

As they moved very close, Reverend Harrison opened his arms. His voice was loud and clear. "Oh, son, we've been so proud of you. How pleased we are with what you've done!" Jimmy's father took the other hand of the young man standing with Ruth. "We are bringing a very special person with us. Meet my grandson . . . your son."

■ ■ ■

The procession of angels passed beneath Seradim, continuing to march out across the globe and into the whole of the cosmos. From out of the millions of angels, one large Guardian stopped and beckoned. Instantly Seradim heard his call.

"Hail, conquering one," Michael summoned. "Join me. You've more than earned your place in our ranks, for you have overcome through the power, not of the sword, but of love. You are a brother to the Crucified One who always reigns from the cross. Come. I would be proud to have you stand by my side."

Seradim was overwhelmed with the joy of total fulfillment. "I am on my way!"

Michael beamed. "You have earned a special place in this procession. Your assignment is complete. You presided over the demise of the last two demons on Earth. Behold the dawn of every tomorrow."

A great voice thundered across creation, guiding the legions of angels forward. "Behold I make all things new.

It is done! I am the Alpha and the Omega, the beginning and the end." Another burst of splendorous light flooded across the creation and Seradim abruptly experienced a heavenly *déjà vu*.

"I know this exact experience of glory!" Seradim explained to Michael. "This is precisely where I began in the highest heaven, worshiping around the throne of God. The realm from above has descended to the world of human beings!"

"All the plans of eternity are fulfilled," Michael answered in awe.

Worship exploded from the deepest recesses of Seradim's being. He answered, "Amen and Amen."

APPENDIX

■ *The Third Millennium* has remained a bestseller since it came out in early 1993. The partnership I began with Robert L. Wise in that book extended to *The Fourth Millennium,* which has been a steady best-seller as well. Using the backdrop of our travels together in Israel, we attempted to put the secrets of the Scripture in an exciting form to help people prepare spiritually for their struggles as the world becomes an increasingly difficult place to live.

We hit some amazing predictions right on the head. In *The Third Millennium,* our characters discovered a number of approaching turning points in history that have now happened around the world. Our book foresaw secret negotiations between Israel and their Arab enemies; in the summer of 1993, Israel and the PLO held secret meetings. Our book also forecast a treaty; an actual treaty was signed at the White House by the Israeli prime minister and Yasser Arafat in the fall of 1993.

If you've not read it, you will find the appendix in the back of *The Third Millennium* to be very helpful in understanding the mathematical and prophetic reasons for these projections and why we thought (and still do) that the year 2000 will be a significant turning point in Bible prophecy. The discovery of the importance of Av 9 in the Jewish calendar allowed me to develop other projections based on Israel's feast days. These events are definitely tied together in an amazing biblical system of prophecy that is the key to understanding the future.

The Feast of Trumpets is the Jewish New Year. For a variety of reasons, and using the prophecies in the book of Daniel concerning "Daniel's Seventieth Week," I counted back seven years from the Feast and landed in the fall of 1993. The calendar offered two options for the signing of the peace treaty (which will actually start Daniel's Seventieth Week some day in the future): November 6 (using the Hebrew calendar) or September 16 (using the Gregorian calendar). Because either date was possible, we compromised and picked the "fall of 1993." However, as a matter of fact, Yasser Arafat and Yitzhak Rabin really did sign a now famous treaty on the White House lawn with President Bill Clinton watching . . . on September 13, 1993, three days before the Feast of Trumpets that year.

To my pleasant surprise, Yitzhak Rabin returned to the United States, on November 6, to sign another yet-to-be-disclosed deal. While the details are secret, *The Jerusalem Post* suggested the U.S. government promised to protect Jerusalem if Rabin in turn would cooperate in signing more ridiculous "land for peace" deals with the nations surrounding Israel. (It sounds strangely reminiscent of Hitler's land-for-peace deals, which led to World War II.)

The Third Millennium also successfully predicted the formation of an economic union within the Arab world; we called it the United Muslim League in our book. In 1994 such a merger was accomplished. I do not claim to be a person with special prophetic insight but have simply memorized verses from every prophetic chapter in the Bible. I try to guess in accord with my best interpretation of the Scripture.

On this basis, we also anticipated that Russia's "flight into democracy" would end in anti-evangelical and anti-Semitic attitudes and laws; this came to pass in 1997 with new legislation that restricts religious organizations. In 1993, after the state had changed hands, I stood in Red Square with a soft drink in hand, toasting the new prime minister with Russian soldiers. I was chanting, "Yeltsin, Yeltsin." During this visit I taught Christian psychiatry at the state university in St. Petersburg. Since then, former communists have become the "black mafia," and they actually continue to control Russia in spite of its democratic window dressing. With great grief, I recognized from my study of Scripture that true freedom of religion would soon be gone in Russia.

No one knows the day or hour of the Rapture or the Second Coming. As a psychiatrist, I know that people who are dogmatic on these matters are both biblically and emotionally unsound. At the same time, the serious Bible student will not retreat from recognizing the nature of our era and the times in which we are living. While we can't hit the final date with the precision of a rocket launch, we still eagerly wait for Jesus' return and can live with an eternal perspective during tough times. Not knowing *the day* does not keep us from having a cause to live for as we look toward the end.

I have listened to the ongoing arguments about future timetables. Different groups predict a "pre-trib," a "mid-trib," or a "post-trib" Rapture. While we lean toward a "pre-trib" view, Robert Wise and I are officially "pan-trib," meaning only God knows when the end events will happen—but we believe it will all "pan out" in the end.

We have had to adjust our speculation about the Second Coming possibly happening in the year 2000. The desecration of the Temple Mount (predicted by Jesus in Matthew 24) would have to have occurred on Passover 1997 to meet that date. *It didn't happen.* A month before Passover, or Purim 1997, Orthodox Jews would have to have stopped animal sacrifices in Jerusalem, *which they haven't even started.* Yet unexpected pieces of the puzzle are coming together. The rare red heifers have now reappeared in Israel and will be available when the political climate allows sacrifices to start again (possibly in the year 2000).

Since the writing of *The Third Millennium,* we discovered another problem. Our first novel indicated a nuclear attack in Israel on July 25, 1996. That future war is predicted in Ezekiel 38 and 39. In the Hebrew calendar the date would have been Av 9. *It didn't happen.*

Why were we wrong? Allow me to reference some of the material I discuss in much greater detail in the appendix of *The Third Millennium.* First I will quickly survey the history of what happened on Av 9 through the centuries, and then I will look at what could have been anticipated on that one particular date in 1996.

Over 3,500 years ago on Av 9, ten spineless Hebrew spies entered Canaan in preparation for Israel's invasion. Because they were faithless, Israel wandered in the wilderness for forty more years. From that point on, the date of Av 9 became a day of infamy. Most of the horrible things that God, in His sovereignty, allowed to happen have occurred at this time. The Old Testament calls Av 9 an annual day of fasting and mourning.

The first temple fell on Av 9, 587 B.C. In A.D. 70 Titus and the Roman legions besieged Jerusalem, killing many priests and stopping sacrifices, finally destroying the rebuilt temple on the ninth of Av. Sixty-five years later, the last Jewish uprising against Rome, led by Simon Bar-Kochba, was crushed on Av 9.

Centuries later, the expulsion of Jews from England in 1290 and France in 1306 occurred on Av 9. In 1492, Jews were driven from Spain on . . . guess what day? The ninth of Av. The Holocaust officially began on that unspeakable Av 9, 1942, when Hitler began loading the crematoriums. As horrible as this review is, the entire catalogue has hardly been touched. This singular day should cause every Jew to shudder every year as it rolls round.

But we picked July 25, 1996, to be the special Av 9 predicted in Ezekiel 38 and 39. The prophet foresaw a future war during a time of false security based on a faulty peace treaty. Israel's enemies will be Iran, Ethiopia, and Libya, with a high probability of Syria, Russia, and several other nations joining them. The clash will probably be short-lived, because God will supernaturally deliver Israel. Ezekiel predicted dead enemy soldiers piled in such quantities that it would take seven months to pick them up and bury them.

We anticipated fulfillment of this prophecy on July 25, 1996, and everything was on schedule right up to this moment. What went wrong?

In the summer of 1997, Robert introduced me to an amazing book written by a secular Jewish reporter for *The New York Times*. Michael Drosnin's *The Bible Code* raced to the top of the charts as it revealed hidden messages encoded inside the Hebrew text thousands of years ago. These messages are now available to us because of the new capacities computers give us. Four years earlier, we had actually used one of these cryptic messages in *The Third Millennium's* chapter thirteen, but we barely touched the tip of an iceberg.

To our astonishment, we discovered Drosnin's *Bible Code* picked July 25, 1996, as a critical moment in Israel's life. On this date, Prime Minister Netanyahu was supposed to be assassinated in Amman, Jordan, triggering Ezekiel's nuclear holocaust in Israel. But this was only the first shock wave.

The Bible Code had another insight. Encoded in the same message were the words, "delayed, delayed, delayed." For some reason, known only in the economy of God, the date apparently was planned and then actually changed, postponed!

A coincidence? Could the Bible have predicted a modern event three and half millennia ago with the exact names and dates by accident? The chances are about one in who knows how many billion.

Michael Drosnin discovered in the hidden code, predicted 3,500 years earlier, the assassination of Yitzhak Rabin. He warned the prime minister a year before his death; Rabin ignored the message. The election of Benjamin Netanyahu was also detailed. In addition, a trip to Cairo was predicted, to be followed by Netanyahu's own assassination in Amman, Jordan, on Av 9, 1996. This prediction was modified by "delayed," the word used not once but three times.

As a matter of fact, Netanyahu *did* schedule a visit to Cairo and had another trip planned on July 25, 1996, to Amman—before Drosnin warned him of the consequences. But Netanyahu was determined to go anyway up to the last minute. Then Jordan's King Hussein became ill, and the trip was delayed until August 5.

Although World War III was postponed for that year, the Bible code indicates we're back on track for Av 9, 2006. We missed it, but we made a good guess (and I emphasize only an educated guess).

Why did we return with a third novel? In the September 1997 issue of *Christianity Today* magazine, *The Third Millennium* was called "the most biblical of the three prophetic novels under discussion." Their only suggestion was that we should have written more about spiritual warfare. We had already anticipated this need and were hard at work on this book. The first two novels were aimed primarily at a secular audience. This book is particularly for the Christian concerned with today's highly demanding spiritual and emotional battles. We have zeroed in on the issues that I, as a psychiatrist, and Robert, as a pastor, find people facing every day.

The book of Revelation warns that demonic activity will get worse and worse as Lucifer reads the signs of the times, knowing that his days on earth are numbered. Look around. Watch TV. What is the content of today's movies. Only the morally blind could miss the escalating assault on every front. Make no mistake: your children are the number one target on the demonic hit list.

We hope our three novels will give you the insight and motivation needed to "retire" from the vain human rat race. Our prayer is that you will get excited about serving God and people and sign on for the "kingdom team."

You'd be surprised to discover some of the people who are already suited up. Occasionally I do Bible studies for the Texas Rangers baseball squad and the Dallas Cowboys football team. One of these genuinely spiritual players is my friend Chad Hennings, defensive tackle for the Cowboys.

A week before the Cowboys beat Pittsburgh in the 1996 Super Bowl, Chad called me up for lunch. The Air Force academy graduate and jet pilot asked me to join him and Cowboys' chaplain John Weber. Trying to keep up with the lunch consumption of a six-foot-six, 290-pound athlete is an exciting experience.

I expected Chad to be nervous about the Super Bowl. Perhaps he was thinking that a Christian psychiatrist could give him some techniques for relaxing before the big game. To my surprise, Chad wanted to have lunch with me so I could give him an update on biblical prophecy. He said, "I love playing on a Super Bowl team, but I'm a lot more excited about being on the kingdom team." Chad's perspective was on target. He had his eye on what would last.

I hope this novel has the same effect on you. Writing it has reinforced those feelings and values in Robert Wise and me.

Till He comes again,
Paul Meier, M.D.
Dallas, Texas
Rosh Hashanah, 1997

ABOUT THE AUTHORS

■ Paul Meier, M.D., is the cofounder and medical director of the New Life clinics, the largest provider of psychiatric services in the United States. He is the author of more than forty books including *The Third Millennium, The Fourth Millennium, Love Is a Choice,* and *Happiness Is a Choice for Teens.*

■ ■ ■

■ Robert L. Wise, Ph.D., is a noted teacher, lecturer, and author of fifteen books including *Quest for the Soul, The Fall of Jerusalem,* and *All That Remains.* He and Meier are the authors of *Windows of the Soul* and *The Fourth Millennium.*

LOOK FOR THESE OTHER BESTSELLERS IN THE MILLENNIUM SERIES

The Third Millennium
A Novel

Guardian Angel Michael's assignment is psychiatrist Dr. Larry Feinberg and his family. As the last days start to unfold, Michael begins his story of how one family struggles to find faith amid chaos and confusion.

0-8407-7571-7 • Trade Paperback • 320 pages

The Fourth Millennium
A Novel

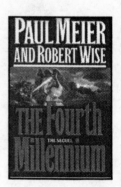

The sequel to the bestseller *The Third Millennium*, this story of the Millennial Reign is based on a literal interpretation of Scripture. Although peace and prosperity have reigned for over a thousand years, Ben Feinberg and Jimmy Harrison discover a trail of clues leading to a dark conspiracy. A compelling tale of Satan's last effort to destroy the kingdom of God on earth.

0-7852-8149-5 • Trade Paperback • 324 pages